Y0-CDN-659

Bad Blood

BAD BLOOD

HUGH DUTTON

FIVE STAR

A part of Gale, Cengage Learning

GALE
CENGAGE Learning®

Farmington Hills, Mich • San Francisco • New York • Waterville, Maine
Meriden, Conn • Mason, Ohio • Chicago

LIBRARY OF CONGRESS CATALOGING-IN-PUBLICATION DATA

Names: Dutton, Hugh author.
Title: Bad blood / Hugh Dutton.
Description: Waterville, Maine : Five Star, 2016.
Identifiers: LCCN 2016024380| ISBN 9781432832551 (hardcover) | ISBN 1432832557 (hardcover) |ISBN 9781432832445 (ebook) | ISBN 1432832441 (ebook) | ISBN 9781432834586 (ebook) | ISBN 1432834584 (ebook)
Subjects: LCSH: Single men—Florida—Fiction. | Murder—Investigation—Fiction. | GSAFD: Suspense fiction
Classification: LCC PS3604.U7757 B33 2016 | DDC 813/.6—dc23
LC record available at https://lccn.loc.gov/2016024380

First Edition. First Printing: December 2016
Find us on Facebook– https://www.facebook.com/FiveStarCengage
Visit our website– http://www.gale.cengage.com/fivestar/
Contact Five Star™ Publishing at FiveStar@cengage.com

Printed in the United States of America
1 2 3 4 5 6 7 20 19 18 17 16

BAD BLOOD

CHAPTER ONE

Pete Cully heaved the cumbersome oak limb onto the pile of deadfalls waiting for Bobby the tree guy to mulch up during his weekly visit. Big old sucker fell in the Oslund girl's yard sometime last night. Missed her house by a short foot, or he would've had a roof repair this morning.

As he rolled it over one last time to get it off the curb, he felt his cell phone vibrate in his pocket. He dusted off his hands and dug it out of his jeans, checked the screen. Yep, Leo again. Only the third time this morning, not as bad as some days. He stabbed the answer icon. "Hey, boss."

"Is there a delay? I expected you already." Pete could picture him tapping his size-fourteen foot and frowning at his telephone.

He glanced at his watch. Only a quarter 'til, and no way Leo forgot they agreed on eleven. But when Leo Burgess gets an itch, it ain't going away until he gets it scratched. Not likely he'd have him an itch over any maintenance update, neither. Gave Pete the skittish premonition that Leo really wanted him to go traipsing around behind whichever Burgess got their ass in a crack this time—probably Nick—and Pete already had a bellyful of that. "No, sir, just taking care of some of the debris from the storm on my way. I'm right down the block, be there in a minute."

"Thank you, Pete." Click.

The other possibility here was maybe Leo found out his daughter and J.D. had a thing going. Pete just did not get J.D.'s thinking on that deal. Sure, Lexy Burgess was a hot tamale all right, but crazy as a snake in a sack, and damn if that old boy's wife didn't look mighty fine her own self. And J.D. had to know Leo would fall on him like a wrecking ball for him being married and all. But that fella just had the hungries, and bad. You could see it in his eyes, the way he looked at other people's cars, houses, and wives. Anything he saw as an upgrade. Pete'd seen it too many times, how that foolishness can get downright dangerous.

Pete tucked his phone away. "But I ain't getting roped into sweeping up after none of Lexy's nonsense either," he told the oak limb.

On his walk up the long driveway leading to the Burgess home, he shook his head at how much sand had washed down the hill from last night's rain. Got to work on that again, though nothing seemed to help. Grass simply didn't grow deep enough roots to hold this sandy soil on the slope of the man-made hill Leo had built for his home site. The old man just had to have his house up on a promontory overlooking the ocean, and Mother Nature didn't like it. Exactly why there weren't any promontories to be found in this part of Florida—something he would've known if he'd bothered to ask a native like Pete, who was born and raised on a dirt-scrabble farm over near Bartow. But Leo didn't hold no interest in any opinion what went against anything he'd already decided to do. Pete did not even want to know how the man got that deal past the county permit people. Or the swimming pool dug in down by the water's edge.

Pete's phone buzzed again. This time he didn't bother checking the screen. "I'm coming, boss, I promise. I'm right in your driveway." Hoping Leo didn't hear the laugh he smothered.

"Have you spoken with the police today?"

His amusement at Leo's impatience died in his chest, a sour taste rising in his throat. So that was the gnat in Leo's shorts—

he'd heard about the latest Peeping Tom sighting. Last night's made the third report of a peeper in Heron Point within a month, and now Leo wanted to pick Pete's brain about Nick. Pete would rather swallow a handful of carpet tacks. Something kind of greasy-feeling about discussing what a sick squirrel the man's own son was. Pete didn't try to pretend he hadn't made this deal himself, jumping on this job when it was basically a payoff, but even an old pet hound dog won't lap up everything you scrape off the table. "No, sir, why, have you?"

"Not as yet, though I anticipate that I shall hear from them. Come around to the Florida room, please." Click.

Pete changed direction and followed the brick walkway circling the house that was as familiar as his own because of the endless labor demanded by Anna Burgess's fickle decorating taste. Two stories, eight thousand square feet, and built long so fourteen windows faced the ocean. Never mind that the brutal Gulf sunsets made those windows useless for five or six months of the year and jacked the power bill up into four figures. The thing almost looked like one of those fancy beach resorts, what with its design stalemated somewhere between Victorian and antebellum plantation style. Leo's image of old Florida aristocracy, Pete presumed. Not that there ever had been any such thing, at least since the Indians anyhow.

Leo, dressed in the white shirt, dark tie, suit trousers, and dress shoes sort of rig he seemed to favor when in the mood to throw his weight around, rose to shake hands as Pete entered the glass-enclosed porch. Nine years of working together and they still started every day with a handshake. Pete reckoned it fit Leo's idea of a man-to-man welcome, though to him it always came across more like Leo patting the faithful old hound dog on the head.

Pete took pride in being a solid muscular man—even at just six months shy of fifty—with the thick limbs that came from decades of manual labor, and damn near six feet tall to boot. But he looked like a runt next to Leo. His giant boss stood six-five at least, and big-boned, built stout as a cement truck. Figure in for that fair-sized gut and he had to go for over two-fifty. Mid sixties, maybe near seventy, Pete knew, but big Leo hadn't lost a bit of his dominating physical presence. Despite almost a decade together, Pete still sometimes felt like he'd been called up in front of the school principal when he talked to his boss.

"Good morning, Pete"—as if they hadn't been on the phone ten seconds ago—"Sit, please." Leo returned to his own seat and crossed his legs. "Tell me what you know," he rumbled in his resonant bass that always reminded Pete of an idling tractor engine.

Now Pete knew damn well Leo meant *let's talk about my son the stalker,* but sorry, he was supposed to be here to discuss repairs. He eased into one of the creaky, rickety wicker chairs Anna Burgess thought of as the last word in sunroom furniture. "Came through the storm fine, everything looks like, and no calls, so no leaks. Thirty-two has another pipe problem. I think it's time to give up and re-plumb the whole thing. It's our oldest plumbing, and I'm patching something every week now. I'll call in a contractor if you agree." He raised his eyebrows in question, enjoying the frustration that showed in Leo's short nod.

"Gonna need an A/C unit at forty-seven, she's grinding," he went on, watching Leo's banana of a forefinger tapping against his chair arm. Of the thirty-three homes in Heron Point, Leo owned twenty-four. Because of the way the street numbers fell, only two address numbers coincided, and this had gradually led to their private shorthand of referencing the other twenty-two solely by number. "I noticed another patched-up window in sixteen. I got a suspicion them Jameson kids are taking that place apart."

"Let us find a rationale for entering sixteen and thus ascertain how bad it is." Leo rubbed his lower lip with the forefinger—a sure sign that he was running out of fuse with Pete's ducking the subject—and then added, "I do not believe they will be here much longer. Their check arrives later each month."

Pete felt a twinge for the kids, even those brats, but he didn't comment. Leo tended to take any tenant's move-out as a personal rejection regardless of the reason, though money trouble was rare in the Point. He glanced up, startled by the rattle-bang of a jay flying slam into one of the glass panes in the cathedral ceiling, and felt an instant kinship with the bird for getting sucker-punched by the unseen barrier. At least the jay could fly away. Before he could keep plugging with more of his maintenance update, Leo held up a hand, palm out.

"See to all of it. You know I will not have our people worrying over basic needs such as plumbing or air conditioning. Now, what do we know of this distressing incident?"

Pete took off his cap and scratched his hairline with the bill, letting his gaze wander the room while he worked on how to get out from under this train wreck. He counted twelve chairs today, enough seating for a Sunday school class, scattered here and there among the potted dwarf palms and hibiscuses. Guess Anna had been shopping again, but what else do you do with a fifteen hundred square foot sunroom? He worked his hat back onto his head and took one more shot at playing possum. "Not much, chief, ain't looked into it. Thought we were going over repairs today."

Leo let that one sail right on by, what Pete would've bet on him doing, and asked, "Was there a letter this time?" He watched Pete unblinkingly, his eyes carrying the opaque, shielded look Pete associated with intense personal interest from his boss. Pete stared back, taking in the big square-cut face on which every feature stood out aggressively—bushy brows, deep-set steel-blue eyes, sharply hooked nose, and a hard-bitten gash of a mouth that never looked comfortable in a smile.

"Not that I know of. Hain't gotten my daily dose of the rumor mill yet, though." One of the peeping victims had received a pretty rank note describing everything the peeper felt while watching her, and the cops said more of them would likely lead to a handwriting slip-up that should help identify the guy.

"Do you still think it's him? Have you found out anything that I should know?" Leo's eyes were hooded now, staring at his hands in his lap.

Pete tasted more acid billowing up and felt it burning in his stomach. He took his cap off again and ruffled his hair, trying to get the thing to fit right. What he got for breaking in a new one on a hot day. By *him*, Leo meant Nick, and no, Pete didn't have any evidence. But his gut said Nick all the way. After all, the boy had him a history. A thirty-year-old cokehead who was too spoiled to get a rise out of good old-fashioned sex is what he was. Pete had tried to tell Leo all this once, and the old man wouldn't hear it, so he wasn't about to say it again.

"I don't know anything more than I've told you, Leo. Maybe send him on vacation, see if it stops. We can't sit around with our heads in the sand." Pete used *we* to keep any threat from showing in his voice, but this was the old man's to deal with.

"Just keep an eye on him, would you?" Leo uncrossed his legs and leaned forward onto his knees. "I'll talk with him again and you monitor his comings and goings, will you, please? Although I must say, I cannot believe him capable of such depravity."

Reckon that's a no to the vacation suggestion, Pete sighed to himself as he pushed up out of his chair. Probably too likely to prove Nick's guilt. And the hell of it was, asking came as close as Leo ever would to pleading, and Pete owed the man that much respect. Fact was, covering up for Nick is what got Pete this lifetime job security to begin with.

"You got it, boss," he said, with a silent promise that if keeping an eye on Nick brought him any proof, he was going to drop a dime on the boy. Calling this nastiness peeping was downplaying it. It had begun to look more and more like stalking to Pete, and he couldn't sit by and let it escalate into another deal like last time. Of course, that meant he'd have to be willing to face one pissed-off Leo.

He let himself out and sauntered back down the drive, squinting against the noonday sun. Yep, just another day in paradise.

CHAPTER TWO

Glancing at the dashboard clock for at least the fifteenth time, Brady Spain let out a groan and coaxed the careening Jeep to the shoulder of the road. He got it stopped and yanked it out of gear, ignoring the chassis' lingering shudders from the violent swerve of a split second ago. Ten minutes past twelve and he hadn't yet reached the entrance to Heron Point. What he did not need right now was another delay. He'd set a noon appointment with the rental agent, and missing her today meant missing her for a week. By then the house would be gone. He needed to acquire a residence, like, yesterday, and this was the one he really wanted. But damn it, he couldn't just drive on by as if nothing had happened.

All of his co-workers made Heron Point sound like everything he'd fantasized about when he moved to Florida to take the job with Beach Haven Resorts. They also warned that he might have to wait to get in, that even people shopping to buy a home settled for renting to get into Heron Point. Seemed the guy who owned the joint seldom sold a house, preferring to keep control of the community standards. Not like Brady could buy squat anyway. He'd been scraping nickels just to make it to Florida. So the perfect and maybe only chance for him to get into a home he could afford in an upscale neighborhood like Heron Point came as such a lucky break the idea of blowing it created physical pain in his belly.

He trotted down the edge of the road, following his skid

marks and glancing frantically along the shoulder. His stomach flopped when he spotted the bowl-shaped silhouette lying inert in the grass. Looked like the same turtle, or tortoise more likely, and he didn't think they enjoyed the upside down thing. Or could turn themselves over, either. Crap, he'd thought he managed to miss the little guy. Correction, big guy actually, for a tortoise. Had to be the size of a dinner plate in diameter, he saw when he came closer.

Squatting next to the motionless figure, he noted that its head and legs had all withdrawn into the shell but the soft underbelly appeared untouched. He reached down and gently rolled it over to look for damage to the shell. His breath caught when he saw the tip of one foot peek out. He quickly backed away, feeling his knees go slack from his adrenaline releasing as bit by bit the rest of the tortoise's feet emerged, followed by its head. After a moment of dazed-looking reconnoitering, it trundled off out of sight into the tall weeds.

"Boy, am I glad to see that hard hat of yours actually works, little buddy," Brady called after it. "But maybe try to stay off the roads, you hear?"

He ran back to the Jeep, piled in, and slapped the spurs to it, thinking of the black smear he'd noticed streaked along one edge of the tortoise's shell. Undoubtedly where Brady's tire grazed it and sent it tumbling. He took one hand off the wheel and crossed the fingers. Close. And now he was really late.

He turned onto Shoreline Drive and forgot his time-panic for a moment, slowing the Jeep to soak up the just unreal beauty around him. The road ran right along the water's edge, with only a single row of palm trees swaying in the breeze between him and the ocean. The blinding blue of the Gulf of Mexico glittering under the July sun, with a lone sailboat out on the horizon, looked like a painting of a dream, only life-size. He watched a little boy in red trunks with hair the exact orange of a brand-new basketball running along the shore, trailing a kite that refused to climb against the gentle wind. Even the racket from a pair of full-throttle jet skis nearby couldn't spoil the awesomeness; it just added a festive summer party sound.

The breeze gusted, lifting the boy's kite and bringing a taste of salt to Brady's lips, and he felt a sudden urgent desire to show it all to Peggy. But she was back in Carolina, a piece of his past. They had drifted apart a year ago, more his doing than hers because of his restlessness, so why did she pop into his brain now?

Twelve twenty-two. Brady found the left turn onto the small, thumb-shaped peninsula Heron Point occupied, jutting out into the Gulf as one arm of a sort of bayou. He crossed his fingers again, this time in hopes that the rental lady had waited.

He'd spent his first three weeks with Beach Haven in a free room on resort property, and though the arrangement came as part of his hiring package, he'd grown antsy living on the dole so long. They had picked up the tab to move him here from North Carolina as the tech guy who could integrate all of their on-property computer systems into a single interactive network, allowing the staff to make reservations for guests at any other Beach Haven property. With seven resorts scattered along the coast from Tarpon Springs to Fort Myers and two more in the negotiation stage, the company also needed a central reservations/Internet sales department. That was the management gig he hoped to land when this current project ended. Brady suspected finding people with good phone presence, Internet savvy, and salesmanship was going to be much more of a challenge than the tech stuff, but he wanted it. So no way was he willing to risk getting the rep of a mooch by overusing his relocation perk.

He zigzagged his way through the neighborhood, pausing to check each street sign against the memory from his only other trip here. The streets all had tree names: Oak, Cypress, Palm, and so on. Just eight of them, two running the length of the thumb and six crossing, but they laid in such a way that most of the homes faced the ocean, which made for a corkscrew route to the interior. Since oceanfront went for a bunch more than those on the inside, Brady was looking at a little green house on the middle row. Not enough paycheck to swing one on the water, and he'd be working too much to enjoy an ocean view anyway. Heck, this rental was a big enough chunk of his check to make him nervous, probably a sign that he ought not stretch it even this far. But this was his big chance, a shot at something better than the stunted aspirations he saw other guys settle for after growing up as poor as he did. And his vision included a home he would be proud to show to Mom; one he might convince her to come stay in. Time to let him start taking care of her from now on. As much as he wanted this for himself, that dream for her never strayed far from his consciousness.

So far, the office scoop appeared dead-on. Not only did all the houses and yards look great, a pair of even better-looking women out jogging in the swelter waved at his passing vehicle, and an older he-man type dragging a tree limb offered a nod and a smile when Brady stopped at a four-way near him. Definitely a friendly impression, such cordiality toward a stranger.

Despite the money worries, excitement flowed through him as he drove, caught up in the feeling of enchantment he got from the rustling palms, the smell of the ocean, the sandy sidewalks, and the cool-looking Spanish tile roofs. Even the relentless heat felt different, special somehow. He shook his head in amazement, remembering himself as a teenager hungering for a taste of life outside of Lee County. The rapt hours lost traveling the virtual world of the Internet, unable to quite believe such places really existed, that people actually lived like this.

And hot damn, here he was.

Brady pulled up in front of twenty-nine Mangrove Street, the house he'd seen displaying a rental sign the other night. He pumped his fist when he spied a car in the driveway.

He hopped out and paused to check himself in the Jeep's side mirror. He had gone with the look he'd often noticed on the locals—khakis, golf shirt, and sandals—but at a lean, not quite lanky six-three and one-eighty, even casual clothes came untucked and got all wanker-jawed when he drove. He leaned down to the mirror and ran a hand through his springy, longish hair, flipping it back. "Can't be looking like some punk-rock roadie when you're trying to rent a house in the high-end district. And dang, you sure are getting a little thin up there for a guy who hasn't hit thirty," he told his reflection.

"Hey, no need for that."

Brady straightened and spun around, heat rushing to his cheeks. He spotted a woman with long black hair, wearing white shorts and a sailor top, walking around the corner of the house toward him.

"No fair to look any better than you already do," she said as she neared. He felt his blush deepen, seeing the impish grin and flirty sparkle in her eyes that said "gotcha."

"Well, no fair sneaking up on a guy who's primping," he said, hoping it came off lighthearted and not too flustered. Try to hang on to some kind of cool.

Up close, she was taller than his immediate impression. Maybe as much as six feet, even subtracting for her high-heeled ankle-strap sandals. The hair and equally black eyes would have suggested American Indian if her skin tone didn't have the unmistakable pinkish glow of a fair complexion with years of tan layered on. Mid-twenties, he figured, seeing no lines in the smooth tan, and beautiful. Which was all like trying to describe a Ferrari as a two-door car with bucket seats. Forget just beautiful—she was hot enough to burn.

"You must be Brady." She extended her hand, her grin incandescing into a full-out smile. "I'm Lexy Burgess. Welcome to paradise."

CHAPTER THREE

Brady took Lexy's offered hand, a long, slender, browned hand with a clear, sort of shimmery polish on the nails, her grip firm and cool. The handclasp brought them close enough for him to catch a whiff of her perfume—something flowery, maybe plumeria—and an intoxicating undertone of sun-heated skin. The energy of her pure raw sex appeal rolled over him in waves, so tangible it made him self-conscious about where to look. Eye contact felt like a come-on, anywhere else and she would think he was smoking her over, and not looking at her was just plain rude. Shit. Then he remembered why he was there and made a vague gesture toward the house. "So, this is it." Boy, wasn't that some fascinating repartee.

"Come on, let's look," she answered, her eyes still teasing him. This girl knew her effect. But wow, what a smile. Enough octane to buckle his knees.

He followed her across the lawn with absolutely no problem deciding where to look now. "Sorry I'm late, hope it hasn't ruined your schedule," he said to her back, hypnotized by the long, lean thighs and the tantalizing tight swell of the white Lauren shorts they disappeared into.

"No problem, Brady," she said over her shoulder without breaking stride. "It gave me a chance to practice the sales pitch I'm going to give you." Her crooked grin told him she knew exactly what he'd been watching. Dang, was that good or bad?

Lexy led him on a tour of the house, which he liked a lot—

hardwood floors, lots of windows, high ceilings with fans in every room. Only thirteen hundred square feet, but it had two bedrooms and two baths, so perfect. Bigger than the cottage he grew up in, where his mom still lived. A cottage that needed a new roof, at least one room re-floored, and some significant paintbrush time put into it, none of which Mom would allow him to invest a dime in. She even had the same furniture from as far back as his memory stretched. Fine, if she wouldn't let him buy anything for her house, he'd cover her future this way.

He had finally stolen some bills from her—medical stuff and taxes she wasn't ever going to catch up to—and paid them off. Part of why he was so short now despite making good money for the last year, but more than worth it. She'd kept working part-time to augment her Social Security, but with shaky health and worse health-care benefits, he couldn't picture her winning the budget war. And of course she'd chided him even for doing that little bit, once she discovered it, though the appreciation and pride in her eyes liked to tore his heart in two.

Meandering through the new place, he felt insecure on what all he should ask—attempting his first venture beyond apartment living—but Lexy volunteered questions and answers for him. From the probing he saw in her sidelong glances, he guessed she was on to his ignorance.

And as nice as the house looked, it wasn't faring too well in the battle for his attention when compared to the captivating flashes of delicate midriff that showed anytime the sailor top swayed, the gentle slope of upper breast visible when she leaned, or even the quizzical expression she used that made one eye tilt higher than the other. He'd always thought Peg owned the sweetest body he'd ever seen, but maybe not anymore.

He smiled, picturing her reaction were she here. Peggy never seemed to get catty about another woman's looks. She'd just be kicking him on the ankle and smirking when she caught him rubbernecking. Bet she'd like the house, though. Funny, she wouldn't even know he moved to Florida if not for the long-forgotten suitcase he retrieved from her apartment. First he'd seen her in a year, going back to when he took the tech job for that nutcase car dealer in Charlotte.

After they looked over, under, and through everything, Lexy offered him a Coke from the fridge and led him out to two chairs arranged around a little table on the screened-in porch, the only furniture in the place. Girl had a seriously smooth hospitality system all laid out.

"See, Brady, you can see the ocean from here," she said as they sat.

He turned in the direction she pointed, and sure enough, between two other homes across the street, he saw the silvery-blue sparkle of the Gulf water. He drew a long breath in reflex, trying for a whiff of ocean smell. Long way from Sanford, North Carolina. Though he had no interest in spending the money waterfront would cost him, Brady had to admit that it was pretty cool to be able to see it from your porch. Next to all this, a sleepy little southern town landlocked out in the middle of nowhere like Sanford offered all the excitement of a dentist's waiting room. People who stayed there liked to talk up the "small-town ties" thing, but to Brady those ties felt more like a noose.

"Yeah, but is it cheaper if I promise not to look?" he asked straight-faced, and got a laugh. "Hey, I know you're a real estate agent, but I noticed you keep saying 'we' and 'our.' Do you also own the house?"

She did a quick shake of that flawless head, hair swinging and glossing in the tree-dappled light. "No, but my father does. He designed and built the neighborhood and leases some of the homes to the right people."

She put so much spin on the word that he felt an automatic

gut-twist of anxiety about the prospect of her ever classifying him as "right." After all, a half-Filipino boy raised by his single mom on a librarian's salary in the rural South didn't develop much expectation of qualifying for anything as exclusive as Lexy made this sound. Just the crazy dreams that never truly felt realistic. He caught himself flicking the two middle fingers of his right hand against the palm, an old nervous habit left over from college exam days.

"What do you mean, 'right'?" he asked, suddenly questioning whether he ought to be feeling ranked off about it. But it couldn't be a race thing; she wasn't blind.

She reached across the table and patted his forearm. How could her touch be cool and hot at the same time? "Oh, you'll see. Heron Point is more of a lifestyle than just a residence, kind of like a club. Everybody loves it here and they hardly ever move, so I usually have a waiting list. In fact, I do now, but everyone on it wants waterfront, which makes this your lucky day." She looked him straight in the eye. "I have had two other calls on this one, though, so do you want it?"

"I think so." He didn't want to seem too easy, despite the thrill he felt at being accepted. And as much as he wanted to be one, something was uncomfortable about the whole "right people" thing. "You can decide I'm the right person that quick?"

"Oh, we'll need a credit check and you'll have to sign off on our policies and regulations agreement, but I believe you are," she said. She smiled again and that flirty look came back. "It's mostly up to me, just being sure it's someone who will be happy as part of the neighborhood here." She leaned in toward him, exposing another glimpse of the soft rise of her breast pushing against a bra so lacy it looked sheer. "I think you'll fit in great. So?"

"Let me see the numbers again," Brady said as a stall. The money did make him edgy.

He scanned the contract again and felt a lurch of dismay. The monthly rent he already knew from the phone conversation, but he had not known that she also wanted the last month prepaid plus a damage deposit equal to another month's rent. Heat climbed the back of his neck. He wished he could slink under his chair and hide, because he just flat didn't have it.

The chattering from a pair of squirrels atop a nearby orange tree broke the silence, like spectators jeering at the imposter exposed, the proof that he didn't belong here. He leaned his head back and scratched under his chin with a fingernail, trying to think of a way to explain this to a rich girl without sounding like a loser.

She brought her right foot up onto the edge of her chair, wrapping her arms around her leg, and propped her chin on the knee. Her eyes searched up and down his face. "Is there something disagreeable about the contract? It's pretty much your standard, boilerplate one-year lease."

He averted his gaze from hers, feeling a little red around the gills. Man, she was tuned in. Okay then, just say it. "Three months up-front is more than I can do right now. Could we make last month's rent due when that month gets here maybe, if my credit checks out?" He gave in to the urge to offer some sort of explanation, and then felt pathetic for adding, "I'm sorry, I've only been here a few weeks, playing catch-up. I didn't expect this much today."

She shook her head slowly, just an inch or so back and forth, biting her bottom lip. "No, it's not something I can change. I know it's a lot, but Dad insists on it." She brought her foot down and straightened out her half-mile of perfect, honey-brown legs, stretching like a cat in the sun. She laid her head back against the chair and eyed him across her cheekbones with a resigned but conspiratorial grin. "Between you and me, he's been kind of retired for a few years, and I think he's a little out of touch with the real world of budgets."

Brady liked the way she said it. He sensed her empathy, but that was that. He stood and shrugged. "Oh, w—"

"Hey, I'm getting a brainstorm," she cut in. Her face lit up and Brady marveled again at how truly stunning she was. "How about this? You make two checks and I'll hold one. Could you do that if I cashed it in, say a month?"

He realized how much he really wanted this house, this neighborhood, and to see more of this woman. Though writing bad checks seemed a dangerous way to make it happen, he recalled the car dealership in Charlotte holding customers' checks all the time. What the hell, don't miss the chance. He ran the math in his head and nodded. "Four weeks will cover it. Can you really do that?"

"Oh, sure, Dad will never even notice." She made a little dismissive flick of her wrist and handed him a pen.

"Yeah, but can I trust you?" he said, only half joking.

She laughed and gave him another taste of the flirty look. "With money, absolutely." Pause. "But not about anything else."

With any luck, that meant he couldn't trust her to keep business and pleasure separate. Brady grinned back at her and got busy writing.

"So, you told me your company gave you a room at Dune-side Villas," she said. "That sounds pretty sweet. What made you decide to move to a house?"

Smooth, the quick change of subject from money once it was settled. Brady finished the checks and ripped them out of the book.

"Well, even though the room offer was part of my relocation package, they didn't mean like forever," he said. "Besides, I don't want to live at work. Not only do I never really get to be off, I feel like I can't ever have a date, throw a party, drink a beer, or anything. It'll just never feel like my own place."

"That makes sense when you put it like that. You can certainly do all those things here, and we hope you will. Although maybe not too wild a party." She winked. "Unless, of course, I'm invited."

Brady had to laugh when she finished by moving her eyebrows up and down like Groucho Marx. He followed her out, trying to decide if she was asking to be invited as his date. Sounded good to him, but he suspected it was just her way and not a come-on. She projected none of the needy aura he usually sensed from women on the make, something he'd seen plenty of when bartending his way through college.

He took a last glance at his new home as she walked him back down the driveway to his Jeep, the euphoria reassuring him that he hadn't just overloaded himself. As long as nothing went screwy on the job, he could handle it.

When they reached the sidewalk, Lexy waved at some people out by the pool beside the house across the street and then turned to him. "Hey, there's a whole pack of your neighbors. Let's go over and I'll introduce you to everybody. You're gonna love it here."

She grabbed his hand and took off across the street, high heels and all. Brady held on tight and entered the social scene of Heron Point at a half-trot.

CHAPTER FOUR

Maggie Davis broke off in the middle of explaining her new bedroom color scheme to Ellie Macken when it became obvious she had lost her audience. Cupping her hand above her brow to block the sun, she tracked the path of Ellie's lasering stare to see what on earth had caught her eye and triggered such a sudden flare of anger. From Maggie's angle, some guy Lexy Burgess had by the hand across the street appeared to be the target of all those daggers. Hmmm. Totally unlike quiet, calm Ellie to show emotion like that. Who was this man and what was the story between him and Ellie?

"Hey, Lexy!" whooped Susan, their unofficial master of ceremonies and always the clown of the party. "Come on. The water's too warm, but there's a nice cold pitcher of Mai Tai to swim in!"

Too sucked into the drama playing across Ellie's face to risk missing the slightest twitch, Maggie let the corner of her eye follow the hasty primping by the other two women there at the poolside table. Susan, whose barrel-shaped body was the battleground of a thousand failed fad diets, stood to adjust her perpetually wandering swimsuit, all the while still waving to Lexy with her free hand. Tall, languid Jill, she of the pithy skewering wit that never missed a bull's-eye, had twisted around in her chair to finger her pool-damp coppery shag into shape by the reflection in the polished steel barbecue grill. The splashing and shrieking from Jill's two pre-teens romping in the pool drowned out whatever Susan was trying to tell them all about Lexy.

But Maggie watched Ellie's quivering nostrils, seized by a desperate longing to feel that passionate about something, anything, even if it was hate. Her own life had stultified to the point where it felt like a fatal disease. God, how disgusting to realize she had sunk to fulfilling all her emotional needs vicariously, like some pitiful voyeur whose feelings had been amputated. She didn't really have to worry about dying from terminal boredom, though. Maggie knew—when sober enough for the thought to sneak in—she was drinking herself to death.

Her body kept warning her; the tremor in her thighs only a drink could quell, the morning blank spots in her memory of the day before, the traces of blood in her vomit after a long night's binge. She knew the signs because she had watched her mother kill herself the same way. She also knew that if something didn't change her life, she wasn't going to stop. Suddenly, the normally happy party smells of chlorine and the coconut sunblock Jill slathered on her boys closed in on her, suffocating and claustrophobic.

She turned to face Lexy and the mystery man as they squeaked the ornery gate shut and approached the flagstone apron surrounding Jill's pool. He looked younger than Maggie's thirty-six, probably closer in age to the other women, who were all younger than she. She liked his dutiful chuckle at Susan's same old weary line about "drinks are on the house, but we have to take turns climbing up to get them." Lexy just rolled her eyes and introduced the man as Brady Spain, the new tenant of the green house across the street.

He was tall and trim, with the kind of sleek ropy muscles Maggie thought of as the sexiest, especially in younger men. His hair was dark enough it would appear black anywhere except next to Lexy's, and he wore it long, almost shoulder length.

Deep complexion as well, kind of Hispanic but maybe Asian too, with chocolate-brown eyes and a friendly smile. Not exactly handsome, but really cute. Lexy, of course, looked great in her little shorts and blow-away blouse. Enough to make you sick.

Not that she disliked Lexy; they had a funny kind of unspoken bond because of their fathers. Maggie and Mark were one of the few couples who owned their home in Heron Point because Leo had been only too happy to sell to the daughter of the late Little Jake Thibideaux, Louisiana banking legend and cruel bastard of a father. Jake's parenting legacy covered everything from holding six-year-old palms against a hot stovetop for discipline to the humiliation of a compulsory medical exam to prove her virginity when she missed her curfew on prom night. Not that Leo would know any of that, whether or not he had actually ever known her daddy as he claimed.

Besides, she got a kick out of having Lexy around, enjoyed other women's reactions to her. Like someone had brought a pet alligator to a party, supposedly tame but no one quite believed it. And all because they suspected Lexy could have any man she wanted, and from the rumors, she wanted plenty. Which didn't intimidate Maggie, she wished someone would steal hers. She should be so lucky. She almost laughed aloud at the idea of Lexy going along with Mark's Friday night routine: Kung Pao chicken and Mongolian beef from Charley Wi's, with sex scheduled promptly at eight-fifteen. Every single Friday, without fail. With that serving as the highlight of romance in her life, thank God for Mai Tais and Häagen-Dazs.

Maggie watched Brady's eyes as he exchanged hellos with Ellie. He showed no recognition at all and Ellie displayed none of the hostile vibes from moments ago. Her face wore its normal friendly-ice-princess contradiction now. Must be Brady just resembled someone Ellie knew. Someone she certainly did not like.

"I'm Maggie," she said when he turned her way. "And I hereby volunteer to climb up and get you that drink." She rose and sidled around the table to the serving cart where the pitcher of Mai Tais sat sweating in the sun, glad for an inconspicuous opportunity to refill her own. After all, it was nearly two o'clock, and it was only her third, she reasoned. She'd just drink less that evening.

"No, thanks," he said with a cute little sideways grin that crinkled his eyes. "I don't think I'm tough enough to handle my liquor in this heat yet."

She got her chance to pour her own anyway when Susan jumped in and asked Brady if he was new to the area. Susan was usually loud, always funny, and would ask anyone any question any time. Maggie settled back in her chair and shared a secret smile with Ellie: here comes the Susan Leland show.

"Yes, I am," he answered with a bit more South in his voice than most Floridians. Closer to the bayou accents she grew up around, minus the Cajun twang. Sort of an "ah yam" diphthong in there. "Moved here from North Carolina three weeks ago."

"Gawd, where'd you get that tan?" Susan brayed. "Here we are broiling like rotisserie chickens and you look like you stepped right out of the South Seas."

"I did, sort of." Brady laughed and his eyes got a playful look. "It's what you call a genetic tan. My father is from the Philippines."

Maggie felt a jolt of embarrassment at Susan's crassness, and heard a little snort from Ellie that meant she did too.

"Don't mind her, Brady," drawled Jill, as she unwound her long limbs from her Adirondack chair and stood, patting him on the shoulder. "That's just her idea of a pickup line. 'Scuse me a sec." She took off in pursuit of a child who was trying to cough up a lungful of pool water.

"Hey, I'm just jealous," Susan cackled back. "It sure is a lot more interesting than 'My dad's from Iowa,' which is all I can offer. Spain doesn't sound Filipino, though."

"Susan!" Maggie had to jump in before this hunk decided they were all uncouth.

He glanced over at her and winked with just enough intimacy to give her a little flutter, but the look in his eyes when they flicked back to Lexy told her that Lexy had already bewitched another one. "I don't mind," he said. "It's only when beautiful women don't ask me personal questions that I get worried. My father's name is Torres, so she's right."

Maggie saw Susan lean in with the bloodhound expression that signaled a serious invasion of privacy, but Lexy slid in before her with a description of Brady's job and the conversation mercifully moved on.

Maggie let the voices drone around her, wondering why Ellie and Lexy never talked directly to each other. Neither appeared to avoid the other or show any ill feelings, they just did not speak. Seems like they used to talk, so it could be Ellie had heard the rumors swirling around concerning J.D. and Lexy. Maggie avoided those rumors because she wanted to avoid getting stuck in a do-I-or-don't-I-tell-her quandary.

She slipped away to pour one more Mai Tai. Stole a peek at her reflection in Jill's sliding glass doors, pleased that the booze still hadn't touched her figure. Only four, right? She could handle it. She was going to be all right. She just needed something to change her life, maybe something like Brady Spain. She never had cheated on Mark, but when she did she wouldn't settle for someone else's husband like Lexy did with J.D. Macken, no matter how good looking he was. No, she would get a young single stud just like Brady there, with his big hands and warm brown eyes.

An unbidden image rose in her mind, in vivid big-screen detail—Brady, his lean hard body all hot and sweaty, climbing up on her like a stallion. She crossed her legs, smothered the fire with a gulp of Mai Tai. Down, girl, you just met the guy.

CHAPTER FIVE

So just kill one of them. Preferably Ellie, if he could hold off until she received her inheritance. Then he'd have the money and could be with Lexy every day. That epiphany came to J.D. Macken as he scrubbed the fourth and final tire on his nine-month-old black BMW 328i, sweat dripping from the end of his nose in the sizzling south Florida sunshine. He rocked back on his heels to check his work, pausing to stroke the car's sleek, glistening flank before giving the tire one last vicious swipe and straightening up slowly to ease the kinks out of his spine.

Okay, a nasty bastard of an idea for sure, but it was becoming ever clearer that he'd never get to have the money and both women. And worse, Lexy might have to be the one to die if she didn't start practicing a little discretion. A mere matter of time before Ellie found out about Lexy anyway. Wives always did when the mistress moved in the same social circles. And there'd be no forgiving; Ellie would kick him to the curb. So he needed her to stay in the dark until that inheritance came, and then kill her for the money. He retrieved the water hose from the grass and sprayed the suds off his wheels and tires, ducking to avoid the ripening grapefruits that had begun their annual sag on the trees lining his drive.

Laying it out cold like that felt kind of queasy, because he did still feel something near love for Ellie. Their sex life was just dead though, with zero chance of resurrection, and who wants to live like that? Such a waste, too, because she had plenty of

33

eye to her. But damn, she kept hanging onto that shorthaired, scrubbed-face college girl look, and J.D. was over it. Christ, didn't she understand that a man gets to thirty-five, he needs a little glamour? Even the trim, athletic body that used to be such a turn-on now bored him. He twisted the spray nozzle to the off position and whipped the hose around in a whistling arc, imagining a machete or a hatchet, listening to the fleshy thunk as the heavy brass nozzle bit into a dangling grapefruit and sent it flying across the lawn.

"Afternoon, J.D."

J.D. dropped the hose as if it had sprouted thorns and spun around to see Pete, the neighborhood fix-it guy, waving at him and dragging a tree limb down the street to wherever Pete dragged such things. J.D.'s heart caromed around in his chest. Could Pete tell what he was doing, what he was thinking?

"Up to a little pruning today?" Pete asked with a chuckle. Thick-bodied and country-faced with an accent to match, Pete always reminded J.D. of his own hillbilly family wallowing around in their Southernness and ignorance back home in Martinsville, living for Friday night bowling and Sunday morning hunting. That weekly paycheck and a twelve-pack of Bud existence would be a fate worse than hell and, truth be told, J.D. wasn't far from it, based on net worth.

As it stood now, even the damn handyman was doing better than him, guy just piddled around all day and owned him a big fancy house to show for it. Two new trucks, too. Kept J.D. wondering why old Leo Burgess, the land czar who owned the whole neighborhood, paid Pete that kind of dough for such work. Though Leo sure could afford it—not only did he own Heron Point, from what J.D. heard the man owned half of this part of Florida. What J.D. would give to have that kind of jack.

"Good afternoon yourself, Pete. Another day in paradise, eh?" J.D. said, his brain scrambling for a plausible explanation.

"Just, uh, tired of banging my head on these things." He forced a laugh of his own.

"Whatever works for you, pardna." Pete smiled, shook his head, and continued on down the street.

J.D. blew out a sigh and returned to his tire rinsing, swatting away at the mosquitoes that showed up for their afternoon buffet. The only hitch in this perfect solution, other than getting away with it of course, was the waiting. He had to hold off until Ellie's mother croaked because that's where the money was. The blessed passing should be soon. The old bat lived in la-la land already and worsened every day. Her death would net Ellie over nine million bucks by last count. J.D. knew because he advised Mama Jean on many investments, her being all impressed with his job in banking. Sure, it was actually just a mortgage house that specialized in mobile home loans, overcharging the very young and the very old, but he hadn't bothered setting Jean straight on it.

Keeping a lid on things until Jean cashed out wasn't going to be easy. Lexy seemed hell-bent on seeing just how obvious she could get, and controlling her behavior was about as likely as reining in a locomotive with kite string.

The rumble of a vehicle slowing in front of his home grabbed his attention, and his heart rate doubled when he saw Lexy's pearl-white Jaguar convertible. She probably felt his thoughts, knowing her.

The passenger window of the Jaguar slid down. Lexy leaned across the console and called out, "Hey there, carwash boy, don't go tiring yourself out. I know something fun you could save all that energy for, say in about thirty minutes or so." She flaunted a raunchy grin, and he felt the instant crushing hunger she could set off whenever she wished.

The memory of the day he met her, almost two years ago now, jumped at him in vivid detail. The perfect white smile flashing against her dark Florida tan and midnight-black hair, those impossible legs bewitching him as she strode about showing the house to Ellie. He got to see her often afterward in her role as their rental agent—which she was for all of her father's homes in Heron Point—until finally, four months ago, she wound up in his bed. He had marveled at his luck in landing her, and now he lived in fear of her blowing his shot at nine million bucks. He tossed the hose aside again and hotfooted it down the drive, the sweat on his neck turning cold from the fear of her shouting something really revealing to the entire freaking neighborhood.

"Damn if that ain't the best offer I've had all day, babe," he said, leaning down against the door to get his head under the closed convertible top. "But remember, Ellie's not working this weekend."

"So? She'll be at Jill's pool party all afternoon. I just left there." Lexy's unreadable black eyes narrowed down. "Besides, I wouldn't care if she did walk in on us."

He glanced reflexively across the Jaguar in the direction of Jill Granary's house and then back at his mistress. "Look, let's don't go over all that, okay, babe? I've told you, soon but not yet, right?"

There again loomed his problem with Lexy. Every conversation brought a new drive for bolder risk-taking, crazy stuff that multiplied their chances of getting caught and jacked up the likelihood of attracting the attention of Heron Point's restless rumor factory. Which would surely get back to Ellie—she belonged to that set. He didn't believe Lexy really gave a damn about him being married; she just got off on seeing him prove how bad he wanted it, if he'd push the limits of caution to have her. But crazy as he was about her—and he wanted her for keeps, like schmaltzy forever stuff—his epiphany included the realization that he'd kill her instead before he'd let her reckless moods or her big mouth ace him out of the money.

36

She tossed her head, swinging her hair over her shoulder, a hint of contempt in the move. Crap like that made him want to tell her to get lost, though he knew he wouldn't.

"Hey, it's not me that got into this with a wife along," she said. "Anytime you're tired of it, just say so, buster."

Her taunting tone sent a burst of anger through him and he opened his mouth to say just that, but the thought of life without Lexy jerked his leash back to heel. Well, plus the certainty of her pulling a big sisters-in-suffering sob scene with Ellie as soon as he ceased being an obedient toy. Good thing Lexy didn't know about the money; she would crank up the true confession drama right away just to see if she was worth nine mil to him. Which she was not, nothing was. Or almost nothing. If only he could believe she would someday grow to feel for him what he felt for her. He would chuck it all and live in one of those trailer parks with his customers if she'd stay with him forever. But he didn't kid himself about the chances of that, it had been asked and answered. So screw it, if he couldn't keep her or dump her without the whole thing getting out before Jean died, Lexy was going to get herself killed.

He reached in across the passenger seat and grabbed her hand. "Look, sugar, I know it's my problem. I appreciate you working around it for me, okay? I just don't want to hand her a gift-wrapped way to take me to the cleaners."

Humor crinkled the corners of her eyes. "You might be surprised, bet it'd cost you less than you think you have," she said.

Whatever the hell that meant, but then that was Lexy for you. A sea breeze drifted in, carrying the fresh smell of the ocean along with the hint of stink from the decayed vegetation and rotting fish carcasses low tide exposes. He let his gaze follow his nose, where the slivers of ocean visible between the trees and houses that separated him from the Gulf of Mexico seemed to be mocking his dream of that most ultimate of accomplishments: his own beachfront home. One like Leo Burgess's would do just fine.

"Well, just to be safe, Lex, can't we hook up at your house?"

She pulled her hand out of his and grabbed the gearshift. "Don't make this a hassle, Jay. I want it on her bed, you know I like that. Her sofa too, maybe even the damn kitchen counter. I'm wearing my slut shoes and I want to make heel marks all over everything, okay? I've got to run some stuff over by Dad's, and I'll see you after that."

She yanked the shift lever and J.D. snatched his arms out before she peeled away and amputated them, because she would. He watched the Jaguar disappear around the corner, the ticklish hollow feeling of anticipation climbing through his stomach as he pictured Lexy on his kitchen counter. Oh sweet Jesus, the things she would do when the clothes came off. Or even with them on, for that matter.

J.D. always got plenty of opportunities with women and knew they found him irresistible—"kind of short but as cute as a Ken Doll," he'd overheard once—and had even come to expect to have his every whim indulged. But this was different. Sex with Lexy made him feel like an absolute god. Woman was only twenty-six, yet light-years older than his plain-brain thirty-four-year-old wife. He shook off the wave of Lexy-lust like a dog coming out of the bathtub and trudged up the six steps to his back door.

Well, what if, just what if, he could have Lexy and the money? The sudden image of her naked in an oceanside pool at his future beach house accelerated his blood to head-rush speed again, sending him to the liquor cabinet for a rum and Coke before his shower. He just needed to figure out how to keep her cool, hold things together for a while. And start making his murder plans now.

CHAPTER SIX

The sudden concussive whump sounded like it came from right under him, startling Nick Burgess. No, scratch that; spooked the fuck out of him. Probably would've bucked his ass straight up over the windshield if not for the snug fit of the bucket seat in his Porsche Boxster. His head snapped around to see what had hit his car even as his brain registered the noise as merely a slamming car door. And right behind him, in an empty lot with a hundred spaces. His pulse hiccupped with a spurt of paranoia that screamed cop as he watched the man walk toward the weekend-deserted office building.

Older dude, forties anyway, round-shouldered and balding. Looked more like a dentist or something, which made sense, this being a medical office. Plus that hilarious Sanasabelt and penny-loafer outfit, so relax. And shit, see there, the guy parked here because it was the closest row to that private entrance Nick hadn't noticed.

You're some kind of jittery, like way wound up, he told himself as he turned the music down, eased the Porsche into gear, and drifted over to a far corner of the lot. *But hey, that's why you're here, to get a little bump to smooth out your nerves. And it's not just your jonesing that's got you all paranoid and shit.* If only the old man would give him a damn break. Okay, so the Porsche insurance jumped eight hundred bucks from one lousy speeding ticket. Why chew his ass, a thirty-mile-per-hour speed limit on a four-lane was a revenue scam anyway. The insurance geeks using it as a way to score a rip-off was no more his fault than any of the other bullshit Pops always blamed on him. Getting suspended from high school for spying into the girls' locker room when other dudes did it too, or burning his baby sister with that sparkler when he was seven because she was the one who ran into it, or even the crazy bimbo in Pensacola claiming she hadn't already offered him some of that cooch, just on and on. It seemed like he was always talking to Pops through Plexiglas, the man couldn't hear a good word no matter what Nick tried.

He rolled both windows all the way down, hoping for a cross-breeze. Had to be a hundred and ten degrees on the pavement. A parking lot was a stupid-ass place to buy blow at six in the evening, but this new dealer insisted on it when Nick called. His regular connection, Cameron, made it easy, lived right there in the Point. But he was gone off on vacation, believe it or not, and swore this dude Jericho was the right hook-up. Nick had never pictured dealers going on vacation like other people. *And what kind of name is Jericho, anyway?*

He leaned down to check out his twitching left eyelid in the side mirror and his cell phone rang. He flinched again, banging his head on the doorframe. *Ow, damn it.* He fumbled the thing twice trying to pick it up with shaking fingers, finally got it, and peered at the screen. Not a familiar number, so maybe the man with the goods.

"Hey." Nick recognized the voice of Jericho. "I'm right behind you. I'm gonna walk up to your window."

"All right." Nick punched off and squirmed in his seat, uncomfortable at the prospect of being trapped at the knee level of a man he'd never met, let alone bought shit from.

The guy who eased up to his window and stooped to face him would have been a totally normal-looking dude except for all the hair. A huge mane of curls swung down around his head as he bent, mingling with a full beard that Nick figured would reach chest level even when the man stood. It was like having a damn Wookie stick his head in the car, only without the fangs, just two little brown eyes stuck in the middle of all the fur. Maybe that was why the name Jericho. Definitely some biblical-looking hair, for sure.

"I'm Jericho," the guy confirmed. He handed Nick a road map and squatted beside the car, at eye level. "You use this to point out directions and get busy explaining all about how to get where I'm going."

"Huh?" For a moment Nick felt as if he had stepped into someone else's movie. "Oh, I get it. In case we're watched."

Jericho just stared at Nick with a "how stupid can you get" expression, and pointed at the map. Pissed Nick off, but he unfolded the map and gestured at it with his finger. That felt stupid, too. "How come the broad daylight if you're so into the James Bond scene?"

"Two dudes hanging out in a parking lot in the middle of the night? Po-lice man can smell that in his sleep, get outta bed, and show up down here in his pajamas," Jericho said, as he held up a fist clutching a wad of plastic wrap that had, Nick hoped, coke in it. "You want five, right?"

"Yeah." Nick felt a surge of excitement just at the thought of it. "Gotta get through a whole 'nother week before Cameron's back." Then he felt like a chump for explaining his needs to this guy and added, "You're lucky I answered the phone. That's a different number than before."

"And it always will be." Jericho paused, suspicion growing in his eyes. He shook his head, and it ebbed, replaced by the, "oh, you're stupid" look again. Pissed Nick off again, too. But the guy had the blow, so chill.

"Then how do I get you if I need you?" Nick asked, picturing Cameron in some plane crash or shit, and getting all panicky about being on a permanent jones.

"Call the same number you did before and I'll call back again. You got something for me?"

Nick passed him the money, folded twice in a paperclip the way Cameron always wanted it. Still curious, he asked, "Well, if you keep using that number, won't they know my number and tap it for your callback?"

"Nope. My landline keeps up with my call history and I never answer a number that's ever called before."

A prowl car siren whooped nearby, scattering birds from the scraggly trees bordering the blacktop, right as another car careened into the lot. Panic cramps convulsed through Nick's body, his mind galloping away with the impulse to blast out of there and leave Jericho holding the coke. The car, a green Ford Taurus, completed its circle and exited in the opposite direction from where it came. A turnaround. He glanced down to see if he had whizzed his pants, then back up to see Jericho grinning at him.

"Easy, dude," he said around the grin. "Gotta be at least a block away."

"Yeah, but don't we need to, like, get the hell outta here?" Nick squeezed from his strangled lungs, wondering why Jericho's serene cool made him want to choke the living shit out of the guy.

Jericho reached in with his free hand and grabbed the steering wheel. "Law want us, he wouldn't be making all that racket, we'd be kissing concrete already. But you go screeching off, you'll change his mind. Chill for a minute."

Nick wrinkled his nose at the grime-ridged fingernails clutching the wheel of his ninety-grand ride, but nodded his agreement. Dude sounded so sure, it felt like getting the word straight from the police chief or something.

"Okay, cool." Jericho nodded and withdrew his hand. "So

anyway, if you want me, best use a different phone so I'll call back. Makes it pretty tough for Johnny Law to get wired fast enough. Maybe they'll triangle me one day, but I like my odds." He shrugged fatalistically and dropped the plastic package over the side of the door while pointing at the map. He twirled his cell phone by its antenna in his other hand. "You'll never know the callback number, either. Never use one of those puppies more than a day or two. You need a taste before I split?"

Nick wanted to in the worst way, not sure he trusted Jericho. But the weight felt right and he just had to come out on top of at least one exchange with this guy. So he fell back on the superior indifference of the rich. "Nah, I'm sure it's okay if you offered. Ain't like it's enough money to worry about."

"Suit yourself." Jericho stood back up and began folding his map. " 'Til next time then." He disappeared the way he came.

Nick checked the rearview to be sure Jericho was out of sight and then ripped into the plastic wrap with greedy fingers. Inside was a baggie full of the white dust that always set him free. To hell with the cops, he could outrun them if he had to. He dug out from his pocket the little spoon, a gift from Cameron, who had said, "Dude like you, born to the silver spoon, a silver spoon is what you need to use." Nick scooped and inhaled, waiting for that all-powerful feeling of invincibility to take over.

As he cruised back toward home, mindful of the speed limit and the felony-sized coke bag in his car, the familiar rush of happiness blew through his veins and started him thinking that tonight would be a great night to look in on some of his bathing beauties. Last night's prowl got cut short by that nosy bitch neighbor spotting him, leaving him still hungry.

He had no idea why watching an unaware woman washing herself was so hot to him, but he preferred it to the hassle of trying to get laid. Seemed like spending time and cash on some cow in hopes of getting some leg was a low-percentage game, and didn't even feel as intimate as watching a woman who thought she was alone, especially one in the shower. Now and then he would lose it, have to bust on in and get off, but mostly just the watching. And he didn't worry about hearing yes or no. He knew that most of them, if not all, imagined someone like him watching and it made them feel all sexy rubbing their soapy hands up and down their bodies. He knew it, he just knew it. So it was already like sex, both of you imagining what you'd do to the other.

Besides, he couldn't face the idea of going home to the old man's droopy-ass face, the sad-sack look that said he wondered what the hell Nick had done wrong now. At least to Mama he was still darling Nicky and always would be. But that wasn't enough to overcome being around Pops. They would probably all be better off if the man croaked, but Nick wasn't sure he was ready to contemplate the idea of life without the old fart around. At least not until he found a way to get respect from the man, some acknowledgment or recognition, maybe even just a lousy pat on the back.

Aah, forget it, feeling too good now to think about that crap. Freak he might be, but Jericho's junk sure packed a kick. Sundown soon, almost time to go creep Ginny Oslund's house. See if she was done with yoga and ready for a shower. Oh sweet bitch, when that girl arched over to dry her legs, what a shot. And always right across from the window. *That ain't no accident.* He cranked up the music and kicked the Porsche a little, figuring he could get away with ten over the speed limit.

CHAPTER SEVEN

Brady Spain hit the office early Monday, anxious to get his move arranged without blowing off work. Never mind that he couldn't think of anything except the fantasy life about to become his; a three-week employee pushing for promotion best not go off playing hooky. Though after two near-sleepless nights and driving out to Heron Point three times on Sunday to look at his new home, he'd be ready for a straitjacket if it didn't happen today.

He'd packed his few possessions the day before, but utilities had yet to be arranged and something done for furniture. By late morning he did get the electricity hooked up over the phone after authorizing a credit check, though the water company insisted he come in person. That burned his lunch hour, and even worse, he had to pony up a hundred and fifty bucks for a deposit. He recalculated his checkbook balance twice to be sure he could cover it. The old piggy bank had dwindled down to loose change after the monster he'd written Lexy.

The cold-fish little accountant gnome who lived in one corner of his brain kept reminding him that an apartment might've been a smarter choice, but damn it, he could do that in Sanford. And forget any idea of Mom being happy giving up both her little house and her gardening. Not going to happen. Besides, he had the salary to afford his new place if he could just get through all the transition expenses.

He took a pause from the miserable, ancient computer he

was grappling with to glance at his watch. Of all days, one of the Stone Age front-desk PCs had chosen today to collapse under the weight of the network Brady was building. The new hardware he had on order hadn't arrived yet. So he had taken his office machine out to the resort for the meantime, and was now mired in coaxing the files they needed to retain from the dying hard drive on this one.

A shadow slid across the PC screen, and he looked up to see Ed Schlatt, his boss, leaning into the doorway. Ed was a poster child for the business dork look, from his Clark Kent specs down to his lace-up wingtips, but a pretty nice guy to work for. "Yes sir, what's up?"

"Why don't you get out of here a little early?" Ed said, jerking his head in the general direction of the front entrance. He tapped out a little drum roll with the fingers he had wrapped around the doorjamb. "Get started on your move before the traffic hits."

"Thanks, boss." A surge of contentment enveloped him, a sense of being in the right place, wanted and accepted. Even if Ed was just eager to lose a nonrevenue houseguest it still felt good. "Believe I'll take you up on that, if I can finish recapturing these files." He rapped a knuckle on the time-grimed keyboard. " 'Fraid once I shut her down, they'll be gone for good."

Ed twitched his nose with the dismissive air of the guy who knows more than everyone else. "Don't worry, we've got backup discs. Company policy, every week."

Well, that was smug enough to make this little nugget fun to share. Brady rotated his chair and leaned back in it to make eye contact without twisting his neck. "Yes sir, I understand that. But this is exactly why we're moving to cloud storage as soon as we can, plus a redundant external drive; because so far no one can find the discs, and this thing doesn't have long to live.

Thought we'd better save everything we can, just in case."

Ed stared at him for a beat, then closed his eyes and let go of one of those suffering sighs only management types can perfect. He popped his eyes back open and did another fingertip rat-a-tat on the jamb. "Sounds like I need to do some records accounting at the other properties before this happens again." He pushed away from the doorframe. "Glad you're on the job, Brady."

He started down the hall and then stopped and turned back. "You don't like giving up on anything, do you?"

"Well, no." Brady grinned at him, still basking in the praise of a moment before. "Let me know if I get carried away and it's a problem."

"Oh no, it's a good trait in business." He smiled back and flapped a hand. "Anything I can do for you, then?"

Brady wanted to say, since you mention it, let's talk about my future in this business, but now was too soon and he had more immediate concerns anyway. As in furniture, and Ed should be knowledgeable on that. "Do you know the best place to go for household stuff around here, especially like a bed?"

"That's right, you said you were starting from the ground up, didn't you?" Ed strode into Brady's office, leaned across the desk, and snatched up the telephone. He paused with the handset halfway to his ear and said, "I think I can do you one better than that. Do you want just new or does slightly used work for you?"

Brady scooted his chair back as far as was possible in his closet-sized cubicle to make room, not sure what all he had just set in motion here. "Anything in good shape suits me, and saving money sure won't hurt my feelings," he said cautiously. He watched Ed punch in a four-digit code unfamiliar to him and listened to Ed's side of the call.

"Dorinda? Ed Schlatt here. Have you finished rotating out

the mattresses? . . .

"Are they still there in the storage room? . . .

"Thanks, keep them there until tomorrow, okay? . . .

"All right, have a good evening." He cradled the receiver and turned to Brady. "Right there where you're staying, Duneside. Glad you asked, or I'd've never thought of it. Look them over, find one you like, and take it. They're all going to charity anyway."

Brady felt his eyes widen and wondered if he was goggling. How lucky could a guy with a two-digit bank account get? Then his exhilaration got cut short by the sudden insight that scoring freebies off the company might not fit the image he wanted. He still carried some scar tissue from his bartending gig in college, which had ended rudely when he got canned for drinking a free beer at shift end. Ironic too, because it was the night manager's little tradition, giving the whole crew a round on the house. How was Brady to know it was verboten? But when the liquor count started showing up short, the classic red flag of a skimming bartender, the owner learned of that tradition and bounced the manager on the theory of a thief is a thief. And fired the entire shift with him.

He shook his head at the memory of how stunned he'd felt when the bar owner dropped the axe. Brady wasn't going to lose his shot at management from the same mistake.

"Quite all right if you aren't interested," Ed said, apparently misinterpreting Brady's headshake. He rapped his knuckles on the desktop and put on one of those rubber smiles that were more of a face stretch than an expression. "Let me know if you change your mind."

"No, no, it's not that." Brady got to his feet, beginning to feel that he looked like the stereotypical slacker techie, all kicked back in his chair in front of the general manager. "If it's like the one in my room, I'm in love with the way it sleeps. I just don't want the company to lose anything on me. I'd rather pay something for it, at least the tax write-off you'd lose if nothing else." Great going, mister bigmouth, with what money? Unless . . . "Maybe deduct whatever that is from my payroll account?"

"There's no need, but if that's how you want to do it, fine," Ed said, his eyes inscrutable through the shrinking effect of his glasses. "Hundred bucks sound fair?"

"More than. I really appreciate this, sir." Best deal he'd ever gotten on a mattress and possibly the smartest hundred bucks he'd ever spent. He leaned across the desk and thrust out his hand.

Ed took the hand, a hint of glitter showing now in the micro-sized eyes, though still unreadable to Brady. "Good, then. You can take their pickup truck to move it if you like." His head turned to the wall clock and back. "Maintenance won't be using it at this hour. Now finish up so you can get out of here."

Brady flopped back into his chair after Ed vanished down the hallway, hoping he had played it right. The guy was more perceptive than he looked, because he couldn't have picked up on Brady's stubborn streak just from today's computer fiasco. Had to be a trend he'd noticed, despite the practiced easygoing demeanor that usually kept Brady's iron-headed side well hidden. He had no answer to why his obstinacy toward conceding defeat at anything should feel so personal that he had this compulsive need to camouflage it. He just knew he felt exposed and vulnerable if anyone noticed how much it mattered to him to never quit, never give in. Maybe because of the humiliating way it became a mantra for him, fifteen years ago.

That was when fourteen-year-old high school freshman Brady had crossed the athletic field one afternoon, long enough after the final bell for the campus to be near-deserted. Three up-perclassman redneck types, the kind who already sported beards and nicotine-stained teeth, approached and surrounded him, announcing that they were "gonna teach this pencil-neck Flip a lesson." Brady never did figure out what their lesson was supposed to be, but he learned one, all right: don't stay down.

Not because he was tough. He'd always been the scaredy-cat type, running from any confrontation. And that day he went down quickly after the first couple of slaps to the head. But once down, he learned that their shit-kicker boots hurt way worse than any fist they could throw. So he got up, and kept getting up, in sheer desperation for survival. Just as he reached the point of believing he wouldn't be able to rise again, his attackers ran out of gas. The leader gave Brady one last half-hearted shove and said, "Forget it. Let's ride, boys. Damn Flip's too stupid to even know when he's gittin' his ass beat."

Brady had lain there in the mud, gulping air and listening to the mutters of "crazy" and "dumbfuck" from the departing wrecking crew, scared witless that they would come back. But they didn't, and for the rest of the year, they crossed to the far side of the hallway or parking lot at the sight of him and avoided any eye contact. Brady never reported the beating, out of embarrassment and the inescapable feeling that somehow he had gotten the best of the three goons. Ever since, he had believed in the power of perseverance over any other talent or advantage. After all, the tortoise did win the race. But he did feel uncomfortable about Ed's ability to see it, good business trait or not.

The blank screen in front of him sprang to life as a cascade of hieroglyphics came scrolling across it and yanked his attention back to the job. Hallelujah. Upload completed. He retrieved the thumb drive and shut the worthless junker down, officially declaring it now the world's largest paperweight, and hit the lights on his way out. "Paradise, here I come."

CHAPTER EIGHT

For Leo Burgess, Monday arrived with a ball of snakes and dropped them in his lap. Justin, a climbing young star in Leo's real estate office, called to warn that Arn Holstad was poised to back out of a contract for the purchase of ninety-plus acres. An annoying time to find the patience for any of Arn's hysterics; Leo had set the morning aside for a sit-down with Nick before this peeping scandal escalated into a full-out manhunt. But business came first.

"I'm very sorry for disturbing you with office matters," Justin was saying. "It's just such a sizeable deal, and I know you know Mr. Holstad."

"Quite all right," Leo allowed. True, he'd retired from active business some time ago, and no longer had any enthusiasm for the daily grind of the speculation game. All he wanted was a chance to savor the power and influence he'd earned and watch his children grow into their birthright. It had been a long climb from the three-room tenement flat in Brooklyn that had been more than enough to surpass the humble dreams and aspirations that led his parents to leave their native Ukraine for a better life in the land of opportunity.

Once retired, however, Leo had soon discovered he couldn't bring himself to delegate away the decision-making control of his personal portfolio, and thus he stayed involved in any deals that chipped away at the remainder of his private holdings. Especially this piece: inland, not on a highway, not on a corner, not near the business district. He'd known it would be a tough sell when he split it off of the subdivision-sized tract it came from, but he'd netted sufficient profit on the prime sections to make it worth whatever he lost on this one. Not that he minded talking business with a young man of Justin's caliber. He could close his eyes and pretend it was Nick who was young and hungry and smart and learning. "Tell me, what's Arn's issue with the loan?"

"It's not the appraisal or his credit; it's that he's stretched thin enough the lender wants more cash participation from him. He's not willing to pony up more, so neither side is budging."

Leo sighed and scratched his ear instead of throwing the phone. Typical imbecilic ego-posturing from Arn. "How far apart?"

"Ten percent. They want to carry seventy, not eighty," Justin answered. Short and boiled down, the way Leo liked it.

He swiveled his chair around to watch the surf lumbering in from the Gulf outside his study window. Any seventy percent mortgage offer for undeveloped commercial property in the current loan market qualified as manna from God himself, tenfold for a project of Arn's. And though Leo owned his own bank, it wasn't set up for multimillion-dollar construction loans. It was there to facilitate selling off scrubland as mobile home parks. Not that he wanted to be the one holding Arn's paper anyway, the man's business model smelled like a bankruptcy waiting to happen. But the trader's instinct that built his empire told him there was little probability of selling this odd lot again for anything near Arn's contract. "Justin, in your opinion, if we had to sell that tract for ninety percent of what we agreed to with Arn, would we take it?"

"I would recommend it," said Justin, showing more caution in his voice now, but at least Leo didn't hear the tap dancing he despised from a subordinate. *Good boy. Ah, Nicolas, why not you?*

"It'd have to be someone who wants to do a strip mall like Mr. Holstad," Justin continued. "Or something similar, and those buyers are hard to come by. Someone who can actually swing the deal."

"I agree," Leo told him. He spun his chair back and let his gaze wander the rich, dark wood interior of his office, each piece handpicked from fifty-year-old memories of the wealthy homes his immigrant house-painter father had serviced. He decided that the most prudent course here would be to risk a little profit and ram this deal through, get the ninety percent in the bank. "Have a personal note for the ten drawn up between Arn and me. Make it for something else other than land, for God's sake, to avoid any secondary lender liability. If he goes under, I want the bank owning the land, not me."

Nick slouched in and dropped into a chair while Leo was wrapping up with Justin. Leo disliked continuing to hash over creative ways to not lose profit after the decision was made, but he appreciated Justin's meticulousness. He did not relish wrangling with Nick either, but it had to be done. So he let Justin finish his questions while eyeing his son. The boy looked poorly, bloodshot and pasty-faced. Pete had hinted about drug use, something Leo could not believe. Nick merely liked the nightlife, as young men often do. Perhaps too much, based on his appearance.

What Leo did suspect, despite his son's protestations to the contrary, was the likelihood that Nick was indeed the Peeping Tom. It pained Leo to think his son capable of such warped behavior, but the boy had similar escapades as an adolescent, skulking around girls' locker rooms and such. Easier to hush up and shrug off the antics of a teenager than to keep a grown man out of jail. One never knew when one might encounter a policeman who couldn't be persuaded financially. Or when one might not luck into someone as penurious and thus susceptible as Pete Cully for the sole witness. They had been fortunate in Pensacola and might not be next time. Leo cradled the telephone and swiveled his chair to cross legs too long for the desk to accommodate.

"You wanted to see me, Pops?" Nick asked, slumping even deeper into the chair. Insolence and wariness fought for control in his voice.

Leo took a deep breath and recommitted to ignoring the boy's galling demeanor. "Yes, Nicolas, I need your help with a matter."

"What kind of help?" Nick's eyes shifted about, signaling victory for wariness.

"As you may have heard, we have received more reports of a prowler in the neighborhood." Leo raised his jungly eyebrows until he got a nod, noting how the skin tightened along Nick's forehead. *Does this subject alarm you, son?* "I am considering hiring a security man, private detective if you will, to resolve this problem ourselves." *And perhaps keep you out of prison.* "I do not feel that this recurrent police activity represents the image we want in Heron Point. I would like your opinion."

"I don't know, Pops." Nick sat up and leaned forward, making the overly direct eye contact of the practiced manipulator, a disappointing proclivity with which Leo was all too familiar. "I'm not sure some broken-down rent-a-cop snooping around is the image we want either."

The uncharacteristic caution in Nick's tone heightened Leo's suspicions. Which, of course, was the real purpose of the questions. He cared nothing for Nick's opinion. Never had, and he'd begun to conclude that he never would. "Then you believe our problem will go away by itself." *Say yes, Nicolas. Please.*

"Hey, we don't even know there is a prowler," Nick sneered. "No burglaries or assaults, right? Just a guy walking around.

Has anyone gotten a good look at him?"

Leo shook his head. *And does this news make you glad, Nicolas?* "My fear is that this man is one of our residents, and therefore my wish is that we don't suffer the stigma of having an arrest here. Hence the idea of our own security detail." *To keep you out of prison, son.*

"Whatever. It's your money, Pops." He flipped a hand and assumed an earnest, responsible expression. "Say, speaking of residents, have you thought any more about letting me have my own house here? I think I'm really ready."

Leo rose and crossed to the far wall to adjust the vertical blinds against the encroaching glare. Time for another deep breath and a slow count. Was the boy too delusional to comprehend the stakes at hand here?

"I will be glad to, Nicolas." He returned to his desk and the only chair he'd ever found that truly fit his oversized frame. "As soon as you find employment. You are well aware that I would be quite happy to find a position for you in any one of our businesses."

"Aw, Pops, I want my own crib first. See, then I'll want to get a job." He collapsed back into his customary slouch. If one could stamp one's feet while sitting, Leo believed Nick would have. "Lexy's got one, and I know she doesn't pay you for it."

It was an old argument, one that Leo bore no interest in rekindling. "Alexandra has a job. One at which she is doing well. And that is still a prerequisite. It certainly would be so for you to arrange residence elsewhere." Exasperated, Leo added, "And need I remind you, she has accomplished this despite being younger than you. I recommend you spend more time worrying about Nicolas and less time on Alexandra."

"I recommend somebody worry about how to keep her pants on," Nick snickered.

Leo slammed his plate-sized palm on the desk, rattling the

windows. "I will not have you speak of your sister in that manner. Do you hear me?" He felt the flames only Nick could ignite licking at his gut and clamped his hands together to control them. He knew his daughter to be incapable of such infamy. He lost the battle for control and smacked the desk again. "Is there nothing beneath your dignity, boy? Now go say good morning to your mother before you go off and do whatever it is you do."

The boy even walks impudently, Leo thought as he watched his son's departing back. And of course, he left the door open. Leo rose and circled the desk to close it, unable to stomach any further exchange. Not boy, man, he corrected himself. A thirty-year-old man who needed to be kicked out of the nest, but if Leo did so, Anna would be impossible to live with. The daffy woman believed herself fortunate to have her faultless, doting son at home. Besides, who would then take care of situations like this for Nick?

Leo continued to harbor a small hope that Nick was not their stalker, and a secondary hope that the mere hiring of an investigator would rein him in if he was. Otherwise, the only clean solution Leo could see was for Nick to be caught *in flagrante delicto.* Then they could address the sickness head-on. But he must be caught by their own man, someone Leo had bought and paid for, instead of by the police. Thus they could handle everything quietly, privately.

Pete would know someone; he understood the extent of loyalty Leo required and the lucrative rewards such service paid. Leo returned to his desk and picked up the phone.

Digger Carrero checked his rearview mirror again, moving just his eyes so no one in the sheriff's car riding his bumper would see him looking. Still back there, for two blocks now. Looked like a female cop, old bitch-pig tracking the Digger man. He twisted the cap back onto his bottle of Mickey's Malt Liquor and eased it under the seat. He glanced at the speedometer to be damn sure he wasn't going too slow. Heat would pull him over for that sooner than speeding, figuring he be poking along so slow because he was roasting some weed.

After another half-block of grandma driving he saw what he needed, a gas station. Didn't need no gas, needed an unsuspicious pull-off to get outta this bitch's way. No hanging warrants he knew of, but he had the open Mickey's and three twists of crystal in the car. And since he wanted to get himself a woman tonight, if that soft-tail badge back there cruised on by, it would be like a sign, proof that she wanted him to have one. Not one of them wore-out beasts from the skank zone he lived in, either. Although he liked the way he could get away with busting them up a little, made getting on that thang all the sweeter. They were scared of him, thought he got called Digger from all the graves he dug for people he'd iced. None of them skags knew he became Digger from picking his nose so much in school. He used to hate that name, but man, some nicknames can't be escaped. He liked it now, with the reputation he had spread around about it.

He slid the Cutlass up alongside the island and reached across to crank up the passenger window against the raw smell of the gasoline that the dumbass at the pump next to him had slopped all over the ground.

No, tonight he was gonna have him one of them ponytail girls, in their spandex and halter tops out jogging or biking or whatever. Digger knew women didn't care about exercising, they can't grow no muscles. They just out jogging and all for one reason. Show off that thang. Especially those prissy ones in the subdivisions, all fixed up like a fashion show. They needed a man like Digger to show them what they really wanted, their purpose in life. And man, he loved the way they cried when he showed them.

'Course, he'd have to slap his ponytail girl around some too, imagine it was his sister Roni, payback for all the shit she used to do when she raised him. He hated the power she still held over him, hated knowing he couldn't even get hard unless he imagined it was Roni begging and crying and giving up some of that ass. But only if he pictured her like she looked at fourteen, making him wear a rubber band around his joint all day whenever he had wet the bed. Now she just another fat ugly bitch with about seventeen of her own kids stinking up the nasty-ass trailer she lived in.

He nodded to himself as he watched the cruiser coast on by, then settled back in the driver's seat and let his fingers tap out a beat on the wheel. Decision made. Got to have him one. Tonight. He turned north onto Shoreline Drive and kept tapping, starting to cook a little rhythm now. Man, he could smell the rich girl perfume already.

CHAPTER NINE

J.D. Macken browsed impatiently up and down the aisles of Goolsby's Ace Hardware, wishing the old lizard in the clerk's smock would leave him alone. There was such a thing as too much customer service. How in the hell was a man supposed to shop for a murder weapon?

"No, really, I'm just killing time before a meeting," J.D. said for the eighty-fifth time. He slid back around to the gardening aisle, trying to refocus his thoughts.

He had decided on a burglary scenario for the dirty deed, and knew that to carry it off he must think like a burglar and go through all the motions of one. Like the method actor concept he'd read about somewhere. So now he stood torn between buying a tool that a burglar would likely carry, one that would also work as an effective weapon, or finding some deadly but innocuous home and garden item a scared intruder might snatch up.

The call had come Sunday, as if in answer to his prayers. Mama Jean had been hospitalized again for her fluttery heartbeat. Now all J.D. could think of was Lexy, how she smelled, how she tasted. His mind kept replaying the wild, wanton, downright depraved things they'd done to one another Saturday. The anticipation of having her every day was about to make him explode. Damn if he hadn't caught a woody right here in the hardware store at the thought of it. But he'd best get back on task right now. Ellie was making noises about flying up to Richmond, though her aunt was with Jean for now. J.D. needed to get his plans set before the woman died, if he got so lucky, because he'd have to attend the funeral with Ellie.

"Hot time of year for yard work, isn't it?" The voice came from right over his shoulder. J.D. flinched and whacked his head on a hanging rack of axe handles.

"Ouch, shit." He clutched his forehead and spun to see the clerk's face sprouting up over the aisle partition like a pop-up genie. "Don't do that. You'll kill a customer someday."

He glanced at his hand for any sign of blood, listening to the old man clomp off muttering. No way that prune-faced pain in the ass would forget this transaction now, so he'd damn well better pick out a common everyday purchase. Good idea on the seasonal aspect, though, got to give it to the geezer for that. J.D. had considered driving to another county to do his shopping, but he knew that would be a serious sign of guilt if discovered later.

Best of all, he believed he'd landed on a stroke of genius with his obituary plan—write up something flowery that mentioned Jean's wealth obliquely and named Ellie as her sole descendant. Get it published in the local paper as a moral support for his wife and, presto, instant burglary motive. Then just wait for the will to go through probate. As long as he could keep Lexy's mouth shut. Otherwise, there'd be a burglary at her house instead.

And oh-ho, what do we have here? A set of oversized barbecue utensils: cleaver, skewer, fork, and tongs. Very seasonal and much too long to fit in any drawer. Perfectly natural to hang them on a peg within easy reach of a freaked-out burglar.

Brady swung the borrowed pickup to the far curb to make the turn into his driveway, forced to go wide around a car parked along the curb out front. It looked like Lexy's Jaguar, with a

60

silhouetted figure in the passenger seat. The setting sun's reflection off her tinted windows obscured any detail, though he saw no one on the driver's side. Seemed an odd place for her to sit in her own car. Then he spotted her sitting on his stoop as he pulled up the drive. He hopped out and circled the truck, heart dropping. What had gone wrong? Was she unable to hold the check? Or, God forbid, had he added wrong and bounced the other one?

"Hey, all right, Brady, nice bed," she called out as he approached, flashing that mind-bending smile.

Well, cool. Her greeting didn't sound like he'd been evicted before he got in. Must be some minor glitch. He glanced back at the mattress set trussed up and riding high in the truck bed. Looked pretty redneck, but hey, it didn't blow off during the trip.

"Yeah, I hate that it looks like the hillbillies have come to town," he said, grinning. "But as much as I like the hardwood floors, I didn't think they'd be fun to sleep on."

"No, seriously, I mean it. Simmons is a good name, and that looks like a pretty deep pillow-top you've got there." She stood and tugged down the hem of her shorts. Yellow ones today.

So maybe she'd be willing to try out the mattress with him? Much as the mere thought of it set his blood humming, he had nowhere near the nerve to ask. "Ought to be, what they charge per night where I work," he answered with a laugh, hoping his face hadn't told on him. "What's up?"

"Oh, I just remembered you saying you were coming tonight, so I wanted to bring a little housewarming gift." She reached behind her and held up a bottle of wine and a vase of pink and red flowers with petals like roses but a shape more like a daffodil. "Welcome to paradise."

He gathered in his loot, feeling shy and awkward. Not so much because of the gifts, more the weird sense of intimacy that came with them. "Thanks. My first time getting flowers from a, uh, lady."

"It's okay, Brady." She winked and patted his arm. "You can call me a girl. And I know guys, so I felt pretty confident you wouldn't bring your own."

"Would you like to come in, help me with this?" He hoisted the wine. "Invite whoever that is waiting in your car." Probably her boyfriend, with his luck, but might as well know now.

"Thanks, but no, I've got to rush." She patted him again and skipped down the steps, nimble as an alley cat. "We'll see each other soon, okay? You've got my number. Call me for anything."

Brady set down the flowers to wave as she motored off. *All right, I've scored some housewarming booze,* he thought, *maybe there's room on a credit card for something to eat.* He glanced at the vase. Leaded crystal, not from ye olde local supermarket. Pretty flowers, too, but he had no clue as to what kind they were. Pink and red whatevers. One thing for sure. This was the nicest place Brady had ever been, and he had only lived here an hour. Now if he could just get lucky on what her "call me for anything" might include. Because he couldn't think of anything he had ever wanted as much as he wanted to hold that incredible body in his hands.

CHAPTER TEN

Pete Cully thumbed his phone off and leaned his head back, eyes shut against the sun's glare. A private eye? Really? To "identify and apprehend" the Peeping Tom? Who the hell was Leo kidding? The old man had a habit of deciding what he wanted the truth to be and massaging the facts to fit, but this was a pip. And for a guy trying to duck anything connected to digging Nick out of the hole he'd made for himself, Pete wasn't having much success. He finished spooling the new line onto his weed whacker and tossed it in the truck bed. Seemed his lawn wouldn't get done today after all.

What it meant was, Leo knew damned well that Nick was the one stalking these women and he figured to keep the cops out of it by a show of diligence. For Pete's money, it was a bad move on Leo's part because not everybody had a blind eye for sale. Which mattered as much as a gnat on an elephant's ass— when Leo didn't ask for an opinion, he didn't want one, and he was the boss. And true, Pete did know a guy. He fired up the truck and nosed into traffic, headed downtown.

The odds said he would have to leave a message for Gerry Terence, but he got lucky. The man was in. A dingy little office in a shabby building smelling of crumbling paint and mildew, but from the movies Pete had seen, that was expected of a private detective. Gerry waved him in and shook his hand in an easy manner, as if he had been sitting and waiting for Pete, though they hadn't even talked in over a year.

They looked each other over as old high school pals do, checking hairlines and waistlines. Gerry was definitely the dumpier of the two, but dumpy the way a roll of chain link was dumpy, Pete knew. Twenty years as a street cop had only hardened the power of the undefeated collegiate wrestler's body. Hard to believe it was five years since Gerry retired from the force.

"So, Pete." Gerry leaned back in his chair and clasped his hands behind his head, eyeing Pete with the same relaxed, neutral expression that Pete had seen more than one of those wrestling opponents misjudge. "Personal or professional visit?"

"I'd like to say personal, bro, and maybe it is, since you're the only guy I can trust with this." And the only private eye he knew, too. "But I'm here because my boss needs to hire you."

Gerry returned his chair to upright with a *sproing*, leaning forward with his forearms on the desktop. He picked up a pencil and slid it back and forth between his fingers, a brief glow showing in the mild eyes that maybe only a friend of almost forty years would notice. "Here for big Leo, eh? What does he need done?"

"Ah, jeez, where to start." Pete took his cap off and finger-combed his hat hair. *Aw, quit dithering,* he told himself, *this is Gerry. Just lay it out.* So he did, omitting his suspicions of Nick out of fairness to Leo.

When he finished, Gerry sat without speaking for a minute, tapping the pencil and staring out the window. "I'm not quite clear yet," he said finally. "Do you want to identify your stalker or are you trying to deter further incidents?"

Pete scratched his head and put his cap back on, etiquette be damned. "Both, I think." That depended on Leo's purpose with this, which he really did not want to know.

"Solving a Peeping Tom case is tough. It's a nonstarter as a criminal offense without a witness who can identify the guy, a witness who'll swear out a warrant and testify. For a deterrent, you just need a security guard." Gerry held up a hand when Pete opened his mouth. "Which I'm not saying I won't do. Glad of the work. But I charge the same to play rent-a-cop."

"That's fine. Leo doesn't want a security guard. He said two or three times that he wants his own detective on the case." Pete frowned. Was it fair to his friend to not at least hint at what Leo's "own detective" might mean? "But I guess I'd better know what it is you do charge."

"Six hundred a day. Plus expenses. Which, by the way, is not padding like gas or food, only job-specific expenses. And you get a real workday for that, not a gate-guard shift."

"I think he'll go for that," Pete said, nodding. He reluctantly decided it'd be just too unethical to spout off his suspicions of Leo's motives while banking the man's checks, but God a'mighty if he didn't feel like the fellow who drops the flag between two cars to start a game of chicken. "Start Thursday night? Like I said, this guy seems to be a weekend warrior."

"Maybe he works weekdays, maybe he knows his targets and when they're home." Gerry shrugged. "We'll see. How sure are you that you have a Peeping Tom and not just some guy out looking for his cat?"

"Pretty sure." Pretty damn sure another poor luckless girl would get raped, too, if something didn't happen soon. "Susan Leland saw him one time, at a neighbor's window, and she's sharp. Got all the subtlety of a bullhorn, but I'd bank on her."

Gerry cocked his head to one side and squinted. "Any description?"

"Nah, it's always in the dark." Pete felt like an idiot for not providing any real help when he wanted to say two words: Nick Burgess. Whatever came out of this mess, he wanted to make sure it included that boy getting his. "Medium height, medium build, medium, medium, medium. They think he's white. That's the best I got."

★ ★ ★ ★ ★

Sara Zeletsky finished changing clothes, gooped herself with bug repellent, and slammed out of the house with twenty minutes of daylight left. Maybe if she gave up her lunch hour and ate at her desk at the Rosenguild law firm where she worked as an associate, she could get home at a decent hour, but there was just no way to shorten the commute. She had tried every route possible.

She started at a mini-trot as she turned east on Palm Avenue on her way to the pedestrian path that ran along Shoreline Drive. She liked to wait until her lungs fully expanded and the sweat popped out before she kicked into full jogging speed.

Running along a busy state route like Shoreline Drive made her nervous, especially at dusk. She worried about a drunk driver careening off the roadway, or a tourist who was unfamiliar with all the curves and lost sight of one in the twilight. But the path was easily the best around, and very picturesque as it wound through the palms along the water's edge. She especially loved it at this time of year, when the invigorating ocean smell combined with the sweet scent of the wildflowers that bloomed after sunset.

The solution she would not consider was skipping her jog. In less than three months of running a minimum of five evenings a week, she had seen tremendous improvement in her figure and particularly her hips and legs. She started this program back in May when the pool parties kicked off. Though she hadn't developed a weight problem, knock on wood, her body was beginning to sag and lose definition. She had noticed her shape molding to her swimsuit instead of the other way around. Gross. Not ready for that at twenty-eight. And she had improved so much, so quickly, now all she could think about was having her butt look as good as Ginny Oslund's. She'd always felt so insecure about bringing any of her dates anywhere near Ginny.

She reached Shoreline and turned up the path, reassuring herself that after all, she was at least ten to twelve yards from the road in most places, and she was facing the traffic. She'd have time to see any danger and jump out of the way, even in the fading light. Besides, the sound of the gentle breakers was so soothing it always made the exercise seem effortless, and the way the shadows of the swaying palm fronds flitted across the phosphorescence of the surf looked romantic enough for a postcard. The thought popped into her head that this would be a gorgeous backdrop for a sunset wedding. She moved up to cruising speed as she followed the curve dipping down around a cluster of barrel palms near the water's edge.

A sudden rush of footsteps behind, and she glanced over her shoulder. A figure, no more than a looming outline in the dusk, closing in on her fast. She tried to accelerate in a spurt of panic, but a wrenching tug of her hair slammed her down on her back. The impact against the concrete sent a hot spasm of pain up her spine. Through a haze of semi-consciousness, she felt hands pulling her up to her knees and she sobbed with relief. Someone was here to help!

Then a band circled her neck, tightening, tightening. Her clawing fingers identified it as leather, the size of a belt. She tried to scream before her air cut off, but a hand reeking of stale beer clamped over her mouth. She stifled the vomit that rose in her throat in response to the rank, callused palm pushing against her teeth, certain that this monster would let her choke on it. Hot breath in her ear.

"Now hush up, bitch," the hot breath said. "You're gonna like this. I got exactly what you been thinking about when you got all fixed up for this party of ours. You look real nice, so I'm gonna give it to you."

A yank at the belt forced her head back, her neck arching in a desperate fight for air. She strained her eyes from side to side as far as she could without tightening the belt's hold, looking for someone, anyone, to please help. How could there be no one on Shoreline Drive within hearing of their scuffling? Then she remembered the cluster of barrel palms and she knew no one was going to hear or see. *Please, God, someone help.*

Hot Breath dragged her along by pulling the belt, Sara scrabbling frantically on all fours to keep some slack in her noose. Deeper into the trees and the beautiful shadows that now became the setting of her worst nightmare, down near the masking noise of the relentless surf. The nightmare man kept making a horrible chuckling sound, and Sara realized that rape might not be all he wanted; she was at the mercy of insanity. A shaft of shame pierced her terror when she realized with abrupt clarity that she so wanted to live she was willing to sacrifice her body, the source of all her pride just moments before.

Chapter Eleven

Ellie Macken was on her way to meet her lover. When J.D. called to tell her he would be working late, she wasted no time arranging the tryst, though she dreaded the painful yearning for more she'd feel when the clock struck and she turned back into a pumpkin.

She detested the cheating aspect, wanted to tell J.D., wanted to shout out her new love to the whole world. But her lover wasn't ready to go public, and Ellie understood they needed time for the bond to grow stronger. After all, the relationship was barely a month old. So even with the apprehension she felt about her mother's condition, she was not going to miss what might be her last day of happiness for a week or more. That thought brought up a mental image of how mortified her mother would be by her affair. Ellie shoved it out of her mind and focused on the happiness.

She turned down the radio, fiddled with the air conditioner, cracked her window, and tried to will the left turn signal to change. Had to be the longest light in Florida. Wading through traffic to get there was always the worst part. But also the best, she reminded herself with a smile. The prolonged anticipation was the most delicious part of sneaking around like teenagers.

No, the worst part of her life was the weekend, when she worked thirty-two hours of double-shift nurse duty at the hospital. Going home to J.D. was no picnic either. She longed for the day when she would wipe that smirk off his face with her news. He might not really care, as she felt sure he too had a lover—probably some bimbo who matched up to his porn fantasies. But she knew J.D., and he was so vain that it would bruise his ego even if he didn't want Ellie any longer.

She'd believed herself so lucky to marry such a gorgeous guy, easily the best looking on the whole UVA campus, believed his cocky confidence held the promise of a romantic, worry-free life together. Ten years later, she knew she should've seen that J.D. just loved J.D. Now she sickened at the sight of him preening and brushing and cologning and prancing around in a towel for ages. Yes, he was a beautiful man, but her lover was way better looking, and without all the rigmarole. Just stepped out of the shower that way. Even rolled out of bed looking great. Ellie had discovered what real love felt like, the kind that was meant to be, her once-in-a-lifetime person, and that was something she would do anything to keep.

Her skin still remembered the indelible erotic sensation from that first magical moment, when her lover had brushed a hand across Ellie's blouse where her nipple pushed taut, stared deep into her startled eyes and whispered, "Don't you think about doing this?" Seized by a reckless urge for something wild and dangerous to happen, Ellie had shocked herself by reaching up and unbuttoning her blouse. The gentle inquisitive hand slid in, the hungry mouth came down on hers and suddenly, the shy, theretofore-faithful Ellie Macken hadn't been able to get her clothes off fast enough.

The turn arrow glowed green at last. She shivered off her goose bumps, slammed down the gas pedal, and swung the Accord onto the highway. To hell with anticipation, she wanted to get there before her thighs went up in flames from all the wonderful dirty things she was thinking of doing.

★ ★ ★ ★ ★

When he caught the news flash on the television at Spahn's, Gerry Terence froze in mid-chew, oblivious to the half-eaten peanuts dribbling onto the bar. Not that one more rape assault shocked him, but having it happen near Heron Point the day he contracted for a job there sure did. He noticed his mess and scraped at it with a bar napkin while keeping his eyes on the report. No real information: this just in, reported moments ago, more details shortly, blah, blah, blah.

"Brian, get me another," he called, still watching as the news program cut to a commercial.

"I'm afraid that would be against the house rules, sir."

Not believing his ears, Gerry turned to face the sly grin of the barman, who placed a fresh Chivas rocks down in front of him.

"Only kidding, Mr. Terence. I've just never ever seen you have more than your one." He struck the pose Gerry had noticed too often for it to be anything but that, leaning on the bar at an angle that accentuated the gym-rat pecs and biceps bulging against his black tee shirt, which fit tight enough for a tourniquet. Just in case any ladies in the joint had missed out on what could be theirs for a night, Gerry presumed.

"Very cute, Brian. Glad to know somebody's keeping their eye on me," Gerry answered absently, his brain gnawing at the implications of what he had seen. "And easy on the Mr. Terence crap, okay? Just Gerry or just Terence is fine." Like he hadn't told Brian that at least a dozen times.

"You got it. I'm just glad you're gonna hang out with us a little." Brian swiped the bar, picked up the empty, and slid away. Not very far though, since Spahn's was a cozy ten-stool bar with only five or six tables scattered around it. Standard hotel lounge décor, deep sound-swallowing carpet, dim Tiffany chandeliers, and shelves of bottles arrayed across the mirrored back wall. Right next to Gerry's office, too, and always clean, quiet, well kept.

Gerry returned to the peanut bowl and television screen, sorting out what this development meant for him. His compassion for the victim and his outrage at the crime were there, to be sure, real and powerful, but automatically shunted to a corner by years of police work. Would this mean no job now? Start sooner than Thursday? Investigate the rape as well as the peeping? Should he call Pete, or Leo directly?

The newscast interrupted his pondering with an update. Still nothing concrete, just a live report from the scene with lots of blue and red lights flashing in the background. They did say the unnamed victim was believed to be a resident of Heron Point, the police were working diligently, and stay tuned for a special report: "Are Our Streets Safe?"

"You know, they've had a Peeping Tom running around Heron Point."

Gerry turned to see Brian standing nearby, watching the report with his arms folded across his chest in a flexed position sure to set off the saliva glands of any women who hadn't caught the bar pose. "Really?" He wondered if the peeper problem was known about outside of Heron Point more than Pete believed.

"Sure as hell do," Brian said, eyes flicking back and forth from Gerry to the television. "My girlfriend's got friends there. They've been worried about something like this. Shoulda caught that creep before this happened." He smacked a fist into his other palm.

"Yeah, it's too bad," Gerry muttered, not in the mood to hear a bunch of cop-bashing. Nor did he agree with the assumption that both crimes were the work of the same man, for the simple reason that so many of your true serial Peeping Toms never graduated to rape. The spying itself was their hot flash. Now, a stalker who peeped to handpick his victim, Gerry could buy that one. Pete had told him of the letter one of the violated women had received; the rape made it crucial that Gerry get a look at it. While he made no pretense of being an expert profiler by any means, he figured he could tell the difference between the writings of a guy just playing in his shorts and a lit fuse describing a fantasy he planned on acting out. The detective team assigned to the case would have a working theory he could wheedle out of them, but if he still had a job in Heron Point, he wanted his own opinion.

Go right now, he told himself. He slipped a twenty under the untouched second drink. Brian always tried the on-the-house line, thinking Gerry still had friends on the force. Which he did, but not enough pull to help Brian if he got his tail in a crack for serving minors or drunk drivers or whatever the motivation behind the obvious efforts to cultivate a cop buddy. Not that he was willing to be anybody's fixer even if he did have the juice for it, and he never had liked the free drinks for cops ploy anyway. Too close to graft and somehow condescending, as if he was their pet flatfoot.

As for his buddies in blue, surely he could find someone working the graveyard shift who knew him well enough to talk to him before the two cases got connected and blew up into a media circus. A crime like this in a neighborhood like Heron Point was destined to be a headline screamer and the brass would put the gag on everybody. But not yet, so tonight someone should be willing to show him that letter if he pretended he might be able to recognize the handwriting.

CHAPTER TWELVE

When J.D. Macken first heard, his gut reaction was, "Oh God, not Ellie." Chad, a neighbor who got off on others' misfortunes and loved any kind of nastiness, rang him at work with the news and told him that his oh-so-worried canvass of the neighborhood had identified Ellie as one of the residents unaccounted for. Nobody knew yet if the victim was dead or alive, either. J.D. blew off Chad and his bullshit pretense of concern and tried Ellie's cell phone. It rolled directly to voice mail; turned off.

He tossed the phone back at its cradle, leaned back in his chair and threw his pencil at the ceiling with enough force that it stuck in one of the little foam squares. Driven by emotions he was unable to sort through, all this worry and protectiveness about the woman he planned to kill, he sprang up and walked out without even shutting off the lights. He was going home and he hoped to God he would find Ellie there, in bed, snoring her skinny ass off.

The hell of it is, he thought, as he blew through three straight red lights, *why did I think of her instead of Lexy?* He grinned despite his anxiety when the answer hit him; any picture he conjured up of Lexy confronted by a rapist ended with her either seducing the asshole into one of her fantasies or beating the shit out of him. Tough, that girl. Ellie was more defenseless, adolescent even, with her moony-eyed romanticism and her head crammed with fairy tales.

But the real bitch was, why did he worry about Ellie at all?

Why wasn't he hoping she was the victim? Damn it. He was going to kill her anyway, so how perfect would it be if someone had taken care of it for him—he'd get Lexy and maybe at least some of the money later, all with no risk for him. Then why in the hell didn't he feel that way? Holy mother, now he was really fucking confused.

Maggie Davis hung up her phone too, pausing with her hand hovering to see if it would ring again. Jill was her third call in an hour to discuss the gruesome event and now Maggie felt a frantic urge to do something, anything, but she didn't know what. The worries and suspicions and finger-pointing she was hearing all sounded normal enough, except it carried a vicious undertone that was new. As if this one despicable act had stripped away an indefinable yet essential illusion for the women of Heron Point. The whole place seemed at a crossroads that overshadowed her inner crisis. And though Maggie had been longing for something to change her life, this wasn't it. It just made her want to crawl farther into the bottle and pull the cork shut behind her.

Jill had guessed the unlucky victim to be Sara Zeletsky, a quiet, shy, younger woman whom Maggie did not know well. Jill had noticed her leaving on her regular jog but hadn't seen her return. And that drowsy-eyed, detached air of Jill's hid an unrivaled radar; she didn't miss much. Anyone who bounced through lovers the way Jill did couldn't afford to.

Maggie hoped Jill was wrong, that Sara was safe. The few occasions she'd seen Sara, she reminded Maggie of her baby sister Kimmy. Sweet little too-young Kimmy, dead twelve years now, drowned in a motel pool on her senior spring break trip. With a blood alcohol level of point two three. Ironic how Maggie was taking the same way out, just slower. It was still difficult for her to think of Kimmy, though it seemed to be even worse for their brother Grant. He wouldn't talk about Kimmy at all. Of course, he wouldn't touch his trust fund either, their posthumous gift from the great patriarchal tyrant. Maggie saw it as better revenge to party her way through her share.

But if not Sara it had to be someone, and she realized that hoping it wasn't Sara was like wishing the horror on someone else. Truthfully, she wanted it to be someone she didn't know, although that thought made her feel like a bad person. She fixed herself a drink, knowing she'd already had too many again, but this was a day that called for too many. Consider it emergency medication. Help her sleep.

From the talk she'd heard, every woman in the Point felt furious that no one had arrested the Peeping Tom before this happened. Though she suspected they hadn't been too concerned about the peeper at the time, because she hadn't. More like something to laugh off. It was real creepy when she actually envisioned it, and she would feel terribly violated if she found out she had been spied on. But under one of the gnarly little rocks in the backyard of her mind, she had imagined it would be nice to be so hot that men would want to spy on her. No more. She had never fantasized about rape and she got really steamed whenever anyone said women did. God, she wanted to castrate the bastard.

She replenished her drink, figuring it only counted as a half since she hadn't quite finished it. She'd lost count again anyway. She took it to bed with her after rechecking the bolted doors and latched windows. Mark was already asleep in his separate bedroom, which was how Maggie liked it. She could finish her drink and think about things without hearing the popping noise he made with every inhalation.

Sitting on the edge of her bed and massaging her feet, she wondered if she was witnessing the end of the Heron Point she knew. Was this a rough patch or would it slide into becoming just another crime-ridden neighborhood with locked doors and strangers next door? Or had she just finally burned out on the same old cesspool of rumor and innuendo, and begun attributing a malignancy to Heron Point that was really her own? Maybe that was why she liked Brady so instantly. He seemed different than the usual new guy. He didn't throw money or his mouth around to prove he belonged. His easy friendly manner felt genuine, not the smarmy fawning of a status seeker, something they had too many of around here.

So what chance did she have of tearing Brady away from a goddess like Lexy? She'd seen the hot flash in his eyes when he looked at Lexy, and longed for a way to tell him how much better she would be for him. She felt like the girl in the old Pretenders song, the one who sings *Look at me!*

Maggie rose and walked over to the closet door mirror. She cupped her breasts in her hands and turned back and forth, giving them the critical eye. Not bad, especially after ten thousand Mai Tais, but no match for Lexy. Maybe she should get implants, or a lift done, but the idea of it always felt as though she'd be giving up on her true self. She didn't want to give up on Maggie yet. And whatever in the world was she going to do with poor old faithful, plodding Mark?

CHAPTER THIRTEEN

Brady awoke Saturday morning to the scent of honeysuckle drifting through his bedroom window, a fragrance so reminiscent of Peggy's perfume that for an instant he thought she was there. He hadn't encountered the smell before at the new house, but last night was his first time sleeping with open windows instead of air conditioning, thanks to a nice steady breeze that had moved in after Friday's dose of the daily thunderstorms.

He sucked in the sweet air and held it, wondering what she was doing at that moment—sleeping in, breakfasting, washing her hair? Was she happy? He rolled over and checked the clock. Wow, nine hours of coma. He'd needed it. Today was party day. He'd spent a lot of time traveling that week and felt pumped about the results. The two properties way down by Sarasota, Mariner's Retreat and Sandcastle, were up and on the new network, the new terminals in too.

He had busted a gut to get those two done by Friday, to have a guilt-free day off. When Susan stopped him in the street Wednesday and invited him to a poolside barbecue today, he'd made a vow to be there. Partly because blowing off his first invite seemed a surefire way to torpedo his social life before it ever left the pier, but his main drive was the hope of seeing Lexy there. He hadn't seen her since Monday, other than in daydreams, of which he'd had no more than, say, fifteen hundred or so.

After he first heard about Sara he thought the party might be canceled, until he learned more details and realized the invitation had come after the assault occurred. So the party-gang parties on. He agreed with the idea of not letting bad news become a killjoy, though he felt a little freaked out over the horrific nature of the crime and also the scoop about it being the guy who'd been peeking in windows for some time now, something he hadn't known was going on.

He took a cup of coffee out onto the porch after his shower and shave, promptly slopping half of it all over the place when he started at the sight of a four-foot-tall heron standing on his stoop. Damn thing stood so motionless that Brady had walked up to within ten feet of it before the bird turned its head and scared his pants off.

"Looks like you got you a friend there."

Brady whirled toward the voice, sloshing most of his remaining coffee down the front of the white Polo he'd selected for party wear. Great.

"You know, you learn to recognize those suckers, you'll see they favor particular hangouts. That one might figure this here is his yard." The speaker was a wide-body muscular type, the tree-dragger from the day Brady met Lexy. Up close he looked somewhere in the forties to fifty range, with close-cut salt and pepper hair showing beneath a Marlins cap and a grin like a picket fence a truck had crashed through. He was standing between the house and the hedges fronting it, next to the tree on the southeast corner.

"News to me," Brady answered, holding his scalding shirt away from his belly with thumb and forefinger. "I didn't see him until I almost ran into him. Scared the hell out of me. He sure doesn't seem too scared, though." And who the heck was this cat, hanging out in his bushes?

"Sorry if I did that to you," the man said, wagging a finger up and down in the direction of Brady's spreading stain. "I thought you saw me when you came out. I'm the guy who looks after things around here. Name's Pete."

"I'm Brady. I've heard how awesome you are, looked forward to meeting you. Something wrong I don't know about?" Like, something worth digging around in the yard at eight on Saturday morning?

The heron took flight without any preliminary move, just a sudden loud leathery flapping of the great wings that startled Brady again.

Pete chuckled and took his cap off, ran his other hand through his hair, and then replaced the cap. "Reckon he decided you're too big to eat, and we're too noisy for good company. They're 'bout the only birds what seem unaffected by all the people. I do believe most of the seabirds, gulls and such, wouldn't know how to feed themselves anymore without hotel balconies to eat off of."

Brady turned to watch the departing bird, feeling a lurch of discomfort at the way that sounded. Didn't sit too well to think he was a cog in the machine destroying Florida's avifauna. Did Pete know where he worked?

"Anyways, I just stopped to check out that laurel tree," Pete went on. "Noticed a diseased-looking side of it from the street angle that I hadn't seen before. Might have to come out of there."

Brady shrugged, the search-me variety. Kind of a downer, thinking about the tree being sick, but he wouldn't even know what to look for. "Anything I can do to help?"

"Naw, I'll just keep an eye on it for a few days." Pete tilted his head a touch, squinting at him. "I hear you're from Carolina, right, Brady?"

"Yes sir." Quite the non sequitur there, and a surprise that Pete knew any of his bio. But something about the guy's laid-back friendliness appealed in a way he hadn't yet felt here. A warm tingle climbed his spine at the thought that maybe Lexy had been talking about him.

"Good folks there. Got kin there myself, up Henderson way." Pete walked around the hedges and squatted down in the yard, fiddling with a sprinkler head that hadn't fully retracted. "Have any women living in the house, Brady?"

Well now, dang if that didn't belong in the none-of-your-business file. Then he remembered the rape and knew instinctively that this amiable, open-faced man was referring to it. "Nope, strictly a bachelor's pad." And this ugliness had thrown a little dirt on the idea of how great it'd be to drag Mom down here to live. "I heard about that nasty business, guess I'd be pretty jumpy right now if I had a family."

He hadn't been able to put his reaction to the news into coherent thought until that moment. Sure, he didn't need to worry, he wasn't a woman and he had no wife or daughter. But his undefined angst over the incident stemmed from a deeper sense of affront, or outrage, than he would've felt from a man-on-man crime. Now, whether that was gender shame, or good old-fashioned chauvinism, he couldn't say. It did feel a little better to at least identify his queasiness, though.

Pete gave the sprinkler a final twist, stood, and stomped it back down into its housing with a well-aimed boot. "Looks like a damn-fool thing to do, don't it, but sometimes that's all they need to hook back into their spring." He squinted up at the climbing sun. "Mostly I hate it for Sara, she's a nice girl. But I'd really hate if it happened again."

Brady was all for due vigilance, but Pete's vehemence made him wonder if he'd missed something. "I thought it didn't take place here in the neighborhood. She just happens to be a resident here, but the actual assault was over there near the highway, right?"

Pete smiled, the haywire teeth oddly charming, though his

smile didn't look to be one of real humor. "No, you're right, this is a nice safe neighborhood, one of the best. But it's just like that laurel there, Brady; it ain't smart thinking to assume there can't be a rotten spot, even in a place like this. I'll take off now, see you around."

Intrigued, Brady reached over and pulled the screen door open, locking the stopper in place. "Why don't you let me buy you a cup of coffee? Need another myself, seeing as how I'm wearing my first one. I'd like to hear more about the wildlife around here, animal and human."

Pete grinned again, a wide easy one with his eyes in it, and glanced at his watch. "Well, I 'spect I've got time for a half a cup, anyway."

CHAPTER FOURTEEN

Brady crossed the street a little after one to find the festivities cranking up. He estimated at least thirty people there already, milling about in scattered little clusters and leaning close to swap war stories over the reggae thumping out of a hidden sound system. He even saw one group floating around the pool in a giant inflatable life-raft-looking thing equipped with armrests and drink holders for eight. From the loose, raucous laughter coming from there, he felt confident in concluding that those drink holders were getting plenty of use.

Jill's pool was a big one by backyard standards, as was the flagstone patio surrounding it, and good thing too. In a smaller venue, he concluded, no way could a party with so many people still give off the lazy, timeless flavor he felt from the moment he walked in. Yep, this was the life, all right.

Snaking a path through the waving elbows and gesturing drinks, he said hey to Jill and Susan, the hostess and the source of his invite, respectively, as well as a couple of others he knew, but saw mostly new faces. He came up empty in his hopes of spotting a sleek, glossy mane of black hair. He nodded and hel-loed his way over to where a thirty-foot awning had been erected against the side of the house to shield the food and beverage from el sol. A guy wearing an apron that read "If you don't like the food, kiss my ass" over his trunks stood in front of the grill, waving a pair of tongs and a sweating Heineken bottle with equal enthusiasm.

Brady nodded to him and snared a Corona from the ice chest, taking it to an umbrella table for some shade. The no-Lexy thing had let a lot of the air out of his balloon, but he still wanted to hang out and soak up some of the feel of his new community. The barbecue smells wafting his way made him think of his mom's cooking for some reason, even though she didn't grill. Similar spicing, maybe. *Some swinging single you are, Spain, homesick at your first party.* He snickered to himself.

"Hey, what's so funny?" asked a voice below his shoulder.

He looked down to see a woman lying on a chaise about four feet from him. One of the bunch he'd met right here the day he signed up, but he couldn't remember her name. And wow, he never even heard her sit there, too busy inside his own skull.

"Oh, nothing, really," he said. "Man's got to laugh at himself now and then. Keeps you sane."

"Do tell." She smiled and rolled up on her side, propping her head on her hand. "I'm Ellie, we met last weekend. Would you do me a favor while I learn more about this personal sanity program?"

"Sure." Brady turned his chair to face her. Dang, she looked good in a bikini. Lean to almost skinny, but with super muscular definition, sculpted quads that accentuated the hollows of her inner thighs and a belly so flat that the bikini bottom showed a gap at the top where it strung across her hipbones. He also noticed her wedding ring, which was not his idea of fun, so never mind.

"If you could shift that table this way a bit, my face will be in the shade," she said, taking a few futile swipes at her neck and brow with a hilariously dainty little cloth no bigger than a Kleenex. "Keeps me a lot cooler when I'm laying out."

"Get skin cancer that way, you know," Brady teased. He got up and scraped the table back and forth a couple of times until the shadow looked right.

"I know, I know." She made an exaggerated pout. "Susan's right, you're lucky you don't have to worry about a tan."

Lucky? Brady sure felt like it now, but too bad she wasn't there in high school to explain it when Betsy Jensen's father forbade Betsy to date a "mixed race boy." Brady had been all prepared to do the defiant stance thing, run away together or Lord knows what, until Betsy said she understood why her dad felt that way. Cured Brady of that crush, though the hurt lingered a while. Not exactly something you share with a stranger at a pool party, however. "Hey, that brings up a good question," he said, going with the light touch instead. "Do us darker dudes get less skin cancer because of our pigment or because we don't sunbathe?"

She shook her head the way people do when they roll their eyes, though he couldn't see hers behind her Ray-Bans. "Did you grow up in the Philippines?"

"Nope, never been there. Grew up around a lot of Filipino culture early on, though." He made a quick scan of the premises, but still no Lexy.

"Really?" She flipped her shades up to the top of her head and leaned toward him as if genuinely interested, though it seemed like boring stuff to him. Neat eyes too, an unusual brown so light they flickered greenish-gold when in motion. "Like what?"

"Well, I spoke Ilocano as soon as English. Still can a little."

"Cool. I wish I had a second language. What else?"

"Hmmm." He struck a thoughtful pose, and then laughed. "It's not very different. Nothing exciting to tell. A lot more people around your house. Seems like all your relatives show up for dinner. I was six before I knew you could eat a meal without rice."

"Seriously?" She sat up and started toweling her back, using the full-size one she'd been laying on.

"Dead serious." He waved an arm at the smoking grill on the other side of the pool. "You take my dad over there and serve him one of those hot dogs, he'll walk right past the buns looking for the rice to eat with it."

She laughed. "You're putting me on."

"Maybe a little." He smiled back at her. "But just in the way I tell it. It really is the truth." He made another quick unsuccessful scan and turned back to see Ellie staring at him.

"If you're looking for Lexy, I don't think she's here." The improbable eyes narrowed. "And maybe I should warn you, she might not be as available as she acts."

Brady felt skinned and spitted and ready for the grill over there, even though he'd suspected as much the other night. And way too embarrassed at how obvious his rubbernecking must've been to consider asking Ellie for any details.

"How do you like living here?" She rushed into his silence, like she regretted that last blurt and wanted a redo. She leaned over and hid her face by making a production of fluffing out her short dark hair. Brady noted the rippling in her biceps. Girl had some serious cut to her arms. And apparently some issues with Lexy.

"So far, it's great," he answered. Except for the pipe dream she'd just stomped flat. "Peaceful, friendly, and beautiful is a tough combo to beat."

"Yes it is. Every day here is another day in paradise."

It was the same phrase Brady had heard continuously. All the residents used it as a greeting, which he had thought was pretty cool, but he was beginning to wonder. After hearing it so much, it sounded more like an incantation from some wigged-out church. Kind of indoctrinated-sounding. Before he could formulate some harmless inanity that would extricate him from the conversation and its soured vibe, Lexy plopped into a chair at his table and slid a new bottle of beer in front of him. His mood shot up like a champagne cork, until he remembered the boyfriend warning.

"Hey, Brady," she said. "I saw your drink was empty, and I figured we just can't have that."

"Thanks." He took an obligatory sip. "Afraid I'm a light-weight, so I don't reload very fast." He watched her give Ellie a cursory nod, and turned in time to see Ellie do the same, but from where his chair sat directly between them it was impossible to tell whether it was a cool exchange or the casual communication of friends. Would've gone a long way toward telling him whether Ellie had been protecting a friend or cat-hissing behind Lexy's back.

"See you later, Brady." Ellie stood and touched his shoulder. "I'm glad you like it here."

"I see you staring holes in her swimsuit, Brady Spain," said Lexy, once Ellie moved out of earshot.

Busted. He laughed and shifted around to face Lexy, who looked just stone-cold blood-stopping in a white one-piece cut high enough he could almost see her lower ribs.

"Hey, I was admiring her conditioning," he said with a wink. Amazing how he felt all hyped-up at the sight of her, despite the boyfriend. He wondered how to bring it up, see if he had a chance. "I was going to ask her to recommend a gym."

"Yeah, right." She punched his arm. "She really is in some kind of great shape, you know. She did a lot of rowing in college, still goes kayaking all the time, I think. She'd be dangerous if she ever realized how good she really looks."

"Maybe I need to try that." He flexed his arm and prodded the bicep with a finger. "Nah, no hope." Boy, was it hard to not try for a sneaky peek at all of the Lexy hanging out from the bottom of the high-cut suit.

"I hope you mean try the kayaking." She wagged her finger, no-no fashion. "She's married. That's the other reason I came over, to keep you out of trouble."

"Not my fault she was about the only one here I know." He shook his finger back at her in mock accusation. "You weren't anywhere to be found when I got here." He felt his mouth go dry, but took the plunge anyway. "Besides, she was just telling me the same thing about you."

"I'm married?" She sat back and wrinkled her nose up in a "do what?" expression. "How come I wasn't the first to know about it?"

Brady had to laugh. How about gorgeous and the quickest wit on two feet? "No, she just said unavailable, I assume meaning you have a boyfriend."

Something snapped like an arcing current from a live wire deep in her bottomless black eyes. "Sounds like she ought to try minding her own business." She reached over and patted his hand. "Why don't you ask the horse's mouth?"

He felt his heart whacking around in his chest as if it had broken loose or something. What about her made him so nervous? "Okay, are you available?" Hoping his mouth didn't sound as sticky as it felt. "Though I have to say, I never thought of you as a horse's mouth."

She smiled, mischief bouncing around in her eyes. "As long as I don't remind you of the other end. Available for what?"

Brady sat back, hiding his self-consciousness behind the old sip of beer routine. She obviously enjoyed dragging it out. He wanted in the worst way to say something like, available to take a shower together? But he wasn't sure she would appreciate the humor or the seriousness of it. "Well, maybe we could get together sometime, now that we're done with business." *Except for a three thousand dollar rubber check, that is.*

She swung her head, flipping her hair over her shoulder, and faced him directly by propping her chin on her hand. "Maybe we can, Brady, that'd be nice. I can tell you, I'm as available as

I want to be. But right now, I need your help with something, if you wouldn't mind."

Even amidst the exhilaration soaring in him from her receptiveness to a date, he felt his scalp tighten up as the sudden husky intimacy of her voice set off his alarm bells. Girl like her just did not ask a guy to help her out of her swimsuit, no matter if she was the man-eater that she came on as. "Sure, anything I can."

"Do you remember Monday night? You were moving your bed and I met you there at the house?" She did her little quizzical eye-tilt, keeping them locked on his.

He nodded, wondering what she wanted and if his answer would decide whether she stayed open to that date idea. "Sure."

"Well, that was the night, and pretty close to the time, that the psycho attacked poor Sara." She paused, shaking her head. "Can you actually believe that happened?"

"I know. Makes me sick just thinking about it. They catch the guy yet?" *And what does it have to do with me, with us?*

"No, and that's why I need your help. Dad says all the men here are going to need to prove where they were at the time." She lowered her hands to the table with her chin still propped on them so that she was looking up at him. "Anyway, my brother Nick told Dad he was with me, and he was, but Dad asked me who else saw us that night. And I thought of you. Do you remember him sitting in my car waiting?"

Brady thought for a minute, replaying the scene in his head. "Lexy, I remember there was someone in your car. But he never got out, and I couldn't see in. Couldn't tell you if it was Santa Claus or Aunt Jemima. Besides, I wouldn't know your brother if he fell on me."

"That's okay, all you do is look at him now, or a picture, and say, 'That's the man I saw with Lexy.' " She turned on the big smile, firing up the charm.

"You're kidding, right? You want me to give your brother an alibi?" It sounded so ludicrous, so B-movie, that he laughed.

Her eyes flashed for a second and Brady knew he had been warned. Girl was serious about putting him on the spot. "Exactly. After all, we're your alibi. Bet no one else can vouch for you, and you're the new guy in town."

Whoa, was that a threat or just a poor choice of words by an overwrought sister? He wanted to believe the latter, since she probably didn't date guys she believed capable of rape. "Lexy, I don't think I need an alibi." Did he? "And if you were with him, why can't you be his alibi?"

"Dad says he'll need more than a brother-sister witness to get the police to believe him."

"Lexy, I think you're overreacting." Then the thought hit him like a tire iron to the head. Duh. Could it be that her brother was the guy? He leaned back in his chair in an unconscious attempt to dilute the power of those hypnotic black eyes. Could the whole "that'd be nice, Brady" answer be a little incentive for him to cover for a guilty brother? "I'm not about to get hung up lying to the police. I'm sure they'll get the right guy."

"That's a damn lousy attitude to take!" She stopped and took a breath, softening her face back into a smile. "I don't want you to lie. I just want you to remember. I swear Nick was there with me. Don't you believe me?"

He watched her eyes for shiftiness and saw none. Just the impatience of someone accustomed to getting her way. Maybe she was telling the truth, but that didn't ease the feeling that she was jamming him. "I believe you, Lexy." Should he? He hadn't forgotten her playful warning to never trust her on anything besides money. "Tell you what, I'll think it over some more, okay?"

"Thanks, Brady, you're sweet." She reached over and squeezed his hand. "I'll owe you and Dad will, too. Maybe we can rework your lease after this is over." She smiled again, gave his hand a final squeeze, and then was gone.

Brady flopped back in his chair and took his frustration out on a mosquito trying to excavate his kneecap. So, decision time. Easy choice on the surface—just fudge the facts a tad, and bingo, a shot with Lexy plus an undefined financial reward. Nothing to it if he ignored one glaring little caveat: the fudging would be to the police. Was she worth it? If the brother turned out guilty, how deep was that hot water? Something about the way she'd boxed him into this must-choose position had him feeling like the proverbial deer in the headlights.

CHAPTER FIFTEEN

Leo Burgess stared morosely through his den window at the animated dialogue churning between Nick and Lexy out in the gazebo. Leo expected screw-ups from Nick but he was quite surprised at Lexy's failure to secure the new tenant's corroboration of Nick's whereabouts. She professed confidence that this Spain fellow would come through, but to Leo's business-sharpened nose, her account of their conversation smelled like a big, fat, polite no. Leo would have to see to Nick's safety himself.

He watched as Nick threw his hands in the air and stalked off toward the pool. Typical. Leo felt certain he knew almost verbatim what Nick was saying. Something to do with everything is someone else's fault. Leo's gaze followed Lexy as she shrugged and walked over to her car, head down and her hands in her pockets. Undoubtedly fed up with whatever moronic tirade her brother spewed this time.

He sensed his wife's presence before he heard her, and turned to face her as she spoke.

"Are they going to take Nicky away?" she asked, holding her hands together in front of her. All but wringing them.

He eyed his wife, half fondly, half exasperated. Still a glimmer in her of the beautiful Anna Kovich he had married, especially the eyes. But in a cold light, she was a short, dumpy, sixty-four-year-old woman who dyed her cap of curly hair a different color every month. "No, Anna. And who are *they*?"

"The police." Now she extended both arms as if she were

handing him a live baby bird. "I heard you talking with Lexy."

The walls have ears, Leo thought wryly. He sighed.

She read his sigh with the accuracy developed over forty years of marriage, and pushed on. "You're afraid they will blame him for this awful thing that happened to that girl."

"No, I'm not. I'm merely attempting to be prepared in the event they question him. If our son is even briefly considered a viable suspect, it will greatly damage the image we have built here." To say nothing of what havoc a conviction would bring, a much likelier possibility than his wife would ever comprehend.

"Image, schmimage." She swatted *image* away like she would a pesky fly. "I don't care. You better make sure nothing happens to my baby. He couldn't have done such an awful thing. This is an act of the devil, not some chippy changing her story afterward like the other time."

Only the years of negotiating for a living kept Leo from dropping his jaw. She could only be referring to the rape accusation he had bought Nick out of ten years ago. Which occurred in Pensacola; how did Anna know of it? "The other time, eh? And how do you come by this particular knowledge?"

"You might be surprised by what all I know, Leo Burgess, if you ever paid attention," she said, hands on her hips, indignation in her eyes. "Don't tell me you believe Nicky is capable of such a sin."

"I don't, Anna." Walls and ears indeed. Quite foolish of him to harbor delusions of privacy in a home Anna viewed as her personal fiefdom. "In fact, Alexandra says Nicolas was with her at the time of the attack. And I can tell when she's lying." *At least I could when she was a teenager. Has that become a precarious assumption?*

She moved closer, tilting her head back to compensate for the foot and a half difference in height. "Then why do we need this other person to vouch for him?"

"I simply wish to be prepared for any eventuality. One's sister may not be considered sufficient substantiation."

She shook an admonishing finger at him, something she knew he detested. "Because the police will talk to that other Jezebel and she'll slander Nicky's character!"

"The police will not know about the other incident." That silence had been bought and paid for.

"Then why are you worried, Huggy Bear? Tell me," she said, gently now, using a pet name from their dating days.

Because I do not trust Pete Cully's conscience to withstand another cover-up, especially if he suspects Nick. And if he discloses why he suspects Nick, a sister's testimony will not be worth a damn. Leo knew he could not tell Anna all of this; she would immediately alienate Pete, and they could not risk any further strain on Pete's wavering loyalties. He circled an arm around her, drawing her close. "I am not worried, pretty girl. I am merely taking care of things as I always have."

"Promise?"

"I promise."

They stood like that for a few minutes, swaying gently together, watching the waves roll up onto the beach below. *Perhaps,* thought Leo, *I can come upon the appropriate leverage to help young Mister Spain's memory.*

Pete Cully tugged again at the carefully measured cable, as strong as he dared this time, and brought it up to the terminal. Still short.

"Dad blame it!" He held the cable up and gave it the evil eye. "What's wrong with you? It can't be me, four inches ain't even a sensible mistake."

Maybe he had cut it wrong in his hurry to get done and get out. The last place he wanted to be right now was the Burgess home, especially when Nick was there. But he could no longer put off replacing the relay box for the sprinkler system. The old relay had grown moody, prone to turn the system on at any time, regardless of what hour it was set for. It had gotten to the point that standing anywhere in the yard meant risking an unexpected enema.

He exited the garage and followed the cable route along the roofline of the outer wall. Aha, right there, hung on that little knothole. Must've snagged when he first pulled in the slack. He stretched up on tiptoe and flicked it loose, relieved that he needn't start over.

As he circled back to the garage door, he spotted Lexy crossing the lawn, her jaw set so tight it made his teeth hurt. He turned in midstride and hurried to his truck to move it from behind her Jaguar.

She waved him back and then paused with her hand on the car door, gesturing at the leftover cable dangling from his left shoulder. "While you're working with that, could you wire up my bonehead brother and zap some sense into him?" she snarled, snapping each word off with a brittle pop. "Maybe shock therapy is the answer."

Pete smiled, despite her obvious fury. "Can't say I haven't had the urge from time to time, but I reckon boss man would call that overstepping my boundaries." He could think of some other body parts on Nick where a few thousand volts would do more good.

A tiny return smile flickered at the corners of her mouth, easing the knots along her jaw. "I swear, Uncle Pete, you are the only man around here with any patience. Can't you do anything with them?"

Assuming she meant Nick and Leo, well, no. He doubted those two listened to anyone, but if they did, it damn sure wasn't Pete Cully, which was why the current situation looked like an inevitable firestorm to him. And though the uncle status the teenaged Lexy had awarded her new handyman years ago still felt special to him regardless of the demons in her head, right now he didn't care for any reminder of how tangled up in this family he really was. "Don't fret, princess, I haven't seen the face-off yet where you couldn't smile everybody into surrendering."

She snatched the door open and slung it wide, darn near tearing a hinge off, and leaned against the top of the windshield with one foot in the floorboard. "You're always good for my ego, Uncle Pete, but I don't know this time. I've got one guy who doesn't believe me and these two don't believe I've tried."

Yep, that sounded like the Burgess men, all right. "Who's the other fella?" he asked, curiosity quickening. He couldn't imagine Leo riding Lexy for anything other than business or family matters, and Nick wouldn't be in on any business talks. He'd heard enough of her jawing with Nick to understand that they were pushing someone to back up a story of theirs. Was this argument over some new strategy for saving Nick's bacon?

She shook her head and fanned a hand like she was shooing away gnats. "Nobody you know, probably. A new guy."

Well now, if she meant new in the Point, it had to be that Brady fellow he'd met earlier. Pete hoped Brady hadn't got himself caught in a Burgess crunch—he liked that boy. He kept his guess to himself though, because if he'd learned one thing about dealing with Burgesses, it was best that they didn't know what all he knew, even Lexy.

She climbed in and banged the door shut. "I'm out of here, Pete. Let me know if you change your mind on wiring him up. I want to be the one to plug it in." She backed the Jaguar around his truck and spun a furrow across the lawn.

"Damn, girl, we don't need to bother with fixing sprinklers if you're going to do a burnout on the grass," he called after her.

She stuck her head and arm out of the window and gave him

the finger, a sassy grin on her face. He shook his head, unable to resist an answering smile. He often wondered what she might've become if she had a father who didn't strangle her like Leo did. Crazy girl would probably be President, the way she could charm a guy.

He returned to the garage, gathered up his tools, and carted them out to his truck. He piled them on top of the utility bed cabinet and began opening the side compartment doors.

"Hey, Cully, if you're done there, how about taking a few minutes to wash down the Porsche?"

He turned to see Nick sauntering down from the house, decked out in one of those retro Hawaiian shirts that look like bowling uniforms, flip-flops, and sunglasses dangling on a cord around his neck. Creep. Boy knew damn well Leo would bust his chops if he heard that crap. "No sir, and I ain't got the time to stop and change your diaper for you, either."

"That's a piss poor attitude to take with your employer, isn't it?" Nick smirked. He crossed his arms, sticking his nose in the air.

Pete turned and grabbed a rag from the front shelf to wipe down his snips, keeping his back to Nick. "Didn't reckon you to be my employer. If you've got a legitimate request, let's hear it. Otherwise, that's all the comedy I can use." Fool had the nerves of a trapeze artist or about the same amount of brains as the trapeze, yanking Pete's chain at a time like this.

Nick snorted and continued down the lawn, mumbling something about "what the hell we pay you for anyway."

Pete ignored him, finished cleaning the snips, and hung them on their hook. For the sake of the Burgess family and his own conscience, Pete hoped Brady could back up Lexy's story. He had not slept well at all since the rape of that poor Zeletsky girl, wondering if Nick did it and pondering his own guilt for Nick being free to do so. If Brady came through, it would be a weight off his back. He didn't put any stock in Lexy. She'd lie her ass off for her brother, but Brady was a different matter. Just a gut reaction from shooting the breeze with him, that boy did not seem like a guaranteed lay-down for sale.

Unlike yourself, he thought with a pang. His daddy always told him, "Boy, if you think it's something you might regret, just don't do it." So simple. And Pete had lived by that advice, up until the day Leo's money seduced him.

Almost ten years ago now, he reflected, as he wiped down the rest of his tools and methodically replaced them in their slots. It was one of those pure coincidences—call it luck, fate, karma, or whatever—that change your life forever. Though he and Leo lived less than ten miles apart, they had never met until that day, three hundred miles away at a cheap motel off I-10 outside Pensacola. Pete had made the trip to visit his ailing Aunt Betty, and took a room there to avoid staying in her cluttered, ultra-finicky home where a man couldn't feel comfortable even sitting down. Leo, with Nick tagging along, had traveled to Pensacola for a business meeting. Checked into a much fancier downtown joint, of course. But he had come slumming that evening to take care of his son's latest screw-up.

Seems Nick had met a girl at some beach party that afternoon and asked her out for the evening. Apparently the girl wanted to play grown-up and, knowing that her parents would be away from the room, invited him to pick her up at the motel. Nick showed up early, found the door unlocked, and came on in. Then, sick jerk that he was, he got his rocks off spying on her as she showered. Until that wasn't good enough. When she stepped out of the shower, he muscled her onto the bed and raped her.

Pete had known none of this then. Nor had he known she was only fifteen. He had gone charging into the middle of the fiasco once he identified the muffled moans coming through the thin motel wall as sounds of distress. The manager showed up moments later, armed and officious, promising to call the police and asking Pete to return to his room. He'd done so, figuring the guy was handling things properly, but only after he made sure the sobbing girl had his business card to contact him as a witness.

The call never came. The police never talked to him either, though Leo had dropped in on him that night to hear his account. Pete had been glad to oblige, given Leo's concerned-parent demeanor and the fact that Pete already knew who he was and his community standing.

Funny, when Leo called a couple weeks afterward and offered the job, Pete didn't make the connection. Or maybe hadn't wanted to, because he surely knew that seventy-five hundred a month for a maintenance guy was crazy money, no matter how ritzy the neighborhood. But by then he had put the Pensacola incident behind him, except for knowing he might be summoned to testify someday, and assumed Leo's offer to be the result of a bad circumstance bringing together two men with matching business needs. A struggling handyman simply did not second-guess a regular job like this one, especially at that salary. Over the years, though, seeing how Leo operated, he knew. And it ate at his core like acid.

So Pete was the only witness to Burgess's nasty secret besides the motel manager, who must've either believed Nick's version or took a payoff from Leo. Pete was also the only person outside of the two families who knew that Leo had bought the girl's silence, an arrangement he learned of later from Nick's loose, bragging mouth. Enough money will buy just about anything, something Leo knew well and exercised often. Bought Pete, too. By the time he figured out the real story, including the payoff, he had grown too fat and happy living the good life on Leo's dime to change anything.

He'd told himself he'd done all he could at the time, that it was the girl's decision. He'd reassured himself that no one would believe him after so much time had passed, or even worse, that he could be on the hook as an accomplice for taking Leo's job. But all that garbage was just one big sorry attempt to ignore an ugly fact: he'd made a lot of money off a little girl's virginity.

Daddy was right. Pete had come to regret not calling the cops that day. It sickened him to think the girl's folks had sold her like that, and he couldn't escape the certainty that it never would've happened if she'd talked to the police right then. So Nick got off free and clear, since without a complaint sworn out, there wasn't a crime. And if Nick had done it again because Pete's silence had kept him out of jail, he just didn't know if he could live with himself.

He shook off the past, closed his toolbox, and walked over to the garage to test the new relay. Wait, he told himself. Wait until we hear what Brady says. If it's no, then lay all this out for Gerry. Because Pete had done something to even the playing field this time, something boss man might not like if he knew. On Leo's behalf, with Leo's money, Pete had hired an honest detective.

CHAPTER SIXTEEN

Brady Spain felt hopelessly juvenile for feeling such a need to talk to his mom, but he finally gave in to it. With thoughts of her lurking around in his mind ever since the pool party, he concluded that his subconscious was sending a message. The more he thought on it, the more his conversation with Lexy felt like a confrontation, a crossroads decision, and talking with Mom always worked as sort of a moral truth serum. Though she rarely offered him direct advice, he usually walked away with a clearer picture of things. After eight rings, she picked up, totally out of breath.

"Mom, are you all right?" Her panting and the eight-hundred-mile distance between them shot a bolt of worry through him.

"Perfectly fine, dear, just a little gardening."

"At eight-thirty?" He carried the phone into the bedroom and opened a window, sucking in the sweet fragrance of the honeysuckle. He couldn't get enough since discovering it, though so far he'd avoided analyzing whether the craving represented unresolved questions about Peggy.

"It's too hot outside until the evening, you know that. And it stays light until after eight." She drew a deep breath, sounding better.

"You've got to take it easy, Mom. You're going to fall over in a flower bed one day." She was sixty-eight now, forty pounds overweight and hypertensive, but she tackled every day with an irrepressible energy that defied it all.

She giggled and he smiled despite his concern. He could picture her—pink-faced from exertion, blowing gray hair up out of her eyes, undoubtedly a smudge right on the end of her nose.

"There are worse ways to go," she said, and laughed again. "What's up, pumpkin?"

"What do you mean, what's up? Can't I call to check on my mother?" He flicked on the ceiling fan and kicked back on the bed, feeling a twinge of guilt for not having made a habit of doing just that.

"If that's all this is, who are you and what did you do with my Brady?" She paused and dropped the banter from her tone. "Seriously, pumpkin, I like being your sounding board. That's what mothers are for."

So much for the casual approach. He could swear she possessed telepathic powers. She'd always been there for Brady, even during the hell of adolescence when he'd acted like a jerk. They'd been poor, scary poor at times, though never homeless and usually not hungry. Hadn't mattered in early childhood, he hardly noticed. By his teen years their situation became a source of embarrassment and frustration for him, sometimes outright anger. So he'd showed his ass over it. Regularly.

Eventually adulthood brought an understanding and appreciation of her decisions that had been so maddening at the time. She knew she couldn't prevent people from knowing or even laughing because he was poor. What she could prevent was anyone ever being able to say his needs weren't met, that he wasn't cared for and loved and actively parented. No telling how important that had been to her, especially as a divorcée. Now his heart struggled to bear the indebtedness he felt whenever he thought back over her sacrifices, what all she went without by putting him first. And here she was, still there for him.

He told her of Lexy urging him to back up her story, presenting it as a choice between telling a small fib and letting down a friend. He skipped any mention of rape or stalkers or held checks, stuff that set off maternal alarm bells.

"I don't know, baby," she said when he finished. "I can't answer your question directly, but I can try to help."

"Okay." He wondered if she was going to serve up another one of her riddles, and hoped not. He realized his phone was slippery with sweat and switched hands.

"First, you have to decide if you're an honest man, honey. Honesty is a trait, what one is, not what one does on a case-by-case basis. There's no such thing as an honest answer or an honest opinion. It would be a truthful answer or a truthful opinion. One is honest or one is not. And an honest person telling an untruth can be a very self-destructive thing. Does that help at all?"

"Yeah, I guess so." Being all blasé about it, but really just hiding the fact that somewhere inside he had known it already and hoped she would tell him otherwise. Fit nicely into one of her riddles, too—the one about the easy way out is usually not a way out at all. "Thanks, Mom."

"And Brady, it sounds like you're interested in your friend, this Lexy." She paused again, and he heard her purse her lips.

Oops. He'd tried to gloss over that part, too embarrassed to admit that keeping his chances with Lexy alive was the crux of the dilemma. Though he could talk to Mom about most anything, heck if he could get himself to say: *Yes, Mom, I think about her all the time, I'm obsessed with imagining what it would feel like to hold her naked in my hands, to find out what her skin tastes like.* He did consider telling her how Lexy epitomized the sophistication and elegance small-town life didn't have, everything he'd left to find. But that would bring out a cautionary tale about how growth and success and satisfaction are found from within, not from another person. Or something along those lines. He felt his ears turning red, but she continued before he thought of a safe answer.

"There is nothing dishonorable about searching your memory and finding something hidden in there that helps your friend. But if she's interested in a man who will lie for her, then she is not a woman you should be interested in. Follow me?"

After a moment of untangling he did, though it chafed, as it felt like one more strike against Lexy. On a wild impulse, he almost told her about the honeysuckle, managing to swallow the urge when he realized he didn't want her answer.

Right on cue, she said, "Incidentally, I saw Peggy at the mall in Raleigh last week." How did she do that? Woman was scary. "She asked how you were doing. Have you spoken with her recently?" He heard the sly smile in her voice.

"Not since I left. I keep thinking I'm going to email or text her to say hey, but I never get around to it." *Because I don't know if I'm comfortable being friends with someone I treated so unfairly.*

Mom, you're a sweetheart and a trip, he reflected after they had said their "byes" and "love yous" and disconnected. *Here I am almost thirty, and you're still more worried about me going for the wrong woman than anything else. And now the million-dollar question: Am I an honest man?*

CHAPTER SEVENTEEN

Roaming around Heron Point on foot during the late-night and early-morning hours provided Gerry Terence with the best feel for the place, both the geography and the people. It didn't take him long to start picking out the boozers, the dopers, the quarreling couples, the cheating spouses. Not necessarily one of the job requirements, but Gerry always liked getting tuned in to his surroundings. Plus he enjoyed the exercise in the cooler night air. The crisp scent of the pines and citrus trees, mixed with the slight tang of the ocean breeze, gave the dark hours a fresh clean feel that washed away the tired, grumpy old ex-cop he'd seen too often in his mirror of late. Besides, he sure wasn't going to get anywhere by sitting in his car waiting for the bad guy to wave him down and confess.

The minimal ambient lighting in the neighborhood—just a sporadic streetlamp here and there—was something he planned to recommend Leo change. The skyline of black shadowy trees, outlined against a brilliance of stars not visible in brighter lighting, made for a setting of surpassing beauty and peacefulness but it also offered the ideal environment for peepers and burglars and all manner of night-stalking lowlifes. And that's what he was here to put a lid on, regardless of the aesthetic sacrifices.

Just as well, probably. A little more lighting might chase away his own bogeymen. Much as he loved the dark—and had as far back as he could remember—it was when he missed Angie the most. Seven years now since she left, finally fed up with the boozing and the black moods he brought home from work.

He knew she'd never come back. Though he wasn't willing to admit he might still be toting the torch, the biting regret he felt for screwing up the best thing that would ever happen to him hadn't eased through the years. Hell, he would've never surrendered the bottle and bagged the job after his twenty if she hadn't made him take a realistic look at himself by walking out. Amazing how Angie could be good for him even by ripping his heart out. And she'd get a laugh out of this, him pounding a beat again like a twenty-five-year-old rookie and enjoying it.

Kind of an odd job though, the way Burgess had laid it out for him, Gerry mused as he cut through a tree-lined gap connecting Oak and Magnolia streets. His wish list was for Gerry to take the peeper down in the act or to at least be able to identify him beyond any doubt. Failing that, to deter any future incidents with his presence.

The first scenario required sheer luck, the second would take forever and probably still be a guess, and the third could be done for much less than his rates. So Gerry feared he had taken a case where the client would never feel like he got his money's worth. Bad for business, referral wise. But he'd signed on anyway, partly because Pete asked him, partly good old curiosity. Landing a client with pockets as deep as Leo's was no minor consideration either, given the number of pencils Gerry had chewed through while doing the books last week.

He followed the pitch-black path by memory, picking up no sounds except the cricket songs and the distant crescendos of the surf, his footfalls now inaudible in the loose sand.

When they had met to go over the particulars of the job, he'd felt intrigued by Burgess's reaction to any mention of the rape case. The old man, as Pete called him, wanted positively no investigation of the rape, in fact wanted it ignored. According to

Burgess, the two crimes were unconnected and—since the rape did not even occur in Heron Point—having his hired man look into it might imply responsibility. No, Big Leo had made his position clear: however unfortunate that the victim was one of his tenants, the police could tend to their own crime-ridden streets while Gerry restricted his inquiries to Heron Point. Leo had also stood adamant that the stalker's identity be released only to him, allowing him to contact the authorities. It was a common demand, especially from clients with hidden agendas, and one Gerry usually refused up-front. He'd taken a wait-and-see approach this time, due to the unlikelihood of any arrest happening anyway, in a Peeping Tom case where no victim could make a positive identification.

He reached the sidewalk and turned shoreward, shaking his head at the memory of the tension in that meeting. Though immune to physical intimidation by his fellow man anymore, he had felt a little awe at the presence of Leo Burgess. The sheer size of him, a hulking, bear-like man with a huge boulder of a head and hands that could crush a quart can. Top it off with a deep rumbly voice that made statements which would sound pompous from another man seem like this inexorable steamroller of omniscience, and damned if you didn't want to believe whatever he said. But that absolute insistence was what got Gerry going, got him asking why. Sure seemed like the man had put his blinders on.

Of course, the other thing he just had to know was, what was eating at Pete? The guy's eyes had been begging Gerry to read his mind the day he had come to the office. Not that Gerry really minded his clients holding out on him. If no one had secrets to protect, no private detective would ever get a job. So, having evasive clients was a good thing, in a twisted sense. But for Pete to be disturbed by something too touchy to tell Gerry, it had to be a live grenade he was juggling. And a lifelong friend was a friend, no matter how infrequent their contact.

Maybe I should get him drunk, he thought, smiling to himself. *Get him babbling. Should only take two or three beers.* Pete had never been much of a drinker, though Gerry used to pound it down. Stopped just short of alcoholism, stayed dry a while, and now he could enjoy a drink again without falling off the edge. Hadn't yet, anyway. Okay, scratch that idea.

If only he could get a look at the letter. He felt undecided on whether the guys at the cop shop had been stonewalling him or if they truly just misplaced the case file. Which did happen, often enough to be believable. That letter could ease his nagging worry over the possibility of the two cases being linked. The fact that window-shade freaks often never graduated to rape—especially longtime peepers—didn't rule it out and he was not about to ignore the possibility just because Mister Leo Burgess told him to. His conscience also knew, friendship aside, he had to find a way to drag Pete's suspicions out of him. Did Pete know who their peeper was? And was that guy the rapist?

Nearing the last cross street that would turn him around and point him back inland, he paused at the blue house on the ocean side of Oak Street to check for visitors. Gerry had already caught on to a pattern of too many vehicles coming and going at all hours there. Probably a drug house. Hard to believe, in the middle of this kind of upscale community, but he had a feeling.

He clicked on his flash, shooting the beam up the drive. Yep, another customer. And my, my, it was a nice fancy Porsche belonging to Mister Nick Burgess. He snapped the Porsche with his camera phone. Well, well. Wonder if Mister Leo Burgess wanted to know that he just might have a dope business thriving in one of his homes, and if he already knew that his son was a user? Maybe it was time to talk to Pete again.

★　★　★　★　★

An exultant Nick Burgess bounded down the steps of Cameron's house, fired up the Boxster, and blew a little of the dust off the neighborhood with a roar of acceleration. That Cameron, man, knows everybody. Dude even knew someone to help him with his current problem, getting this Spain guy to see the light. A little pain and fear would make that gomer get his story straight and Nick was taking charge of making it happen.

It would show the old man that Nick knew how to handle problems, every bit as good as King Leo himself. He laughed, slamming the Porsche around a corner, making it squeal. Probably not the way Pops would handle it, but to Nick it was clear that the old man's style of thinking had fossilized. Not enough action.

He wished he could be there when this action went down. See Spain's face. Wished his fast-pants sister could see it too. It was obvious she had the hots for the dork, and Nick liked the idea of anything that crapped in her breakfast. Though it would probably be an even better punishment for Spain to just let Lexy have him. She liked to play a man like a cat with a crippled mouse, toy with him until she got bored and then eat him up and spit out the bones. Spain would age at least ten years by the time she got done with him. But no, that would be fun for her, and that would not do. This way was best.

The sweep of his headlights around a turn caught just enough of a walking man for Nick to recognize him. The rent-a-cop, Gerry what's-his-name. That was a problem, too. Nick had thought he'd talked the old man out of this idea, but here the dude was. Kind of a weirdo, if you asked Nick. Guy spent all his time walking around, talking to everybody. Stupid stuff too, like what do you do, when do you work, what kind of car do you drive? Like he was making friends at a keg party or something, not detective questions. So dude was a loser, more proof that the old man had lost it.

Nick had cooled it on visiting his girls, what with this doofus around, but now that he knew the guy for a moron, he was going to pick it back up as soon as he figured out the timing of the dumbass nightly rounds. The idea of looking in on his girls while the great detective was on the job really appealed to him. Get the reputation of being a supernatural ghost; flit in and see his girls and then disappear again. Good thing that action last week had been enough to hold his hunger for a while. Man, he could still see her shocked expression, the fear in her eyes. Boner city, just thinking about it.

And when his plan brought this Spain putz in line, he'd finally have the old man's attention, have him rethinking Nick as a man of action. He looked forward to carrying more status and say-so around here, specifically over Lexy and Cully.

He eased the Porsche up the drive as quietly as possible, hoping to keep the old man from humping it down the stairs to check out his eyeballs. Like Visine was never invented or something. Pathetic.

CHAPTER EIGHTEEN

Sara Zeletsky looked up in response to a tapping at the doorway of her hospital room and felt a jolt of surprise to see her landlord.

"May I come in, Sara?" Leo asked, ducking his head under the doorframe to peer in.

It took a couple of breathy attempts at groping for a voice, and her, "Yes, please do," sounded like a croak when she did get it out. As flattered as she was by his visit, she felt horrified by how she must look. She still carried the raccoon-eye bruises from the broken nose her rapist had given her—for no reason, since she had obeyed his demands—and she knew that the neck brace made her resemble a girl Frankenstein. Then she realized she didn't care. Though she'd never been quite able to think of herself as pretty, looking her best and being at least attractive had been important to her. But the monster had taken that, too.

"I was very distressed to learn of you still convalescing this long," he said, passing her bed to deposit the spray of roses he had brought onto the window table. "But I must say, you look much better than I feared. We have been worried about you."

"Thank you," she whispered, eyes filling with tears. Since her nightmare began, she had become prone to fits of uncontrollable crying and unfocused bursts of anger, especially when someone did or said anything kind to her. She couldn't understand it, couldn't stop it, and it all just made her want to cry more.

He turned away from her, making an obvious show of reading the cards on the other flowers while she swallowed her misery.

"I'm sorry," she said finally. "Please sit."

He did so, settling into the chair that was usually occupied by her mother, who had thankfully taken a break from her bedside marathon of constant fussing over every tiny detail of Sara's existence.

"No need for apologies, my dear." He held up a hand as if pushing away her words. "It's a terrible thing you have had to endure. How are you feeling?"

She stared at him for a beat, thinking, *how the hell do you expect me to feel? I've been strangled, beaten and raped. I'm alive by an inch. Even if I survive all this, I feel filthy and dirty and it won't wash off. I'm beginning to believe I'll never get out of this hospital. How do you think I should feel?* But voicing it would make her cry again, something she did not want. So she just dropped her gaze and murmured, "I'm alive."

"When will you be released?" he asked, scaring her a little that maybe he could read her mind. Probably just the normal next question, she decided.

He looked so kind and genuinely interested that she launched into the description of internal injuries that were all gobbledygook to her and the spinal fractures they wanted to monitor in hopes of avoiding surgery. She wound down when she saw he wasn't really listening; his eyes had assumed a faraway, glazed-over look. *Because he's a damn man,* she thought with a violent flash. *Just like the damn shrink they send in here.* She'd asked that guy if he'd ever been raped, and when he said no, she knew that all his sympathy and questions about her feelings were just so much bull. Bet he didn't stop every time a woman told him no. Burgess either; she wished he would just leave.

"Well, I am pleased to hear the prognosis is so promising," he said with a smile. Proving he hadn't heard a word. "I would like for you to know, as a way of offering our sympathies for this tragedy, we are waiving your rent payment until such time as you can return to a normal life. You may also be interested to know we have engaged a private investigator to help apprehend the person responsible for this heinous attack as well as to prevent him from repeating it."

Big deal, was she supposed to thank him for that? How was an investigator supposed to help her? It was too late for her, though she felt a fierce stab of hope that he was sincere about making sure no other women went through what she had. As for the rent waiver, nice as it was, it meant nothing. She wasn't ever stepping foot in Heron Point again. She was going home with Mama.

"Thank you, that's very kind," she said anyway. Her voice sounded sarcastic even to her, though she did think it a generous gesture, considering he didn't owe her anything.

She expected him to go now, but he leaned toward her, elbows on his knees, his eyes getting a metallic shield-like gleam to them. "Did you recognize the man who attacked you?"

She shook her head, gently against the brace. Did he really think someone she knew would do this?

"Can you describe him, then?" he asked. The metallic eyes watched her without blinking, reminding her of a giant owl she saw at a zoo once. It was the same focused, unblinking stare.

"No, I can't." She shook her head again. *Except that he has hot breath and drinks beer. Every horny male in America.* "The police asked the same thing, but I can't."

"Not even a general description?" He placed his palms together, leaning in further.

She had forgotten how big a man Burgess really was, having only seen him at Christmas parties and the like, but him looming over her that way was scary. And big forceful men were not high on her warm fuzzy list right now. She found herself tilting back against the bed, retreating from his intensity. She wanted the man in her nightmares caught as badly as anyone could, but this was starting to feel eerie. "Mr. Burgess, I didn't see him, I wouldn't recognize him, I don't want to remember it, and I'm not going to think about it, okay? Sorry."

The air whooshed out of him like a punctured beach ball. "Quite all right, Sara. I hope my questions have not upset you." He patted her hand and stood. "Please tell us if there is anything we can do for you."

She managed a feeble nod and let her shoulders slump back against the pillow once he'd gone, wondering why she didn't feel good about his visit and wishing Mama would come back and sit with her.

CHAPTER NINETEEN

Brady Spain flicked his phone dark and with the same motion tossed it into the passenger seat. Maybe he shouldn't have called her, but he felt ready to get it over with, see if they could move past this thing hanging there between them. Lexy, however, had refused to talk about it on the phone. Said she would stop by after he got home. No chance of this being a pretty scene.

Pulling up to the house, he parked at the curb to let her use the driveway. If she was cool with his answer, he wanted to ask her to stay. As he switched off the ignition, he noticed a gray-haired man in an aloha shirt striding down the drive. Brady opened the door and stepped out, leaning around the corner of the windshield to ask the man what he wanted. He never got the words out. The man circled the front of the Jeep with a sudden burst of speed and slammed full tilt into the door, pinning Brady against the frame.

Stunned, wind knocked out of him, Brady's knees gave and prompted a wrenching pain through his left shoulder and collarbone. He struggled to straighten back up against the pressure of the door, laboring for the breath to tell the guy there must be some mistake.

Another man, younger, brown haired and wearing a bright yellow golf shirt, sauntered up from behind the Jeep. He reached out and grabbed the middle two fingers of Brady's left hand, which was trapped dangling outside the door. With an easy, practiced twist, the man bent the fingers back, almost touching the wrist. Had he gotten his wind back, the scalding pain in his knuckles and forearm would have ripped a scream out of Brady's guts.

"Shit hurts, don't it?" said the man holding the fingers. He winked and smiled cheerfully at Brady. "Can't answer yet, huh? Don't worry, you'll get your breath back in a minute. But save it, okay? This here is gonna be a one-way conversation, got it?"

Must be the pain making me hallucinate, thought Brady. The jolly buddy-buddy approach from a man tearing his arm in half while a human bulldozer crushed him to death was too surreal to be anything else. He didn't know whether to cry or join the lunacy and laugh.

"I need an answer, Brady." The man rotated his forearm slightly, and the fresh jolt of pain made Brady's knees buckle again until the resultant agony in his chest shot him upright. "Just nod, okay? Remember, no talking."

So Brady nodded.

"Good, good." The man eased the pressure on the fingers and broke out another affable smile. "I'm Frank. The big ape leaning on your door there is Art. Do you know why we're here, Brady?"

Brady shook his head. His wind was back, and he sucked in his diaphragm, lessening the grind of the door into his abdomen. So much for the big mistake theory—the smiling madman knew his name.

Frank patted Brady's shoulder. "That's all right, that's all right, I can tell you. What I understand is you got a little amnesia. Notice we ain't hit you in the face or head, right?"

Brady nodded energetically, the price of slow response still fresh in his mind. Of all the days to not see a single neighbor out and about, wishing him another day in paradise.

"That's so you can remember better, see?" Frank beamed at him as if they had just discovered gold. "All this visit is for is to help you remember whatever it is you forgot that's important to someone else. Got me?"

Brady nodded again. This had to be about the alibi thing. He just couldn't let himself believe Lexy was in on it, no matter how impatient she'd seemed. So who, Nick? Daddy Burgess?

"Now, you seem like a nice fellow, Brady," Frank continued. "I'm really impressed with how smart you are, the way you're handling this. I got a son not much younger than you, he wouldn't do half as good. What you don't want is for us to have to come back. Show him, Art."

Art grunted and pushed. Brady heard a whistling squeal, dimly recognized it as his voice. His vision darkened. Art let up, and when the moment of near-blackout passed, Brady opened his eyes to see Frank peering at him with an expression of curiosity.

"Damn, that smarts, huh?" Frank said, nodding with satisfaction. "That's why you don't want us to come back. It gets worse. Believe it or not, when we turn you loose, you won't feel much pain very long. Just some little aches that'll get better. 'Cause it's only our first visit." He slapped Brady's cheek gently with his free hand.

"We're professionals, see, not dumbass Saturday night muscle," Frank went on. He slowly brought Brady's fingers back down, inch by inch. "Now, you might want to put some ice on that hand, keep the swelling down. The ribs, you just gotta be patient, they'll heal."

He grabbed Brady's chin and pulled his face around, locking their eyes at less than a foot apart. Dark, cheerful brown eyes, without a glimmer of empathy in them. "Art's gonna come off that door, and you just ease down, sit a bit 'til you get your breath good, and don't make any moves toward him, me, or anywhere but down. Got it?"

Brady nodded, squelching an urge to thank the man. What

kind of craziness was that?

Frank patted his shoulder again, giving it a little squeeze. "Good deal, Brady. You take care of that hand, and hopefully we won't be seeing you. Come on, Art, I'm dying for a milk-shake."

The abrupt release of pressure against the door was pure ecstasy. Brady slumped to a sitting position on the step plate while Frank the happy goon and his silent stooge clomped off to wherever crazies go. Brady did not even turn to watch; he was too busy savoring air, beautiful air. Though it hurt to breathe. Sure as hell didn't feel like a little ache that would go away.

"Hey, are you okay?"

Brady swiveled gingerly toward the source of the voice and saw a woman bent over with her hands on her knees, staring at him. He struggled up onto his feet with the help of the very same door that had nearly killed him.

"Are you okay?" she repeated. Her brow was scrunched up in an expression of concern, though she had a wary look too, like he was a dog that might bite.

"I thi—" He cleared his throat, tried again. "No, but I think I'm going to be." He did feel a bit better standing up. Ribs hurt less, anyway.

"Did you fall? Do you want me to call an ambulance?" She straightened and edged closer, eyes full of alarm. Guess he looked incapable of biting, after closer inspection.

Pretty eyes they were, too, he thought woozily. Bright gray, but hidden behind a haze of alcohol. And it would be a pretty face, with her short, curly blond hair and soft doll-like features, if not for the sagging skin and puffy eyelids of a habitual drinker. Which was what led him to recognize her. Maggie. He'd met her twice before, and both times she had been riding that edge of drunk but not yet bombed.

"No, really, I'll be all right." He tried for a deeper breath and made it. "Thanks for checking on me, Maggie."

She lit up at her name. "Well, of course I would, Brady. You looked awful all crouched down there. I thought you fell or something. I saw these two men. . . ." She raised her hand to her mouth, eyes widening, the significance connecting behind the eighty-proof fog. "Did those two guys just mug you? They did, didn't they?"

"Sort of," Brady admitted, too exhausted to argue.

"Are you hurt? Should I call the police?"

He shook his head, wanting to make that determination himself, and she jabbered on. "I can't believe, right here in Heron Point. What is happening to this place?"

"Just another day in paradise, eh?" he said, managing his first grin. He recalled thinking of that phrase when Frank was tearing his arm off, and realized he was glad she hadn't shown in time to help. No telling what those two freaks might've done to her. And though he didn't feel as flip as he probably sounded, damn it felt good just to be alive and not dismembered.

"But honestly, Brady, muggers?"

"No, no, not really muggers." Trying to sound soothing, picturing the Heron Point grapevine cranking into high gear. "They were only here to see me, no one else is in any danger, so I'd appreciate it if you kept this to yourself."

Her eyes narrowed now, sobering up. "You owe people money, Brady?"

He swallowed the laugh, figuring the ribs couldn't handle it. Must be something broken in there. "Boy, do I. Lots of people. But not those people. It was something personal."

She frowned. "You don't seem like the kind of man who would have personal business with that kind of people."

"I didn't think I was either, Maggie." He tried a tentative step. Everything worked. Maybe Frank hadn't lied. "I'm just going up to the house and rest, okay? Thanks again."

"Here, let me help you."

She scooted over and slipped an arm around his waist, snuggling closer than he thought necessary for support. Exactly what he did not need right now, Nurse Erotica.

"No, I'm good," he said, extricating himself gently. "It's very nice of you, but I'm fine, okay?"

"Well, if you're sure." Her voice went up a half-octave. "I'd love a chance to help you."

He turned at the disappointment in her tone and was startled to see a hurt look in her eyes. Where'd that come from, he barely knew her. And he wasn't in the market for a chronically sloshed married woman. But his heart did pinch a little because of the shy wistful way her eyes talked to him. No prowling cougar here. "Hey, hey, look, you're wonderful, you're a lifesaver, all right? But I can handle it from here."

He headed up the drive, then stopped and called back. "Between us, right?"

"Okay, Brady," she said, all forlorn looking, standing there on the sidewalk with her hands in her pockets. Then she added with a grin, "I promise I'll try, anyway."

The obvious honesty of it made Brady smile back, and endeared her to him more than did her sympathy or whatever that other stuff was all about. Reminded him of his mother's advice. Maybe Maggie, boozehound and all, was an honest person. He waved and wobbled on up the driveway, in search of ice for his hand, maybe a beer for his belly.

CHAPTER TWENTY

The house felt way too claustrophobic after being pinned in a car door. Brady wrapped his hand in a baggie full of ice and took the promised beer out onto the stoop, under the lengthening shadow of the umbrella trees. Try to enjoy the pending sunset and pretend life was normal. Should he file a police report, or was it all too ludicrous? The police would probably fall out of their chairs laughing. Scheme up some appropriate payback? But how, do what? Stuff like this just didn't happen to harmless, taxpaying computer geeks.

A Jaguar convertible came zipping to a halt in front of him, breaking his trance. Lexy. Damn, he had forgotten about her coming to discuss the alibi. Move that to the back of the agenda now, first he wanted to know whether she had known about the goons. It didn't seem like her style, but obviously somebody named Burgess arranged it. And boy, was her timing convenient.

"Hi, Brady." She swung up and out of her car, smooth and graceful. Today's decoration was a filmy white sleeveless deal, deep-necked and V-cut to her belly button, giving it the effect of two silk sashes crossing her chest instead of a blouse at all. More erotic than showing up naked, as was the black miniskirt that made the unbelievable legs seem to go up and up for miles. She was so beautiful, the fear that his decision would destroy his chances with her made his throat ache, despite his slow boil over the Frank and Art show.

He waved at her with the ice bag hand, finished his beer with the good one. *Here we go.*

"Beautiful day, isn't it?" she said, tossing the long black hair behind her and sliding to a seat on the steps next to him. "Hey, what's with the hand? Did you hurt yourself?"

"Well, I had a little help." He studied her. She seemed genuinely casual, not put on. He told her the basics of it, went into detail describing Frank's lecture about his memory. As he talked, her eyes grew wider and wider, with what looked like real concern filling them. But who could tell with an artist like Lexy? By the time he finished, the eyes glittered with anger, her lips compressed to a thin line.

"That asshole," she said, biting off each syllable. She snatched her phone from her waist and jabbed at it three times, meaning a speed-dial call or a stored contact. "I am so sorry about this, Brady," she said around the phone. Apparently no answer, since she punched it off without speaking and dropped her face into her hands.

"Who's the asshole, Dad?" he asked the back of her neck. Soft little black hairs grew in tiny vees down the line of her vertebrae.

A muffled blurt of laughter came from the buried head and she raised her face back to him. "Don't be silly."

"Then who, Nick?"

"No, what makes you say that?" she asked, totally straight-faced. Bingo.

"Duh. Two guys try to cripple me and tell me to improve my memory. Gee, I wonder what they were talking about?"

She grabbed his hand, thankfully not the left one. "I don't blame you for suspecting us, but this has to be an awful misunderstanding. No one in my family would even know how to 'order up thugs,' as you put it."

He laughed. That was way weak for Lexy. "You're losing your grip, girl. You forget, you just made a phone call to whoever

Asshole is, after I told you about it. If that's the best you can do, I think I should call the police."

She turned his hand over, palm up, and dragged her fingertip up his forearm. Cool nail tracing a line of fire. "You know, Brady, there are other things I can do to make you feel better."

So there it was, the ultimate bribe. He watched her finger climb his arm, hating himself for liking it and feeling all rational thought fade as the greedy justifications crept in. Why not just help her out of the sash blouse and the little skirt? It wasn't a bribe if he didn't lie for her, right? She was a big girl who made her own decisions, he hadn't promised her anything.

He jerked his eyes away to break the spell, and caught her watching him. Watching him with the same exact expression lions on those nature shows have just before they pounce on some luckless antelope. Her eyes changed to warm in a click, but Brady knew right then that he did not want to be an antelope.

"Look, Lexy." He slid his arm away from her. "The reason I called you is to tell you that I can't say I saw Nick. Maybe if you tell him that, he'll leave me alone and I'll just forget about today." *Unless I can come up with a way to hose him up but good.*

She hugged her knees to her chest but kept her head turned toward him, the glossy hair swinging to the sunset side of her face and shimmering like black diamonds in the softening light. "Brady, I don't blame you for being angry. I am, too. But please don't make that decision now. Give it a few days. We'll talk then."

He sighed and averted his gaze, staring off in the direction of his thin slit of ocean view. Paradise. "I made my mind up before your two thugs made the scene, Lexy. I saw someone in your car, but I can't say that it was Nick. I'm sorry."

"Well, trust me then," she said. She leaned further around to catch his eye. Hers were wide and guileless. Looking, anyway.

"I'll handle this other mess, I promise you. Don't you believe me?"

"You know, I probably do, but it doesn't matter. I still didn't see him." Whatever anger he'd felt toward her had dissipated; she was just stuck doing the dirty work for the whole family. He hadn't imagined ever seeing her desperate, she'd always looked like she had the world in her palm.

"You're not going to help me at all?" she pleaded, all hurt little girl sounding. Which was pretty tough to buy into.

He just shook his head, ready for her to go, ready to be alone.

She stood and brushed off the back of her skirt. "Well, I'm sorry, too. Like you said, I'm sure we'll be all right without you, but it would have been nice to have your help." She walked around her car and opened the door. "You look out for yourself, Brady."

He watched her drive off, wondering if Advil would help the ribs and if her parting words were a warning.

CHAPTER TWENTY-ONE

Leo Burgess slammed both palms down on his desktop, the sound reverberating like a pistol shot in the closed room. "You are an absolute imbecile," he roared.

Nick's face immediately settled into the familiar defensive scowl. "What, Pops?" he whined.

"Don't *what* me, you idiot. You know perfectly well I am referring to you assaulting one of my tenants, and right here on our property."

Nick slouched back and crossed his legs in a show of nonchalance. "What are you talking about? I haven't assaulted anybody."

The sight of Nick's smirk dumped gasoline on Leo's fire. Snatching up the closest thing to his hand, a stack of mail, he hurled it at his son. "Shouldn't you be asking, 'Gee, who was assaulted'?"

"Okay, who?" Nick answered, dodging a magazine.

Leo counted to ten, listening to his heart pound. Maybe this would be it. He would fall over dead arguing with his brainless progeny. Perhaps Nick could be convicted of murder if the prosecutor could prove that the weapon was lethal stupidity. He inhaled slowly and tried patience. "This is not the way to do things. Never mind that it represents subhuman intellect and poor taste, it is illegal. Do you not realize that if Mr. Spain explains this to the authorities, we will be the only suspects?"

Nick sneered. "Oh, so it's that Spain guy, huh? What, he got beat up and you think I did it?"

"No, I know beyond any doubt that you did," Leo shouted. "No one else would concoct such a witless strategy." He took another deep breath. Patience, remember. How could his son be so fatuous?

"Well, if I did, and I'm not saying I did, it would've been done by somebody else with no connection to us." Nick straightened his legs and crossed his ankles and then his arms, sinking deeper in the chair. "And if I did, Spain wouldn't go to the cops, 'cause he'd know he'd get another dose," he added smugly.

Leo lunged across the desk and raised his hand as if to slap his son. Though aware he could not reach far enough, he wanted to make the boy cringe and lose his smirk. Screw patience. "I cannot believe how simple you are. Number one, the police will assume you hired it done. They will find your hooligans, who will surely turn on you. Or they may arrest you without that, because they don't even need it. You—have—the—only—motive." He slapped the desk between each word. "Has that penetrated yet? You have committed a colossal blunder. So listen.

"Number two, you have no idea what kind of man Brady Spain is. Nor do I. Some men do not scare. They become tougher. It is always foolish to embark on a course of action before you know your man. And his weak spot."

Leo paused, hoping for an acknowledgment that any of this had found its way through his son's thick skull. But no, Nick remained sprawled insouciantly in his chair, gazing out the window as if deaf. *Lord, help me,* thought Leo. *Perhaps I have not yet made myself clear. Perhaps it is time for this boy-man to risk something more than his father's wrath.*

"Pay attention, Nicolas. I am going to say this once." He held up a sausage-sized finger at arm's length in a manner he knew to be intimidating. "If the police investigate you for this assault, they will also take time to investigate you for rape. And for stalking." He paused again, seeing the boy's eyes begin to flicker from window to Leo, window to Leo. The gears grinding at last. "What we want from Mr. Spain is to help us avoid that investigation. Your reckless actions may very well achieve the opposite. That is why you do not interfere with the processes I put into place. I handle these things. You do not. Because you are not capable.

"Furthermore, if the police do investigate this family because of the calamity you have created, I will not, as you would say, take the rap. Nor will I allow your mother or your sister to become suspects in a criminal investigation. In short, I will give you up. Do you understand?"

He watched his son's eyes fill and his mouth open, but Leo cut him off with a wave of his hand. "Having said that, I will continue to attempt to reason with Mr. Spain. I will even accelerate my schedule of doing so, in the hopes that we can come to an agreement before you bring scandal to this family. On one condition: you will do nothing further in this matter whatsoever, and I mean nothing. If you do, not only will I let the police have you, I will wash my hands of you. Have I made myself clear?"

He stopped there, remembering that his walls had ears, and cognizant that even he had no guess as to what lengths Anna might go in order to protect her only son.

Nick stood, rubbing his hands up and down his pants legs like a little boy caught playing in the mud. "Just like that, Pops?"

Leo turned away from him and stared out the window, unable to look into the face of the man who was the child he'd brought into the world thirty years ago. He waved a hand of dismissal and listened for the door to close, feeling as if his heart was being ripped from his chest.

CHAPTER TWENTY-TWO

After twenty years in law enforcement and five more as a private investigator, Gerry Terence no longer fell into the trap of premature back-patting when good methodical detective work began yielding results. He'd seen too many convincing leads fizzle to consider anything short of arrest and conviction as true progress. But he couldn't deny a feeling of cautious satisfaction when things started clicking together and pointing a case in a specific direction.

Which is what he was feeling about the Heron Point case, both aspects of it. Not only had the window peeping ceased since he started patrolling, which met Leo's minimum description of success, Gerry had developed a suspect. Now he needed to figure a way to nail his guy down with some hard evidence. Nothing but catching it on film would do because of who it was.

The trail started with Susan Leland, the resident who'd caught a glimpse of their guy as he sprinted across a neighbor's lawn after being spotted at a window. Though eyewitnesses tended to be about as reliable as a dice roll, Gerry agreed with Pete on Susan. She was sharp and funny, freely describing herself as a nosy gossip-hound and pointing out that anyone who paid as much attention to other people's business as she did would notice and remember things. She could offer little detail, but stood firm enough on what she did see to give him a working parameter.

He took her description of white, skinny, medium height with dark hair, and began eliminating residents. He came up with a dozen possible matches, including teenagers. Alibi questions phrased as casual get-acquainted chatter boiled it down to two guys who were around at the time of each incident. One of the two was such a blatant homosexual that Gerry crossed him off without even talking to him.

Therefore it came down to two ifs. If Susan was right and if—a big if—the peeper lived in Heron Point, Nick Burgess was his guy. Okay, so it was a stretch. But it fit too good, felt too right in his gut. Nick was a squirrelly sort, carrying a dope habit, and he did not seem to have much dating life, especially for a rich guy. Fit the whole voyeur profile just fine for Gerry. Also explained why Leo Burgess hired him instead of putting more heat on the cops, but he hoped Leo hadn't hired him to go along with a wink, wink, nudge, nudge, boys-will-be-boys thing. That was going to piss Gerry off. Meanwhile, he drifted along behind Nick whenever he could, figuring sooner or later he would catch the punk with his pants down. Literally.

The other half of his investigation—work he'd been scrupulous about pursuing off the clock, since Leo wanted nothing to do with it—was the rape of Sara Zeletsky. The extra hours meant nothing; since Angie left he'd had little interest in anything except his work. And despite the added handicap of keeping it hidden from the Burgesses, Gerry had decided he just couldn't ignore the possibility that it might be the only way to solve the case Leo did hire him for.

Even less so once he talked to Joy Witt, the lady who had gotten the letter. Although Gerry never did get to see that letter, Joy remembered it vividly and wrote it down for him word for word. If she was even close, the man who wrote it seemed capable of rape. What she repeated didn't sound like the ramblings of some lonely weirdo pounding his pud. It was violent and degrading. Which made nailing Nick Burgess a must. But if he was the rapist, Gerry wanted him to go down for that, not peeping. He'd even put off talking with Pete on the drug situation until he got a better feel for whether he would be asking about a Peeping Tom or a rapist.

It was a question he hoped to answer soon, as he'd developed another angle to explore that might lead to closing the rape case first. Though he knew the major crimes division had assigned a lot of muscle to the Zeletsky assault—and running afoul of those guys was another thing he had to avoid—it didn't appear as if they were working it from a Heron Point outward approach.

So Gerry beat on doors until he dug up a guy living on Shoreline Drive who remembered seeing a car parked in the trees near Heron Point at the time of the attack on Sara. This guy, name of Kerry Gann, also saw the car drive off and was sure of the time within fifteen minutes.

Gann said he rarely paid much attention to cars in that area because "people park there all the time to fish or go for a stroll, blah, blah, blah," but this one was different. This car reminded Gann of his favorite car he'd ever owned: a seventy-eight Chevy Monte Carlo. He had watched it drive out simply because he rarely saw one old enough to bring back those happy memories of his. This heap looked just like his old car, only with narrow taillights. And he was sure about the Florida tag and that it was "that same God-awful brown that GM painted everything in those days."

Gerry researched it. General Motors built that body style from the late seventies to the late eighties. Boy, did they build it. Millions of them. Of the four models that shared the design, only the Oldsmobile Cutlass Supreme had narrow taillights. He begged a registration list from a vice detective he knew by promising a drug bust, thinking of the dealer in Heron Point and gambling he was right about that place.

The list of twenty-five to thirty-five year-old Cutlasses still running around was longer than he'd expected. Gerry found it hard to believe there were that many out on the road, considering he'd limited his registrations request to a fifty-mile radius. He was betting the perp was a local, not a transient who stopped off for a quick rape. And he knew scouring the entire state would be an impossible task for one man anyway. Of course, even if he was on the right track, he was nowhere if the car was stolen, borrowed, or repainted. Or if Gann was wrong.

He started in on his list, trimming it down by phone before heading out to pound on more doors. By then he'd need to find out whether the detectives assigned to the case were working the Gann lead. They would crucify him if they crossed paths interviewing the same witnesses. As he worked his way through his Cutlass owners, he mused about Pete's secret. He felt ready to take odds Pete knew, or at least suspected, that Nick was their window fogger. Sure fit everything else. But he struggled to swallow the concept of Pete covering for a rapist, even one named Burgess.

CHAPTER TWENTY-THREE

Brady found the escape he needed by burying himself in his job. He doubled the programming and training schedule and then ran like a mad dog for twelve to fourteen hours a day to keep up, which kept his thoughts away from Lexy and the embarrassment he felt for building that big dream castle around his own ideas of who she was.

By the end of the week, he'd gained such a lead on his project timeline that Ed had begun openly discussing the creation of the Internet sales department with him, all but assuring Brady that he'd be heading it up. So today, seeing as he was the only idiot haunting the place on a Sunday afternoon, Brady decided to shut it down and get out of there before dark for a change. Go take in a sunset and that ocean view he was paying for. Maybe even get to see one without any visits from hired gorillas or bullshit artists in miniskirts. He scooted across the blistering blacktop and managed to slide into the Jeep without touching any of his skin to the searing vinyl interior surfaces. He flipped the air conditioning on high and drove with fingertips while the air conditioner labored to pull the temperature back down below the blistering point.

He hadn't spoken to Lexy since that day. He'd trusted her promise to take care of the thug threat, though he hadn't lost the jitters and still kept his head in constant rotation every time he went anywhere. Nor had he reported the assault, reasoning that she'd be more likely than the cops to get results. With no

132

visible injuries or evidence other than an ambiguous hearsay reference against a family with much more clout than him, he suspected the cops would think he was nuts, and file his report in the dumpster.

He let himself in the house and tossed the week's worth of mail on the counter, thinking a beer would be nice and maybe a pizza. He bent down to retrieve an envelope that fluttered to the floor. It was from his bank and it did not look like the monthly statement. That was never good news. He opened it, noticing another envelope just like it in the stack on the counter. He unfolded the opened one and read it.

He had bounced a check. Number 146. No way, no how, he always triple-checked his math. He snatched the checkbook down from the cabinet he used for financial papers, riffling through the register with panicky fingers. And oh shit, number 146 was the three grander to Burgess Properties, LLC; the check Lexy had promised to hold. Got to be an oversight, no way she'd go so low because of her brother, would she? He wrenched his phone out of its belt clip and punched in her number.

"Hey, Brady, what's up?" At least she wasn't ducking his calls, though the hopeful note in her voice ticked him off.

"What's up? What's up with the check?" he asked, heart pounding as if his chest was just a hollow space for it to leap around in.

"What do you mean?" she said. Still cheery sounding, but cautious.

"You cashed my check. The one you were going to hold?"

"Of course we cashed your check. What do you mean, hold?"

"You're kidding, right?" He was too stunned to come up with anything else.

"I'm not sure what we're talking about, Brady. You wrote a check, we deposited it. That's what you do with checks." Her voice had assumed the brisk, professional tone he remembered from their first conversation, when he had called inquiring about the house. "Are you saying it isn't good?"

Brady backed into a chair and sat, leaning over and banging his forehead gently on the table. Once, twice, three times. He could not believe she was doing this, she was actually going to do this to him. "So you don't remember our conversation where you said you would hold that check for four weeks? Hell, it was your idea."

"I certainly don't recall any such conversation," she said, putting a little pop into the come-hither voice. "And I would never agree to hold a check, anyway."

"Really." He didn't know whether to laugh or cry.

"I'm sorry, Brady. I turn all that over to Dad. You'll have to talk to him." Totally cold now, like she was reading a teleprompter.

"That's funny, before you said he never handled this stuff. I can't believe you're going to pretend none of it ever happened. You're amazing. How do you sleep at night?"

"Like a baby, sweetie. So I suppose I should tell Dad to expect that check to bounce?"

He did laugh then, an uncontrollable bark. Maybe to keep from crying. "Boy, we've come a long way in just three weeks, haven't we, Lexy? Talk to Dad, huh?"

"That's what you need to do," she said firmly, then added, in a softer tone, "I am sorry, Brady. I really am."

The sincerity in her apology was unmistakable, perhaps a hint that she didn't approve of this complete freaking screw job, but it did nothing to mollify his anger. Because he could picture her, punching off her phone, swinging her long black hair over her shoulder in a regretful shrug and moving on, with no more thought given to him than she would the Tibetan stock market. So he clicked off first, without another word, and tossed the phone over on the stack of mail. Right on top of the other envelope from the bank. No, damn it, there were two more.

His heart started galloping again, his mouth suddenly dry and sticky, as he ripped open what was sure to be more financial disaster. The bank had bounced the same check, number 146, a second time. Three days after the first bounce, he noticed. He had never heard of bouncing a check twice. They charged him both times, too. And holy smokes, thirty-eight bucks apiece. The third letter told him that check number 161 had also been returned, the same day as the second charge for 146.

He examined the checkbook register again. It made no sense, 161 was only sixty bucks, the phone bill. Then he realized the seventy-six dollars in charges had run his balance too low. Usually he kept a little cushion for emergencies or addition mistakes, but he had felt so pleased at being able to pay every single bill with his last paycheck, he had run it right down near zero. Now, with a hundred and fourteen in service charges, he had a negative balance. And no cash to deposit. Maybe he had room on a credit card for a cash advance. He sure to God hoped so.

Then he felt the blood draining from his head as he realized that the sixty bucks his balanced gained from 161 bouncing would not be enough to stop another one from bouncing. At least one. Oh God, which was worse, the embarrassment of having his checks returned all over town, or the thirty-eight-dollar charges that would keep multiplying like bunnies? Great. He wadded the whole mess up and hurled it at the wall.

He walked around the neighborhood a few hundred times, his brain pinballing from anger at Lexy to anger at himself to terror over his finances and back to Lexy again, all the while drawing curious stares from the detective dude. A quarter moon followed his every step, its hooked nose and pointed chin sneering down at the self-inflicted failings of Brady Spain.

In time, his feet cried uncle and he drove aimlessly through town, trying to figure a way out of the Burgess drama without giving in on the alibi. No answer except talk to Dad, which smelled like a guaranteed disaster, based on Lexy's flip-flop. He went home, stretched out on the bed, and counted the palm tree shadows made by the streetlights on the ceiling. He paged through his checkbook again, trying to estimate what the final damage would be. Sleep never came.

Eventually, he showered, dressed, and went on to work. Paced the floor of his cramped office until nine o'clock came and the bank opened. He called and got a lady named Julia who claimed to be customer service but sounded more like customer discipline.

"Normally a check would not be returned twice, sir, you are right. But this check was presented on different days by separate institutions. So you must have presented this check twice. We had no choice, since the funds were not available at either time." This last part said with the appropriate inflection of distaste reserved for deadbeats with no funds.

"But you shouldn't charge me twice."

"I'm sorry, sir. The cost of each transaction is the same, as outlined in your account agreement."

"What if I had postdated it?" Wishing he had. "Would that have kept it from bouncing?"

"We don't recognize postdating, sir. We recommend that you never write a check without sufficient funds. Not only is it illegal, it is a breach of your account agreement."

"Wow, you sure are helpful. How do I keep it from bouncing every day for the rest of my life and you guys scoring thirty-eight bucks every time?"

"You may stop payment on the check, sir. There is a fee for that, and since you have a negative balance, you will need to stop by one of our branch offices to pay for it. Although I will say that most banking institutions do not accept checks for deposit that have been stamped 'non-sufficient funds' as yours has."

"Boy, you just can't make a sentence without bring up the non-sufficient funds, can you? I got it, okay? I got it."

After a while it became monotonous, and he gave up and disconnected, after promising to stop in and fix the negative balance. He could admit his predicament was not the bank's fault, recognizing it as his own for trusting Lexy. No matter how much guilt he wanted to lay off on her for betraying their agreement, it was his fault for taking the risk. But it would be nice to have someone at his own bank at least act sympathetic, not just tell him what a dumbass he was.

He slogged through the day, alternating between exhaustion and anxiety. Possibilities bouncing around his head like ping-pong balls. Moving out from Heron Point seemed the best solution, but he suspected it would have no effect on the pressure for him to alibi Nick. If they wanted, they could force him to stay or pay, he had signed a year's lease. Come to think of it, if Burgess let him out of his lease, he didn't have the ready funds to get a new place anyway. And he sure didn't want to ask for his room back at work. Qué embarrassing. Maybe he should just go into it cool, play the apology card, and give Burgess a chance to wave it off as a misunderstanding. If that bombed, he would go to the cops and take his best shot at siccing them on Nick.

He slipped out at three-thirty, angered by the realization that now the Burgess double-cross even had him compromising his professional commitments. He swung by the bank, squeezed a hundred bucks out of his Visa, and headed for his showdown with Dad.

CHAPTER TWENTY-FOUR

Brady had seen the Burgess mansion, of course, but not up close, and brother, it was stout. Standing in front of it with the conscious perspective of the wealth and power of this man who might be an enemy felt kind of knee-knocking. He rang the bell and waited, glancing around to see if he was on camera.

The woman who answered the door would have fit the stereotype of a Russian grandmother if not for the funky pinkish-red dye job. She led him to a room decked out like an executive conference suite, all leather and cherry wood. She left, closing the door behind her, and he wandered over to a pair of oversized windows facing down Palm Avenue. He couldn't quite make out his house, but he could pinpoint where it was behind the trees.

"Good afternoon, Mr. Spain," a voice said. A voice so deep it sounded somewhere between Herman Munster and a diesel engine.

He spun around to see a man standing behind a bar in the far corner on the other side of the door, stirring a glass of something. Older guy, craggy-faced, black hair shot with gray, and big.

"Would you care for a drink?" the man asked, holding his glass up. He crossed the room before Brady answered, extending a hand. "I'm Leo Burgess."

"Nice to meet you," Brady said, though the jury was still out on that. "No thanks on the drink." At six-three, he didn't have to look up at many people, but he did for Leo Burgess. Seriously big dude. His face made Brady want to stare, the bones were so projecting and heavy-looking. Like Mount Rushmore or something. Hard to believe Lexy's exquisite features came out of this man.

"Well, have a seat then," Burgess said, waving him to a grouping of chairs near the windows.

"I came to apologize about my returned check," Brady said once they sat. "Apparently there's been a misunderstanding between Lexy and me."

"The matter of the check is easily forgivable, these things happen. Naturally, I will require you to replace it with certified funds or a cashier's check." He smiled genially at Brady. "Now what is this about a misunderstanding?"

Okay, so far it's all cool, thought Brady, *maybe I overreacted.* He went through the entire lease-signing conversation for Burgess, careful to make Lexy sound courteous and helpful in his telling, but emphasizing that the hold check idea came from her. Which hopefully explained why he could not produce a cashier's check yet.

"Quite a tale, Mr. Spain," Burgess said when he finished. Still genial, but with a hint of amusement in his expression that worried Brady. He crossed his legs, dangling the largest loafer Brady had ever seen. Big enough to need a license plate. "I must tell you, I have spoken with Alexandra and she has no recollection of any such conversation."

Brady bit back a groan. *Lexy, Lexy, why, girl?* He felt the two middle fingers of his right hand flicking his palm and covered it with his left. "Does this sound like something I would make up?"

"Immaterial, Mr. Spain," Burgess said, waving the question away. "Memories are quirky and unpredictable things. If the two of you remember it differently, then I have no choice but to believe one or the other. I choose to accept Alexandra's version of events. You can understand that, can't you, Mr. Spain?" The amusement came out of hiding now, a hard-edged grin splitting the heavy jowls. "For example, you have suffered a recent memory loss of another incident, have you not?"

Brady could only stare in response, feeling his pulse jumping in his neck. How about the pair on this guy? Guess that was it for the misunderstanding gambit.

Burgess chuckled. "Surprised I wish to discuss our differences so openly? Why not? I have learned, over many years of business negotiations, that little is gained by talking around a subject. You should agree, I hear you have quite a promising career in the making." He waggled a finger. "Something you do not want to jeopardize. Now, are you prepared to redeem your fraudulent check?"

"No, I'm not." Brady sat up on the edge of his seat, leaning forward for emphasis. "You know I'm not and you know why. And you know it's not fraudulent." To hell with this guy, his millions and his bigger than a damn mountain self. To hell with him.

"Actually, it is." Burgess rose, moving back to the bar. "I am in contact with my attorney, who advises me that you have committed a fraud if you cannot satisfy the debt. I can swear out a warrant if I wish, and you will be arrested. Then you will be facing a fine and probation, certainly, perhaps a prison term." He returned to his chair with the new drink, sat back, and crossed his legs in the opposite direction of before. "What you and I have to decide is if I am to swear out that warrant."

Brady sprang up and went to the window, squelching the impulse to run screaming from the house and away from the craziness. He couldn't, not until he knew more. Fraud? Prison? Had to be a bluff, he could explain everything. But what if no one would listen? "What do you want from me?"

"Me?" Burgess chuckled again. "It's not a question of what I want. You wished to rent a home and thus entered into a contract with specific requirements. I am merely asking that you fulfill those requirements or I will take the appropriate legal action. However, I can assure you that if your memory were to improve, Alexandra's would as well."

Brady whipped around to face him, feeling his every muscle stiffen from the anger crawling up his back. "You mean testify that I saw Nick with Lexy."

"See? You do like plain speaking. Good for you." Burgess set his drink down and held up his hand, palm out. "I doubt testifying will be necessary. Merely confirming the fact if you are asked should be sufficient."

"Why are y'all so fired up about this? Why do you need me? Did he do it?" Brady asked, anxious to know just how deep this quicksand was.

"No, he did not," snapped Burgess. The blue eyes glittered like an icy lake, and Brady realized this man would ruin him with about the same compunction he'd feel crushing a cockroach. "Why we need your corroboration is not your concern. Your concern is deciding what is best for Brady Spain."

"And if I don't change my story?"

"Then you will be arrested for passing bad checks. It will mean the end of your career and a permanent criminal record. To say nothing about prison, which I understand is not the healthiest place for a young man such as yourself. Have we reached an agreement?"

Brady took a deep breath and held it. Scared as he was that Burgess might not be bluffing, it was too late to turn back. *Okay Mom, here goes. Looks like I'm not one of Lexy's "right kind of people" after all.*

"This is your agreement," he said. "I'll have your money in a week, just like I told Lexy. What I saw, or didn't see, on that day, is the same. No Nick."

"One week, eh?" Burgess smiled at him, not genial at all now. More like an alligator in a meat locker. "Frankly, that is unacceptable. If you are of the opinion that you can prevent your imminent arrest, I believe I can proceed if the warrant predates attempted restitution." He paused and cocked his head to the side, locking the frozen blue eyes onto Brady's. "And if you are planning to leave the city, please know that my attorney assures me such action will guarantee your being convicted of the charges. I think you will find you have no options except improving your recall."

Brady stood, the lower half of his face numb with disbelief, but he'd said his piece and there was nothing else to learn here. He could forget about talking this thing out, the man was dead-set.

Burgess stood too, and waggled a forefinger the size of a salami in Brady's face. "Furthermore, you may as well forget this notion of filing a police report that implicates anyone in my family or employ in the assault on you. No, do not look surprised that I anticipate such an obvious countermeasure. I would like to point out that anyone who has a habit of writing bad checks should expect to have problems with unsavory creditors. Especially if there is a witness who heard your assailants mention such a debt. See how memories work?"

He strode to the door and pulled it wide. "I don't particularly care whether or not you are convicted. The damage to your life is sufficient to satisfy my pique, and your refusal to corroborate Alexandra will be readily accepted as a petty attempt at revenge by a disgruntled felon. Have a good day, Mr. Spain."

CHAPTER TWENTY-FIVE

Ellie Macken was on her way to meet her lover again. Except she couldn't seem to get out of the house and on the road today. All J.D.'s fault, what else?

"I'm telling you, it's not here," she shouted at her phone where it lay atop the counter on the far end of the kitchen, on speaker mode.

"Look again, babe, it has to be there somewhere," J.D.'s voice echoed across the room. She could hear the exasperation even through the tiny speaker and it made her want to tell him to go screw himself. Seems he'd lost his precious iPad and now Ellie had to take the house apart in search of it. If she gave in to her temper and told him off, he might come home to look, and that would not do.

"I have looked and looked. Did you try your car?" *And please just hang up so I won't be late,* she thought. Her date was the third this week, a first. A tantalizing taste of heaven that just made her want more. Today's rendezvous was extra special because she intended to bring up that very subject. When could they be together? When could she leave J.D.? Could they move in together? She wanted everyone else to see how lucky she was.

She felt sure her timing was right; getting this much of her lover's busy schedule simply could not be a coincidence. And Mom was home from the hospital and feeling better, lifting the big worry off Ellie's mind that her shocking news might endanger Mom's health. Though Ellie was peeved with J.D. for acting so irritable when she tried to share the news of Mom's recovery, that too was just another sign. Time for him to get told what's what, go somewhere and be crabby by himself. Fate was sending all the messages that this was it: the most important day of her life was here.

"Are you sure you didn't borrow it and misplace it somewhere?"

She strode across the kitchen, snatched the phone up, and banged it against the wall, hoping it broke his eardrum. "I'm not your child, J.D., don't speak to me like that."

"Damn it, Ell, this is important," he yelled.

Ellie shoved her fist in her teeth and bit it hard enough to make her wince. *Calm down,* she cautioned herself, *because he's wrong. You need to keep your eye on what really* is *important.* "All right, I'll keep digging around, and I'll text you if I have any luck, okay?" she said once she'd lassoed her temper.

She punched off, and with one last glance in the mirror banged out the door. And stopped and stared at J.D.'s iPad lying on the patio table. *So that's where the stupid thing's been hiding.* She wrinkled her nose at it. Well, too damn bad. Can't have him coming home to get it, and no way she was taking it to him. She jumped into her Accord and flew down the driveway.

Her excitement burned so hot that she was bringing two gifts to mark the special occasion. Gift number one was a fabulous new cologne she had found quite by accident while shopping, a rich spicy scent that had instantly reminded her of her sweetheart. The second present was a bit more daring. The hot, steamy fantasizing she'd done while waxing her bikini line emboldened her to go much further than normal, shaping hers into a little Mohawk like she'd heard lingerie models did. Painful process, but erotic, too. Now she felt shy about it, hoping it would be a real turn-on, maybe even a little kinky.

She turned right onto Shoreline and jammed down on the

gas, prompting a satisfying squeal of rubber. Almost there, she thought, feeling her stomach begin fluttering. Sex with her lover was so much better than she'd ever imagined possible—simple, with no poses or roles to play, just tenderness and discovery. They shared an intimacy that J.D. wasn't capable of; they could talk about things he wouldn't even begin to understand. She'd been such a moron, settling for J.D. all these years. Ellie laughed out loud at how wonderful it was to feel like a teenager again. Funny to think she used to believe she knew what love was.

The overdue sleep came at last, once his exhausted body rebelled and cut off the adrenalin supply to Brady's racing brain. He woke after just four hours of it, however, with his thoughts back to running laps around his head at light-speed. So he spent the rest of the wee hours like any good computer jock would—googling for answers. What he found wasn't pretty.

Burgess had not been bluffing. The amount of the bounced check classified the offense as a third degree felony, for which he could be sentenced to no more than five years. The phrasing annoyed him. What, was the "no more than" supposed to make him feel better?

The only gray area the law provided as a possible out required him to prove the payee had reason to know or suspect the check was bad. And he could forget that ever happening if Lexy and Dad presented a unified front denying any such knowledge. Nor had Burgess bluffed about the restitution thing. Even if Brady made the check good, the felony charges could proceed. It seemed preposterous that any court of law actually would, but how could he take the chance? Surely there was some defense available to a guy telling the truth, wasn't there? He needed a lawyer. And how was he going to pay for that? Great, just friggin' great.

He still wanted to believe Lexy's conscience would not allow her to shaft him if he was really headed to prison, but talk about your classic case of wishful thinking. After meeting Leo Burgess, he guessed she would have to toe the line or get crushed too, daughter or not.

That thought made him thank God for Johnny Torres. The all-night drunken karaoke parties were the closest things to poor parenting Brady could remember from his father, and those seemed like all good fun back then. The divorce had been painful, losing his fun-loving playmate Dad. Brady was only six at the time. Not that he ever second-guessed living with Mom, knowing with a child's inner survival instinct that Johnny was incapable of single parenthood. But he couldn't help every once in a while wondering if Johnny would be proud of his success.

His crash course in the ruthless nature of the real Lexy Burgess also provoked an uncomfortable yet unavoidable comparison to Peggy. Just as Lexy was everything Peggy wasn't, Peggy had everything Lexy didn't. And it sure would help right now if Lexy had some of those unwavering down-home morals.

Served him right, didn't it? He was the one who just had to escape the confines of small-town life on Tobacco Road, get a taste of the highlife and the beautiful people. Well, he was getting it, all right. The whole Norman Rockwell image of two hayseeds hitching up and never leaving the farm had suffocated him. And he'd pulled away from Peggy simply because she was part of that picture, not because of one single damn thing wrong with her. Didn't that rationale feel embarrassingly shallow now? She looked pretty wonderful compared to this bunch here in paradise. Not that any of it mattered, his next romance would be with some giant convict named Bubba unless he figured a way out of this mess, and soon.

The spiraling effect of all the negative thoughts feeding on each other began to remind Brady of a toilet flushing, swirling around until they dragged him out of sight. Going on in to work was the only therapy he could come up with that might keep him from jumping out a window or something, and he did owe the job a couple of hours after yesterday.

Good decision, too, because driving through the gorgeous sunrise did wonders for his funk. It was a new experience for him, as he'd never timed his drive in just right before. The kaleidoscope of changing colors as the sun broke the horizon had a clear, almost painful beauty that would boost a dead man's morale. He opened the Jeep's windows to let the cool overnight air rush through, fresh and clean and smelling like the promise of everything good. Just dodge the doorbell and screen his calls for a week, and then send Burgess a certified check with a letter giving the thirty days' notice required to break his lease. He would take his chances on Burgess being able to put him in the slammer after that.

He soon felt even more pleased with himself for going in early, since he had an e-mail from Ed Schlatt: See me as soon as convenient. He took the steps two at a time up a floor to Schlatt's office, his heart jumping like a wild thing. Forget the Burgess hysteria, this could be it, the opportunity he was waiting for.

"Ah, Brady," Schlatt said, looking up from a file spread open on his desk. "Come in, have a seat."

Brady did, trying to keep his face ho-hum, not expectant. Schlatt leaned his elbows against the desk and formed a globe shape with his hands by matching up the fingertips. Brady recognized it as Ed's "important company business" posture.

"Brady, I have the unpleasant task of informing you that we have decided to go in a different direction with our sales and reservations." Schlatt cleared his throat. "Effective immediately, the company will no longer require your services."

Brady sat frozen for a moment, replaying the words for something he had missed, searching Schlatt's face for signs of humor. No way, just no damn way. "Excuse me, did you just fire me?"

"Well, I wouldn't call it firing, but yes, we are terminating your employment," said Schlatt, and cleared his throat again. "As you know, you are still in the probationary period of your contract, when we may choose to terminate our agreement at any time with no notice. I am sorry it has to be this way, and we wish you the best of luck."

What, did he practice this pompous garbage in front of the mirror or something? Brady felt his blood racing with adrenalin, his hands shaking, even his lips numb and quivery. Just no damn way. "I don't get it. Didn't you tell me just the other day how great it was going, how enthusiastic you were about building and expanding on what we've done?"

"Yes, I did, and I won't retract that statement. In fact, no one at Beach Haven has found your work to be anything but exemplary." Schlatt paused and squirmed around in his chair. His eyes showed a glint of apology, guilty conscience maybe, the first sign of the Ed Schlatt he had worked with for nearly two months. "Sometimes financial considerations and the long-term future of a company take precedence over individuals. That's where we find ourselves."

"Financial considerations? What, you suddenly can't afford me?" And then bang, he got it. Burgess. Had to be. The fattest wallet always wins in business. But how? The man certainly did not own Beach Haven Resorts; Brady knew all of the principals. "Okay, then, whose idea was it, Ed, if my performance is so exemplary?"

"Now, Brady," he said, tapping his fingertips together in unison. "You know I cannot discuss that. As I said, I'm sorry."

Then the rest of the equation hit Brady. Burgess and money. No job, no money. No money, no chance of escaping Burgess. He did the math, staring blindly at Ed's bogus sympathetic expression. *One week, eh?* Burgess had asked him, laughing. Without a full paycheck, Brady could not make his check good and pay the rent. Burgess totally had him by the gonads. Unless . . . "What about severance pay, Ed? Surely I'm due something."

"I'm afraid not. There is no such provision in your contract for probationary employees." Schlatt winked and showed him a chummy smile. "However, I will see to it that you get paid for a full half-day today so you will have time to clean out your desk."

CHAPTER TWENTY-SIX

Digger Carrero kept the door cracked until the crazy fuck disappeared from sight, then slipped out without even bothering to pack a bag. He needed to vacate his crib, get gone before old cop came back. Needed to stay gone for a while too, hook up with somebody who would let him domicile at their crib. Dude claimed he wasn't Law, but damn sure acted like it, looked like it, smelled like it.

Maybe not, though, 'cause the man asked some weird-ass questions about his car, offering a reward if Digger could prove if he was a witness to some shit. All smiling and friendly-like too, talking through the door chain like they were old buddies. Not the way any Law Digger had ever met acted, but dude had to be some kind of cop. Said his name was Gerry Terry or some such bullshit. Well, Digger wasn't waiting for him to come back. He could be Vice, they was all crazy anyway, and Digger was carrying a nice supply of meth he had just cooked up.

The real worry was if old fat-ass, cheap-suit-wearing freak had come by because he knew about Digger's last ponytail girl. Shouldn't be, she never scratched him or pulled his hair, nothing for the DNA man. And he had worn a sock on his junk, so nothing there either. It was just the car thing had him going off. Maybe he would dump the Olds on somebody else, hook himself up with a new ride.

First things first, though. He could call Roni, stay there, but being around her would get him thinking on things and he'd need to find him another bitch. He hated all them whiny kids of hers anyway. Better to go out clubbing tonight, socialize, get up with somebody let him hang at their place. Then maybe go get himself another ponytail girl after all, now that thinking about Roni done fired up the old king cobra. Damn, that last jogger-girl was sweet. Another one just like her.

Pete Cully used his key to let himself into the home of Lexy Burgess, per her instructions, following up on her report of a leaking water heater. Two steps in, he locked up like a rusty chainsaw, shocked into complete immobility. He just stared. And stared. And stared, his brain unwilling to accept what his eyes told him. Beautiful, crazy, and oh so damn young Lexy lay on one hip in front of her fireplace, with her back twisted to where both shoulders touched the floor and her head turned to one side. Nude. A gaping jagged gash torn across her throat, wide enough for tissue and cartilage to show. A bloodied fire poker lay beside her, silently telling its part of the story. And lots and lots and lots of blood.

Flies had found a way in somehow, and when he saw them, Pete Cully's muscles finally unlocked. He doubled over and vomited violently right in the middle of everything. The realization of what he had just done to the crime scene and the spasm that said he was close to doing it again sent him scurrying outside to pollute the lawn instead.

Lexy, Lexy, Lexy. The powerful sense of loss that hammered at him came as a surprise. She had been absolutely wild and temperamental, self-centered as you could get, and promiscuous to the point of deviancy. But seeing her there ripped open, gone for good, reminded him of a different Lexy. The high-school senior he had met nine years back, full of fire and wanting a piece of the world. Wild even then, but always with a sweet side for Uncle Pete. That teenager was whom he saw in his mind now. He dearly wanted to go back in and cover her up, but he knew that was the wrong move if he wanted the cops to catch her murderer.

He jabbed out 911 on his cell with quivering fingers, and promised to stay where he was. *Wonder which boy-toy killed her,* he thought as he waited. Macken was the only current one he knew of, but trust Lexy to always keep a string of at least three or four. Rage came boiling up through his sorrow, and he said a quick prayer for a chance to stomp the life out of whichever bastard did this. Such a miserable waste. He coughed, cleared his throat, spat, blew his nose, spat again. Picked the phone back up from where he had dropped it. Time to call boss man.

Maggie Davis set her vodka tonic on the kitchen sink sideboard and flipped her phone around to see the screen. "OMG, did you hear she was naked?" the text read. She closed her eyes and made a gagging motion with her finger.

The news of Lexy's murder had ripped through Heron Point with the speed and impact of a tidal wave. Not only did everyone know Lexy personally, it seemed impossible for such a tragedy to strike a Burgess. But as usual, no one could retell the story without adding his or her own rumors, theories, and embellishments.

Most of her circle believed it to also be the work of the Peeping Tom, that he had moved up to rape and ultimately murder. They were angry at the police for failing to catch the psycho early on, and even angrier with the security guy, Terence, for what they saw as total incompetence. Maggie disagreed with the popular theory, but that wasn't the reason behind her disenchantment with her gossip network. It had been coming on since the rape anyway, and she just found the image of Lexy's death too horrifying to serve as tasteful chitchat material. She couldn't stomach the undertones of delight in their voices at having such a gruesome topic to chew on. She kept picturing people discussing Kimmy's death with the same breathless hunger for more lurid details. Her disgust slapped her in the face with the nasty truth that she was one of them, forcing her to realize she did not like the person she had become.

In her opinion, Gerry Terence was on the ball. After years of developing the knack of noticing who was doing what with whom, at least when she was on the early side of her drink count, she recognized the trait in someone else. And that man didn't miss a thing. Which told her that the murderer, whether the same guy or not, lived in Heron Point. Otherwise, Gerry would have seen him. Which in turn just reinforced her premonition of Heron Point crumbling to pieces, something rotten at the core collapsing. Just like her, rotting from the inside out.

In a moment of clarity normally beyond her reach, Maggie knew she was done. Gone, leaving Heron Point. She also came to the startling yet equally decisive insight that, despite their differences, she loved Mark enough to want him to go with her. It wasn't his fault she hadn't been giving the marriage a chance, making him the scapegoat for her despair at what Maggie Thibideaux had become. And though she had the shameful thought that Lexy's death could open the door for her with Brady, her rush of clarity included the recognition that Brady's fine body wouldn't fix anything either, appetizing as it might be. She had to stop the merry-go-round, and the only way to do it was to leave the carnival. So for her own survival, she had to get out, with or without Mark.

The phone rang. She reached for it like one of Pavlov's dogs, and then slowly drew her hand back. *Done is done.* She waited for it to quit ringing and picked up her drink for a swallow. Halfway to her mouth, she stopped. *Done is done.* And Maggie Davis did something unthinkable up until five minutes before. She leaned across the counter and poured the rest of her drink down the drain.

153

CHAPTER TWENTY-SEVEN

Brady decided to bail out, reaching that conclusion during his morning shower ritual. Not because of the murder of Lexy Burgess, although it had surely knocked any remaining glitter off of life in paradise. His sadness at the news was so complete that his anger toward her vanished in light of the terrible fate she had suffered. He felt haunted by how vibrant and alive she had been. Then zap, all gone. Unplugged. Regardless of how she'd betrayed him, no one deserved that. He had no idea if she had hooked up with a violent boyfriend or something, knew nothing of her personal life, but based on his experience with her he had to wonder if her other business dealings were as treacherous. Could be she crossed someone who had a vicious streak.

No, he was moving out because he had no choice financially if he was to have any defense in a legal battle against Leo Burgess. In the two days since Schlatt cut him loose, he had job-hunted enough to believe he could land one, but found no start-right-away propositions. And he feared the long reach of Burgess would torpedo any background check. With the end of the month looming and too little money to come up with both the rent and the needed replacement check, forfeiting his last month's rent in lieu of notice stood as his only chance. At least then, he would be able to show that he left no debts hanging.

If he used these last three days to pack up what he could and scoot out under the radar, he might be able to find a place he could get into with what little cash he had. He couldn't think of anyone to hit for a quick loan, especially when he couldn't venture the vaguest guess as to when he might be able to repay it. And the butt-kicker was, even if he got the money he stayed on the hook for fraud, the way he understood the law. Nor did blowing out of Heron Point mean he could leave town. Even considering such an action gave him visions of a national fugitive chase, with his picture hanging in the post office captioned, "Have you seen this Filipino?"

The hope came to him, so cold-hearted and self-centered he felt dismay at even thinking of it: maybe he could just get lost in the uproar over Lexy's death. Maybe no one would care whether Nick had an alibi for the rape. But then the same wise-ass little voice pointed out that as soon as Burgess realized Brady now represented Nick's only chance at an alibi, things were going to get even uglier.

The coffee finished brewing with a gurgling rush of steam, and he took his cup out on the porch with him. He expected to see Pete out and about early, having pegged him as a guy who would use work as his method of coping with tragedy. Brady wanted to tell Pete of his plans, the guy was his only friend here, but he could not afford for Burgess to know yet. Friend or not, Pete was Burgess's right-hand man. Brady had no idea how much Pete might know of the squeeze he was in—neither of them had ever brought it up.

He eased out to the porch without slopping his coffee and glanced around, but no Pete. Instead, what he did see was a black BMW parked diagonally across his lawn, its nose crumpled against a palm tree. He set his cup down and came on out to investigate what the hell this deal was. As he neared the car he saw a man inside, slumped back at an angle in the driver's seat with his head resting against the side window. *Oh, that's just great,* he thought, *all I need now is a dead guy in my yard.*

He tapped lightly on the passenger-side glass, but the man did not move. He knocked harder. Still nothing. Figuring there couldn't be a law against opening a car in your own yard, he tried the door. It opened, and a dry, raspy snore told him the man was a long way from dead. The foul odor of stale whiskey made it clear how he ended up in Brady's yard. So what to do now? Was there any such thing as a drunk-removal service? He did not have the heart to call the police on the guy, in light of his own current predicament.

He looked the sleeping man over. Probably a neighbor in paradise, but he was a stranger to Brady. A few years older than himself, dressed in crumpled business attire, he looked like he would be the pretty-boy type when not passed out on someone's lawn. Brady's stint as a bartender had taught him never to wake a drunk sleeping in his car. Some of them wake up mean and you never know which one is armed.

Before he came to any decision the guy's eyes popped open, milky and bloodshot. He peered at Brady, looked around the car, moved a sticky-sounding tongue around in his mouth, and peered at Brady again.

"Hey, man, what're you doing in my yard?" the guy asked. It all ran together as one word, meaning forget hangover, he was still bombed. Late night or lots of booze. Probably both.

"Sorry for the confusion, friend," Brady said in his best bartender style. "But this is actually my yard. Where do you live?"

The guy closed one eye and shook a finger at him. "Are you screwing my wife? Trying to sneak out?"

Uh-oh, hope he isn't one of the armed kind. "Buddy, I don't even know who your wife is. Maybe we can call her. We gotta get you home."

" 'Cause if you are, I don't blame you. She's still pretty hot. And I'm done with her."

"Trust me, I'm not. What's your name, friend?"

"Jefferson Davis Macken," he said proudly. He pounded his chest, setting off a coughing fit. When it subsided, he said, "I go by J.D., though. Don't want everybody thinking I'm a diehard racist like my parents." His eyes watered up. "Can you believe they could do that to a little boy? Name him that?"

"Sounds terrible," Brady agreed. Crying drunks were better than shooting drunks, but not exactly fun either. "Look, J.D., I'm Brady, it's nice to meet you. Where do you live, partner?"

"Are you sure you aren't screwing my wife?" The tears started rolling now. " 'Cause it's okay if you are. She deserves better than me anyway."

"I'm sure. What's her name, let's call her."

"Then what the hell are you doing in my yard?" J.D. demanded belligerently, his tears shutting off like a tap.

"J.D., we covered this, it's not your yard. Here, get out and look for yourself." *And walk some of this off so you can get out of my life.*

J.D. nodded solemnly and clambered out without quite falling flat. He cast a suspicious glare around, blinking against the morning sun. "Well, no damned wonder I parked in the yard. Somebody moved the driveway to the wrong side of the house. And holy shit, what happened to my car?"

He attempted a quick move toward the front of the BMW, promptly stopped, and threw up on the lawn.

Brady sighed, turning away from the nauseating smell. "Gee, thanks, dude. That's really going to help the grass." He took advantage of the break in the comedy to paw through the dash compartment. Here we go: J.D. Macken, thirty-nine Cypress Lane. Just one street over and one block off. Heck, he could walk back.

Hearing that the worst of the retching had stopped, he walked to his Jeep, grabbed a bottle of water, and handed it to his wobbly nuisance, holding his breath as he did so. Pee-yew.

"Here, J.D., try some of this. Then when you're up to it, hop in and we'll go find where they put your driveway. Car looks okay to drive."

He expected argument, but J.D. just folded himself shakily into the passenger seat. Brady felt like cheering when the car started and pulled free of the palm. He eased it over the curb without banging the bottom, and they were off.

During the short drive, J.D. turned all weepy again, mumbling repeatedly about his "sweet Lexy girl" and "life wasn't worth it without her." Brady realized with a start that this guy had been having an affair with Lexy. The thought made him look over at J.D. again, wondering if she ever saw him in this condition. The massive binge made sense now; Brady might go on one himself if someone murdered his lover. J.D. had a wife he had cried about too. What a mess that sounded like. Maybe he killed Lexy. Sure acted tore up about her death, but maybe that was how murderers were. Brady had no idea, never met a murderer that he knew of.

He got the guy home and up to his door, then beat feet out of there. Enough Samaritan routine for the day.

Turning the last corner to his soon-to-be-former house, he spotted Pete squatting down in the yard, inspecting the scarred tree and explanatory tire tracks while talking on his cell phone. Brady waited at the corner to describe the accident, not wishing to interrupt the phone call.

"No, no, I'm not saying that," Pete said into the phone. "I don't think he could do that to his sister. Hell, he wouldn't have stood a chance against her anyway . . ."

"Gerry doesn't believe it's the same guy and said the cops won't either, that's why . . ."

"No, I don't want to bother you with this right now. You called me, remember . . ."

"I haven't said a thing, and I won't unless we get a better picture of things, I promise . . ."

"I'll get on it soon as I knock out what I've got here . . . Okay, boss." He punched off and half-turned to stuff the phone in his back pocket, eyes widening as he faced Brady. "You make a habit out of listening in on other people's calls?"

"No, I don't. And I didn't pay any attention to yours," Brady lied. He walked up and punched Pete's arm. "I didn't hear a word of you explaining to your girlfriend that you had a vasectomy so it couldn't be you."

Pete grinned. "You're all right, Spain, you know that? Least for a Carolina boy." He cocked his head, looking at Brady sideways. "They find me in a ditch someday, you remember everything you didn't pay attention to, you hear?"

They stood there in a freeze-frame, Pete's grin a little strained, Brady not sure if he was serious. Pete broke off eye contact and waved at the tree. "The hell happened here?"

Brady laughed, more of a nervous release of pressure from the weird tableau than any real amusement. He described his morning with J.D. and went on to point out the gunk Pete should avoid stepping in.

"Well, old tree's gonna be okay, don't know about J.D.," Pete said, shaking his head. "Can't help but kind of feel for the guy. Even give him sort of a pass on being married. Guy like him didn't have a chance of resisting Lexy, God rest her, once she set her mind on him. Unless he did it, then I'm gonna do something ugly and Stone Age to him."

He paused, kicking the ridges of dirt down into the tire marks and smoothing it with the sole of his boot. Then he looked back up and said, "Look, Brady, I don't want to be minding your business, but you need to understand there's some things I can't control. And you need to know there's some things you can't control. Hell, there's stuff nobody can control. You find yourself in a spot like that, Gerry Terence is a good man at sorting things out fair."

★　★　★　★　★

Anna Burgess listened until she heard her husband hang up the receiver, then soft-footed back to the den for a rest. She felt completely bloated, her body swollen with grief. Her baby had been cruelly snatched away by the forces of evil. Little Lexy, so called because it was as close as Alexandra could come to saying her own name as a toddler. Anna crossed to the dimmest corner of the den to lie down. Even with the shades drawn she still needed to cover her eyes with a towel, as any light at all made her head throb.

The police would not let her have her little girl's earthly remains yet, disturbing Anna's deepest convictions. She had grown up in an immigrant Ukrainian family to whom funerals were sacred and ritualized events. More evil delivered unto her. And she feared she was going to break in half from the additional agony caused by her certainty that those same dark forces were after Nicky, now her only baby. Anna had always wished for many more children, the big family Leo promised during their courtship, but her body had not been blessed with the capability.

Imagining a houseful of kids and remembering Lexy's infancy evoked memories of her own childhood. When she would spend her afternoons at her father's Esso station to escape the chaos of life in a family of twelve. Hanging around, watching him work and generally making a pest of herself. An irreversible resolution rose in her heart. Those memories surfacing at this very moment could not be coincidence. It was a message to her, telling her what must be done. She knew whom Leo had been talking to in there, heard what he said. She now had to hope that God would forgive her for taking the only path she could see clearly.

CHAPTER TWENTY-EIGHT

Gerry Terence had been surprised when Pete called and asked to meet at his office, but he instantly guessed the why. Pete asked to meet at five, which was about the time Gerry started his rounds at Heron Point. So he expected to be pulled off the job. Probably for the best anyhow, since he felt uneasy about attempting to continue his pervert chase in the middle of a homicide investigation, and all of Heron Point would soon be under that spotlight. Too, getting canned would give him a free hand to push the hot-potato questions he had for Pete.

He arranged the chairs like before, knowing how Pete liked routine, pleased when his friend sat without hesitation upon arrival.

"So, Pete, lay it on me."

Pete grinned, took off his cap, and scratched his hairline. "I knew you'd figure it out. The old man says it's time to shut her down." He replaced his cap and sighed. "My fault, bro, I opened my big mouth and told him you didn't think Lexy's murderer was the same guy what attacked Sara. He didn't like that, so he sent me to give you the axe. Sorry."

Of course Big Leo would never go for that theory, Gerry thought, it kept his son in the suspect pool for the rape. Since sharing his opinion with Pete, Gerry had learned that Lexy's clothes were removed after the fatal wound was inflicted. Blood spatter don't lie. Nor did they find any conclusive sign of rape, which made sense with the blood evidence, though recent intercourse was indicated. None of this could he tell Pete, because the one sure way to lose access to police information was to repeat it. No matter how much you might trust someone, and he knew better than to trust Pete's confidence where the Burgess family was concerned, anyway.

"It's okay," he said instead. "I'm sure the family has a lot more important things on their mind, losing a daughter like that."

"You got that right," Pete said. He shook his head and stared at his lap. "I can't get over it myself. Man, I just keep remembering her as a kid, a teenager." He looked back up, eyes blinking rapidly against his emotions. "But look, Gerry, just between you and me, I want you to stay on the rape case. Bad as I feel about Lexy, I don't want what happened to Sara to slip through the cracks. I'll pay you myself."

Gerry cocked an eyebrow. *Well, well, either Pete truly thinks Nick did it and wants to prove it, or he truly thinks the boy is innocent.* "Not to worry, cops don't let rapes slip through the cracks," he said. "Besides, how can I stay on it when I was specifically told to not get started on it?"

Pete snorted. "Yeah, right. I know Gerry Terence better than that, unless you went and got yourself a lobotomy. Whaddaya say, will you do it?"

Gerry picked up a pencil and bounced it on its eraser a few times, undecided on which direction to blindside his friend from. He flipped a mental coin. It came up yes. "So you really think Nick Burgess did the rape, huh?"

Pete sat still and silent, turning white around the mouth. Bull's-eye.

"The answer is no," said Gerry, "to taking your money. We'll spend what Leo already owes me. I don't want to quit on it either, even though for the record I never started."

Pete opened his mouth and Gerry held up both hands. "I

don't want to know anything you might know, okay?" Enough was enough. He'd planned on digging into his old pal's brain, but now he knew what he needed to know. Whatever mistakes or guilt Pete was carrying, this was not a guy who deserved taking an obstruction rap. A licensed investigator had to stay clean with the law, and Gerry did not want to choose between risking his own ass and rolling over on Pete. He liked the inculpable position of truly not knowing what he might have to deny. Criminal statutes did not always deliver moral justice, he had learned.

Pete nodded, went through his hat-off, hair-scratch reflex again. "Let me say this, then. With Lexy gone, Nick is all Leo and Anna have got now. I guess it would be nice to not have any questions in my mind about him."

"We both know he's your Peeping Tom," Gerry said. "No, don't answer. That ought to be enough of a question for you there. It's not going to magically cure itself."

Pete nodded again, his face a picture of misery.

"I've got a line on the Zeletsky case," Gerry went on. "One that could get Nick off the hook. You realize he's going to get a walk on the peeping. Just about gotta catch him on film to make that stick."

Pete made a fish mouth, started over, and found his voice. "Either way, I want you to do it. For Sara. You sure about the money?"

Gerry had to smile. "I'm sure, bro."

Pete stood, tugged his jeans up, and adjusted his cap until he had it comfortably in its regular groove. "Send Leo's bill to me, that way it'll get done faster." He moved toward the door, stopped, and turned back. "I 'preciate you, G."

After he'd gone, Gerry went to the window and watched him cross the street to his truck. Seeing how troubled Pete was over Nick, and watching him talk around Leo's involvement in his suspicions, had Gerry rethinking his client. Instead of just eccentric egomania, maybe the man was up to something that crossed the line. Tough thing about his daughter, but since when was that a license to control the investigation? As for smarmy-ass sick Nick, even if he got a free ride on the peekaboo act, Gerry hoped to have a surprise for him. Gerry just had to get his timing perfect on the bust he had promised the Vice guy.

Brady found a place to live, but no amount of pragmatic self-talk could blunt the embarrassment and alarm he felt at how far he had fallen.

His new residence was a weekly-rate motel beginning to slide off the edge of respectability. Its flat-roofed, single-story cinder block design did possess a certain quaint old-school flavor he actually liked, though, even down to the flamingo-pink paint job. Their advertising still tried to promote it as a family vacation resort, but who were they kidding? Day laborers, itinerant contractors, illegal immigrants, and drug dealers appeared to be the clientele. But the room looked almost clean, it had its own bath, and it cost two-fifty a week with no deposit other than a week up-front and a manual imprint of his maxed-out Visa.

What appalled him most about his situation was that the driving force in his life was fear. Scared of prison. Out of money and scared to apply for any position because of the reference he would get from Beach Haven, due to Burgess's influence. Scared to chance it because he would quickly get the rep of tainted goods. A small community, the tech business, and he wanted a future if he ever got out of this mess. Scared to go elsewhere because Burgess had promised to swear out the warrant if he did, and Brady had always heard that flight was evidence of guilt.

Nor did he have any doubt that Burgess would know if he

blew town. Guy apparently knew everything. Probably knew to the dollar how much Brady had to his name. That was why Brady's promise of one week had amused the man. He knew he could cut off Brady's only avenue of escape. So it had been a big joke to him.

Brady had found the connection, too. Maybe not proof, but good enough to convince him Burgess was behind the boot from Beach Haven. A few hours on the web was all it took, accessing the avalanche of information available to anyone and then sneaking into Beach Haven's network and the county records site. Turned out the two properties Beach Haven was negotiating for sat on the same strand of beach. Guess who owned the surrounding land and the shoreline access between them? Burgess Investments, LLC, of course. Who had also sold other properties to Beach Haven in the past. Heck, the suits at Beach Haven would fire their own mothers for a chance at a mega-resort complex on that kind of beachfront acreage.

He burned the first hour of his new life as a motel resident by sitting on the floppy, musty-smelling bed and watching a news segment on Lexy's funeral. The picture they showed of her alive and smiling gave him a throat-clearing moment. He still wanted to believe she would have come around. With her gone, there was no support for his story, just a bad check. Hell, with her gone, he was guilty. Open and shut, as they say.

The funeral coverage deepened his dismay when he saw the list of bigwigs and politicos attending in support of Leo Burgess. The power and influence of the man pounded home the point that Brady could not win. He had to find a way to get Burgess off his back, because no public forum would ever believe Brady over the pillar of the community they saw when they looked at Leo Burgess.

Finding work was an absolute must. Anything, even some anonymous manual labor, just something to pay the rent. He might make it a month at the motel on what he had, if he quit eating. Whatever the next step down from the Suncrest Motel would be, he did not think he could go there without blowing his brains out. Somehow that once-suffocating picture of Brady and Peggy reenacting Green Acres didn't seem like such a bad future after all.

A chilling new thought surfaced, connecting flight, guilt, and the clout of Leo Burgess. Would sneaking away from the house and checking into a roach motel so soon after Lexy's death make him a suspect in her murder?

CHAPTER TWENTY-NINE

Nick Burgess slammed the door as hard as he could, hoping the old man would hear it. Hoping it pissed him off. God, he could be so freakin' mule-headed. All Nick had done was present the idea that Brady Spain had killed Lexy. After all, Spain was hacked off at her for sticking up for her brother. They had probably been doing the nasty, too.

But Pops had shaken his fat-ass daddy finger at Nick and said: "I will not discuss Alexandra's death with you. I will see to it the proper steps are taken to answer for it, and I do not want you to speak of it again."

When he told him that Brady had packed his shit and hit the road, Pops said, "Very well." Just like that.

Nick pressed his case. "Don't we want to find him?"

"I am not interested in talking to Mr. Spain until he is ready to talk to me," the old man answered. "He will not leave town, I assure you."

Nick didn't like getting blown off, said as much, and Pops had gotten a little red around the neck. "Remember our agreement, Nicolas. You stay out of this affair. I am handling it. We need none of your juvenile strong-arm fantasies. If it comes to it, an accomplished attorney can expose Mr. Spain as a hostile witness who bears a grudge against you and is using a family tragedy as an opportunity to renege on his original statement. Now, I have work to do."

So Nick busted out of there wishing the glass in the door had broken when he banged it. The old man was just wrong. Spain needed someone to lean on him. You could just tell how smart-ass the punk was, with his George Washington "I cannot tell a lie" bullshit. Without Lexy to swear that he was with her, couldn't Pops see how important this shit had gotten?

He decided to skip the Porsche, walk down to Cameron's. His stash wasn't low, he didn't need a buy; he just wanted to hang out with somebody cool. Somebody who treated him cool. No blow, no getting wired, just burn a little weed and drink a few beers, mellow out.

Bet Cameron could come up with a way to put a hurt on Spain without the old man knowing. It looked like the smart move to Nick, but the thought made his stomach knot up. The old man would for sure cut Nick's nuts off if he found out, and he seemed to find every damn thing out.

What he could not understand was how come Pops didn't treat him better, more like an equal. Nick was the oldest, the only son. Now that he was the only child, shouldn't he be getting the respect Lexy always got? Something had to change. Nick was ready to start making the decisions. So, sit back and fire up some Jamaican, sip on a few cold ones, and get Cameron to help him come up with a plan of attack. He liked the sound of that, a plan of attack.

On the last day of the month, Brady made a final trip to the house on Mangrove Street, one more walk-through to collect anything personal he had missed. Sadly, the bed would have to stay, as would the one and only table he had been able to afford. The two chairs already sat in his motel room, and he had decided the television could survive in the Jeep for a while. With so little time or means to acquire much, the rest of his possessions fit easily into a few cartons, also already divided between the motel and his Jeep. Never know, maybe he could reclaim the big stuff later if he ever got out from under the Burgess steamroller. Might mention that to Pete, should he ever come across him outside of Heron Point.

He was standing in front of the open refrigerator, mulling over a suitable transport container for the milk jug and four leftover beers, when he heard a tapping at the front door. He spun around and craned his neck to peer through the glass without exposing himself, his skin crawling like a nest of centipedes. Somebody short and blond was all he could see, which did not match any Burgess he knew of. Nor Frank or Art, the merry hoodlums. He sidled up to the door and swung it open while standing off to one side.

"Brady? Is that you?" asked a voice he didn't recognize, female, friendly sounding.

He stepped out and knew her then. Air rushed from his lungs and he felt the prickles on the back of his neck subside—Maggie, his boozy rescuer from the hired goon fiasco. But not quite the same Maggie, he noticed. Stone-cold sober, this Maggie, and not just a day's worth of sober. Eyes clear as those of a child, her skin losing some of the grainy slackness of the whiskey queen. Wow. No wonder he hadn't recognized her voice.

"Hey, Maggie, how are you?"

"I'm fine, thanks." She leaned to one side, eyeing the bare interior of the house. "Moving, huh?"

"Uh, no, I just haven't picked up much stuff yet," he said. *Great, all I need is a gossip-hound right now.*

She cut her eyes at him. "Whatever. I won't tell anybody, Brady," she said, and then laughed at his expression. "Really, I won't. Mark and I are moving, too."

"Oh? Well, I'm sorry or glad for you, depending on why. What brings you by? I don't have any muggers for you to chase off today." As starved as he was for any amiable interaction with another human being, he didn't know her well enough to trust her motives. His memory of the obvious overtures she'd made on thug day loomed as an uncomfortable possibility.

"Have you seen the news?" she asked, biting her lip.

"No, why?" The crawling sensation returned to the back of his scalp. Had to be bad news. About him or someone else?

She glanced around as if she expected people lurking in the bushes. "Look, can I come in for a minute?"

"Sure." He moved back, wondering why the cloak and dagger act. As yet, he picked up no come-on vibe from the sober Maggie, so maybe not that. "Though, as you guessed, there's nowhere to sit."

She smiled. "That's okay. We can sit on the countertops and pretend we're at a cocktail party."

He led her to the kitchen, charmed by this different Maggie. "I can even offer you a beer to complete the picture, but it's all I've got."

"Thank you, but no, believe it or not," she said with a wry grin. Then her expression turned serious, kind of urgent-looking. "This is a really stupid question, and I can't think of a good way to say it, but I've got to ask. Did you kill Lexy?"

"Huh?" He couldn't have been more dumbfounded if she had asked if he ate babies for breakfast.

"I didn't think so," she said, visibly unwinding. "But I couldn't just assume it, you know?"

"I guess I'm glad a simple 'huh' gets me off the hook," he said, his surprise shifting into irritation.

"It's not the 'huh,' it's my years of being around people who lie all the time that gets you off," she said with an impatient wave. "Obviously I didn't think so before I asked, or I wouldn't be alone with you."

"Do I get to know why the hell you would ask that?"

"You need to watch the news," she said. "Channel Seven, local segment. I'm not even going to try to explain it, just watch it, okay? There's more to why I came, though."

"Well, I'm going to take a wild stab here, and guess that it can't be any worse than that murder question," he said, guessing at what the news was going to drop on him. Police in a manhunt for fugitive Brady Spain? Did Burgess file his charges? Dear God, was he wanted for murder?

She crossed her arms and ankles, propping her weight against the counter. "Look, Brady, even if I hadn't seen the news, and you'll see what I mean, I know you're in some kind of jam with Leo and Nick." She smiled when his eyebrows went up. "You have to understand, Nick's got a really big mouth."

"Say you're right. That doesn't make it my favorite cocktail party topic. And if I am, what of it?" Where was she going with this? Sent by Leo to keep tabs on him?

"Let's just say that I had a father just like Leo Burgess." Her eyes clouded up, lost in her own past. "Well, maybe not quite as rich as Leo, who is? But he was the exact same kind of man."

Brady waited when she paused, sensing that she needed no response yet. He propped his hips against the opposite counter, in a posture mirroring hers.

"First, I want to tell you something." She looked down at the floor and then up at him, her face hot pink. "I had a thing for you, I'm talking fantasies and crazy stuff, so I just want to apologize if I got weird or anything." She hugged herself with the crossed arms, her color darkening to a dusky rose.

Brady felt his own face reddening, feeling as awkward as if he'd walked in on her undressing, despite having already surmised something along those lines. "No need to apologize, you were cool, and hey, you might've saved my life for all I know." Realizing that his awkwardness had to be about like an ant on a battleship compared to hers, he added, "And just so you know, I think it's one hell of a compliment."

"Thanks, nice guy." She nodded as if he was a student who

gave the correct answer. "I know this is embarrassing but it's something I need to do, talk about my own embarrassing stuff instead of everybody else's."

Her eyes focused into the distance again, and she shook herself like she wanted to escape it. "Anyway, you're too nice a guy to understand Leo Burgess. All that matters to a man like that is money and prestige. And the power that comes with it, I guess. Trust me, that's all he cares about, believe me, I know. So if you plan on fighting him, you've got to hit him in the wallet or the image." She reached into her back pocket, pulled out a slip of paper, and handed it to him.

Brady took the note. *Grant Thibideaux,* it read, followed by a telephone number. Handwritten, feminine, presumably by Maggie. "So who is this?" he asked. "What am I supposed to do with it?"

"That's my brother. He works for the Feds, some kind of watchdog department, mostly banking and stocks. I'm not sure exactly. But if you can find any dirty laundry on Leo, call Grant and tell him, he'll know who you are. He's the guy you want, he loves a crusade, and the bigger the fish the more he loves it."

"He loves crusades against guys like Leo?" he asked, trying to judge whether this was a put-on or a set-up. His every instinct said she was as straight as anyone he'd ever met, though maybe using him as a way to exorcise her own demons. Then again, his track record on instincts sucked lately.

She gave a sad little smile of acknowledgment. "Yeah, well, like I said, we had a father just like him. Some of us chase our ghosts and some of us try to drown them in a Mai Tai."

"Okay, supposing your brother is my get out of jail free card, and assuming I can get dirt on Leo, which I don't see how, why are you doing this? I thought you were one of the Heron Point disciples, you know, just another day in paradise and all that jazz."

"I was, I really was." She reached up with both hands and flicked her short blond hair back, behind her ears. "But I don't need to tell you things are going crazy around here. Like some horrible disease catching up to us. I can't get over what happened to Lexy. She was okay, you know? Whatever she was wasn't her fault. And I know Leo Burgess is too busy feeding his ego by proving he can walk all over anyone he wants to even stop and grieve over her, because deep down he doesn't really give a shit."

She stopped for a breath, touching her fingertips to a spot between her breasts. "I know, because I watched it happen just like this to someone very close to me, and it's just not right."

"Well hey, thanks then," he said, startled by the husky passion in her voice and the sudden flood she was blinking against. "That sure is a heavy load you're carrying around in there. You going to be okay?"

"Yes, I am." Another hint of a smile flickered at the corners of her mouth. "See what I mean? You're a nice guy, Brady, too nice to get ground down by one of these cold-hearted, phony patriarchal types who should spend a little of his precious time loving his daughter who already has to survive carrying his bad blood inside her. Makes me wonder how I ever thought the Burgesses were so great." She shuddered and pushed away from the counter like it was a starting block, patting his arm as she breezed right on out the door. "Good luck, Brady," she called over her shoulder as she went.

Thanks, I think I'm going to need it, he thought, *and good luck to you too, Maggie.* He glanced again at the note and tucked it in his pocket. She did seem to mean well, but what kind of Federal finance regulator would be interested in the sad story of a jobless, penniless, homeless dude with a felony hanging over his head? The emptied house felt depressing after Maggie's animated presence, like a gutted testimonial to his failure. Time to get the hell out of here.

CHAPTER THIRTY

Brady ignored pretty much the entire traffic code in his drive back to the Suncrest, making it just in time to catch the news. His belly churned at the possibilities of something so dire that Maggie wouldn't tell him. Was he a fugitive? She'd asked about Lexy, did that mean he was wanted for murder? He felt giddy and lightheaded at the idea. It was all too Monty Python to be real.

He waited through the weather forecast and some idiocy about how local drivers were coping with rising gasoline prices, pacing his cramped cubicle. His mind wandered, speculating on what a lawyer might cost, until the sound of his own name snapped him back to the television. The face of Nick Burgess filled the screen, looking all clean-cut and wholesome in his white shirt and Ray-Bans, talking to a reporter.

". . . can't understand why the police haven't talked to Brady Spain about my sister's murder," Nick was saying. "This man had motive and opportunity, and I am deeply disturbed to see our law enforcement community so far behind in their investigation."

"Can you tell us if the police have any other suspects in the case?" asked the frosty-blond talking head sharing the screen with Nick.

"To my knowledge, no," Nick replied, his delivery projecting the perfect image of a righteously outraged and grieving brother. "And this Spain character is unemployed, with no permanent residence. He's not even from this area. He could disappear on us if something isn't done quickly, and I want justice for Lexy."

"Can you describe their relationship?" Blondie asked, a bogus expression of concern creasing her plastic brow.

"Spain had a bad debt my sister was trying to collect. He wouldn't pay it, and it's pretty well known that they argued about it. Doesn't that sound like motive to you?"

"Asshole," Brady screamed, unconsciously echoing Lexy's reaction to Nick's scheming. He flopped backwards onto the bed and hurled the remote at the wall, making a dent that would never be noticed among all the others.

The reporter went on to recap the facts of Lexy's murder with no further mention of Brady, probably to ensure that the slander liability was all Nick's, then moved on to another topic. He got up to retrieve the remote and used it to punch off the set, then hurled it at the wall again.

Okay, Brady me boy, what now? It might not be a police manhunt yet, but it sure was all but. And who said money can't buy everything? Only someone like a Burgess could get a news station to interview him about who the hell he wanted investigated. That asshole Nick was such a weasel too, and here he comes off like John F. Kennedy on camera. The worst part was that everything Nick had said was true. It sounded terrible laid out cold like that. Homeless, unemployed, and debt-dodging, like some migrating serial killer. *Oh boy, you are so screwed now, Brady. And dear Lord, please tell me they cannot get that news channel in North Carolina.*

Pete Cully swung full speed and put his shoulder in it, burying the hammer so deep into the ground that only the handle showed. Damn it, damn it. He had hoped to finish repairing this blasted fence of Leo's today, but now he completely surrendered the idea. Hard to give a crap about something like this in light of what happened to Lexy. You would think Leo would be unable to even notice this kind of thing right now, but he had been nagging Pete nonstop. And now, after two days jacking around with it off and on—even leaving his truck overnight to skip the hassle of unpacking everything twice—he wound up right back where he started.

Getting the posts to stay true required cementing, something he had tried to avoid. Should have cemented it to begin with, but that made it a bitch to ever move the cussed thing and you never knew when Leo would want him to. Lightweight decorative fence like that ought to be fine without it, but it was another victim of the hill they had built for Leo's house to sit on. Come a good rain, the water sucked the sand right out from around the posts, and she'd start leaning. And soon as she started leaning, Leo would be wearing out his redial button until Pete fixed it.

What griped him the most was that concrete meant a trip into town. No mix on his truck, and he had to go right now or closing time would slip on by. He yanked the hammer out of the sand, wiped it off, and wrapped all his gear in a tarp in case of a sudden thunderstorm. Fired up the truck and hit the gas.

Passing Mangrove Street on his way to Shoreline reminded him that he wanted to check out twenty-nine, see if Brady moved out. Funny he didn't mention anything, but the house looked vacant from the street. Pete hated to think the boy left, they needed more folks like him. He'd seemed some upset about the murder. Which they all were, Lord knows Pete could not stop seeing her lying there. In fact, he had a recurring nightmare that she had still been alive, that she died while he was out puking in the yard, that he could have saved her. But Brady didn't know her very well, did he?

Also odd that Leo had not told him to inspect the place if Brady was gone. Usually Pete got sent in right away. Nobody got a deposit back until he checked the house over. Did Leo put it off in an attempt to avoid Pete becoming privy to the heat they had on Brady? Knowing Leo, probably. Damn if it didn't sound like him.

Time had made it clear; Brady was not going to back up Lexy's alibi for Nick. The only reason Pete held off talking to the cops was Gerry. Gerry would handle things right. Said he had another suspect in mind, too. That would move a big load of guilt for Pete. And truthfully, no matter how resolved he believed himself to be, his guts got a little weak and watery at the thought of crossing Leo Burgess.

When he pulled up at the intersection of Palm and Shoreline Drive, Pete noticed that his brake pedal sank almost down to the floorboard. Felt spongy too, as if he had lost pressure, or maybe fluid. Wonder why the warning light hadn't come on? He turned south on Shoreline, toward town, mindful not to tailgate in case he had a problem here. By the time he came to the sharp curve where the road veered away from the coast, he knew he did. Had he not eased into that curve he would've driven right into the drink. He managed to bring the truck to a stop on the shoulder by standing on the brakes, finding just enough pressure to keep it out of the Gulf.

The shoulder was too narrow there—his door would open right into traffic. He slid across the seat and exited on the passenger side, giving that door a disgusted bang when he closed it. "Well, that's just peachy," he bitched to himself. What could possibly go wrong next?

He glanced back the way he had come and thought he could make out a trail of fluid there, but he had no intentions of going for a closer look in the middle of Shoreline Drive. He walked around the front of the truck, toying with the idea of crawling up under it to see if he could find a quick fix. Decided that lying on the ground that close to that road was just asking for death by tourist. "Better safe than sorry," he grumbled.

He edged around the front left corner on the truck, wary of idiots whipping into the curve, and made his break for the sidewalk on the inland side of Shoreline. What he did not see was the Georgia-tagged carload of partiers ripping out of a side street without giving the stop sign there anything more than the briefest tap of the brakes.

CHAPTER THIRTY-ONE

Brady took it as a good omen when he found Gerry Terence's office without trouble and scored a parking space right in front of it. He had felt goofy calling the guy, but in his desperate thrashing about for what to do next he'd remembered Pete's recommendation. To his surprise, Terence said he would make time available, come right now.

He climbed a narrow, musty staircase to the second floor and zigzagged the dim hallway until he found a time-stained door that read Terence Investigations. He tapped on it and entered when he heard a summons from within.

He'd seen Terence around the neighborhood enough to recognize his short, stocky appearance, but it was Brady's first contact with the quick gray-brown eyes that seemed to examine him thoroughly in a glance. Nothing shifty and oily about him the way Brady expected a private detective to be, instead more of a serene, placid air. Once they swapped names and shook hands, Terence sat and regarded Brady expectantly.

"I don't know if you can help me," Brady said, "but Pete Cully said if I ever got jammed up, you were the man." Terence's quick smile of genuine friendship at the mention of Pete's name helped erase any lingering doubts Brady had about coming.

"Pete may have exaggerated my talents a bit, but that is exactly what I do for a living," Terence said. He clasped his hands on top of his desk, leaning into it. "Why don't you tell me about the jam you're in?"

"Oh boy, where to start." Brady fidgeted for a minute, then made a snapshot decision to not skate over the worst parts in an attempt to pretty up how he'd screwed himself. He just told it, all of it—the job, the money, the murder, Nick's interview, Nick's alibi, even the Suncrest.

At the end of the saga, Terence settled back in his chair and fixed the probing eyes on Brady's. "The first step is this; if you're guilty of more than bouncing a check, anything you haven't told me, you need a lawyer, not a detective."

Brady waited for more, but the guy just sat there watching him. So he answered, "No, there's nothing. Speeding, maybe."

"Fine. You may need a lawyer anyway, but I hear you on the money situation. Step two is some pretty personal questions. Ready?"

Brady nodded.

"Did you ever, even once, have a sexual relationship with Lexy Burgess? And I mean even Clinton stuff."

Brady felt the blush coming, unable to stop it. Too young to have much memory of that scandal, he nonetheless knew enough to catch Terence's drift. He shook his head.

Terence picked up a pencil from his desk and slid his thumb and forefinger down the length of it, flipped it over, and slid them down the other direction. His eyes stayed on Brady's. "You sure?"

"Well, yeah. How could I not be sure about something like that?"

Terence cracked a smile. "You'd be surprised how many people will tell you they simply forgot, once they're stuck trying to explain a picture of themselves in the act. That'll help, that you didn't. I know alibis are a sore subject, but do you have one?"

Brady thought back, feeling stupid for never considering it. Remembered. "No, that's the day I got canned. I can show that

I was on my computer, but I was alone. No way to prove it was me using it."

"Better than nothing. At home, right?" said Terence, making notes as they talked. Or maybe just doodling, for all Brady knew.

He nodded and Terence asked, "Are you checked into this motel under your own name?"

Brady nodded again. "Is that bad? I didn't think of it, and they make you run a credit card anyway."

"No, that's good," said Terence. He shook his head and laughed softly, as if to himself. "Mr. Spain, I do believe you might be an innocent man."

"Well, good. I mean, I am." Pleased as he was that Terence seemed to believe him, he somehow felt like a kid listening to grown-up jokes. "What about this news thing with Nick? Should I do anything to address it?"

"No, ignore it for now, see if anything gets made of it." He flapped a hand, and then eyed Brady with a curious expression. "You realize if you had reported the assault, Nick wouldn't have dared to shoot his mouth off like that, don't you?"

Brady just nodded dumbly. He had figured that one out, been kicking himself ever since. Reporting it now would look like some lame attempt to discredit Nick. And not having reported it right away made him look guilty of something, as if he was avoiding all contact with the cops. Probably what Terence thought.

"Well, forget about it now." Terence flipped his pencil up in the air and caught it, a glint of malice in his eyes. "I may have a little special something cooking up for old Nicky-boy. So do I understand you right, you're just about flat broke?"

"Yes, but I'll sign a contract or IOU, whatever you want," Brady said, not wanting to get blown out now. This felt too much like his last hope for any help. "You can run my credit report. It'll show I'm good for it."

"That's not what I'm getting at," Terence said with another fleeting smile. Evidently that came across funny too. "You said you need income to survive while we hash this out. I agree, because regardless of the bad check problem, you do not want to skip town if you are even remotely considered a suspect in a homicide, not even to find a job. Are you willing to work, and I mean hard work?"

"Sure, anything," Brady said, but his mind filled with visions of washing bedpans or prepping bodies for embalming. Oh well, gotta do what you gotta do.

"We'll figure out the money later. Your situation might be tangled up in something else I'm working and there wouldn't be any fee. If not, we'll work something out. Be at the plant nursery on the corner of Riverside and Eighth at seven in the morning. You're looking for a fellow name of Chaz Martin. He'll be driving a white truck, I don't remember the brand, but it'll have JTA Greenscapes on the side of it. He'll put you to work if you can hack it. And he'll come on tough, but underneath he's practically Mother Teresa. I'll call and tell him you're coming. Fair enough?" He stood and held out his hand.

Brady rose too, and took the hand. "More than fair, I owe you one for this," he said, flashing back to Lexy using the same phrase on him. "Do I call you if anything else happens?"

"You mean as in your one phone call from jail?" Terence smiled. "Yeah, anything critical or newsworthy, call. Otherwise, I'll find you."

During the drive to the motel, Brady worked the Pollyanna angle, telling himself to stay positive about the future with Gerry Terence in his corner, but that closing reference to jail kept popping up to remind him how bleak things really were. At least now he had a job, regardless of anything else Terence could or couldn't do. As he walked past the office on the way to his room, the manager, a big fat chick with a Winston wheeze and at least fourteen rings on her fingers, stuck her head out the door and called to him.

"Hey, you're lucky I don't believe everything I see on the news, Mr. Spain, or you'd be outta here. But I'm warning you, the first time any cop shows up looking for you, you're gone."

Wonderful. Now he was considered a lowlife even in a garbage can like the Suncrest.

CHAPTER THIRTY-TWO

Leo Burgess sat in his Florida room, eyeing the thunderheads building up inland with the promise of a coming deluge. The air already carried a heavy, sticky smell. He felt old and enfeebled, weary from replaying the same depressing scene with his son, this time blistering the boy for violating his directive regarding the Brady Spain affair. Yet his anger had been a pretense, for privately he viewed Nick's news conference as a bold, expedient strategy, one he might have concocted himself. Perhaps genealogy had not failed him after all. But he did believe he should be unforgiving for Nick's disobedience, thus the show of temper.

In reality, the publicity helped the agenda. It would certainly cripple any attempt on Spain's part to present himself as anything other than the disreputable malcontent Leo's legal team would describe. The only potential backlash Leo anticipated was publicity itself, anything that drew attention to Nick at a time when the police seemed to have eased their focus on the rape of Sara Zeletsky. They were concentrating their energies on solving Alexandra's murder, which was exactly as Leo would have it, indeed as he insisted. It was even possible Nick's public challenge could further increase that diligence.

Alexandra. His stomach burned as if he had swallowed a live coal whenever he attempted to acknowledge that someone had actually dared to perpetrate this ultimate of trespasses against a member of his family. Had subjected his entire family to this nightmare. That burning hole in his gut demanded vicious, ruthless consequences for the miscreant who stole his daughter.

Obsessing over vengeance had become his anchor to sanity. Any effort to absorb the idea that Alexandra was gone, gone forever, exposed a cold empty spot deep within him and a continuous nagging worry that he had somehow missed an opportunity. But what? He'd given her everything she asked for, everything a daughter could want, everything he never had himself.

The first audible rumble of thunder rattled the glass-top table as the conflicting shore winds wrestled over which direction the storm would turn. He ignored the crackles of lightning, just as he ignored these indefinable emotions he could not rationalize, instead devoting his thoughts to securing suitable retribution for her death and protecting Nicolas. Which had grown ever more crucial with her gone. Not only would another scandal be more than the family name could withstand, he did not think Anna would survive. Should anything happen to her remaining child, Leo would have to commit her to a psychiatric facility or put her down like some crazed animal. If that added up to destroying Brady Spain, so be it. Much of his unresolved anger had begun finding its way to Spain anyway, this young nobody who would defy Leo Burgess.

He also recognized the need to do something to snap Anna out of her despair, and soon, before sanity slipped away from her. As if the brutal murder of her daughter was not enough to bear, the media, and even some of the investigating authorities, had hinted of multiple dalliances in Alexandra's past, of a lewd, loose lifestyle. Leo refused to hear such defamation, but Anna listened, and it devastated her.

Perhaps a community cookout around their pool would provide some sense of normalcy for Anna; allow her to play the hostess and accept condolences from the many people who cared. It would be good for the whole family to socialize, ensure that their people regarded them as sympathetic figures. He felt certain Alexandra would approve of exploiting the opportunity to gain public sentiment. So plan it for Labor Day, just a few days hence. Though it had never been an annual event, he had thrown Labor Day parties often enough for it to be in good taste, perhaps even laudable.

Leo sighed. He missed the days when outsmarting the negotiators on the other side of the table consumed him, instead of his family. He heard the telephone in his office ringing, so he grunted himself up and out of the too-low settee in the Florida room and went inside to answer.

By the time he made his way to his desk, the ringing stopped, but he picked up and accessed his voice mail. Leo detested people who did not immediately return calls—time was money. Absorbed by his Labor Day plan and the compassionate goodwill it would generate, he never comprehended exactly who it was leaving the message to inform him of Pete Cully's fatal accident.

He dropped the receiver into its cradle, stunned, sharply struck by how much he had come to depend on the man. He knew their association was nearing its end. Leo could not abide a member of his inner circle whose loyalty to the family was suspect. In fact, he had already instructed his attorney to research the statute of limitations affecting the Pensacola incident. That vulnerability had to be eliminated before he could safely cut Pete loose. So despite his personal sense of loss, Pete's misfortune had solved a problem for him. But he had wanted to make that move on his timetable, when he felt no further need for Pete's services. Was there no end to this conspiracy against him?

CHAPTER THIRTY-THREE

As best Brady could tell, he was the only guy standing around in the plant nursery parking lot who spoke native English, maybe the only English speaker period.

Lots of guys there, though, mostly Hispanics and a few using languages he'd never heard. Must be the unofficial employment office for all the day labor in town. Everyone seemed to be segregating into little nationality cliques, with of course no American section. Or even Filipino for that matter, but what the hell, he wasn't thrilled with the whole segregation thing anyway. Too similar to how the movies portrayed prison life, and he avoided thinking about anything that reminded him of prison. He picked a deserted corner of the lot to wait, wondering why he had worked so hard to obtain a business degree in computers for this future.

When the JTA truck arrived, the man who got out was short and wiry, dressed in a muscle shirt, camo pants, and a baseball cap. He was very dark-skinned, like the color of French roast coffee, but his features looked different than those of an African black. Brady saw why when the guy adjusted his cap. The upper half of his forehead was much lighter, as if someone had added a heavy shot of cream to the coffee, making for a startling two-tone effect at his hat line. *Now that is some serious sun time there,* thought Brady. Gave him a pretty good idea of why Terence wanted to know if he was afraid of hard work. He went over and introduced himself.

Martin shook his hand and looked him over critically. "Well, you look like you might survive. This ain't no job for a whiner, though. Gerry says you're ready to go to work."

"Yes, sir," Brady answered. Dude had a grip like a steam wrench. He looked down at the ropy brown forearm and saw the egg-shaped wads of muscle that flexed and slid with every gesture. Work indeed. Martin waved him into the truck and off they went.

"Know anything about landscaping or lawn maintenance?" Martin asked as he drove, eyes moving back and forth from Brady to the road.

"Nothing except what you learn doing your own," Brady admitted, still seeing the hungry, disappointed eyes of the remaining hopefuls in the labor pool who watched them drive away.

"Guess that's as good a start as any," Martin said. He brought the truck to a halt at a red left-turn signal and looked over at Brady with a grin. "Don't worry, anyone can use a blower or a shovel or a rake, plenty of stuff. We'll teach you the rest.

"Here's the deal," he went on. The green arrow lit up, and he made his turn onto a four-lane boulevard that Brady didn't recognize. Couldn't make out the sun-faded street sign, either. "I can pay you ten an hour, but you gotta bust ass for me to afford it, okay? You're going on the books as Brady Spain Enterprises, so no withholding. How you handle your taxes is your business, but know it's gonna be on my books. And not as hourly either, no overtime. You and I will figure it up and book it as a contracted fee. That way I can give you all the work you can stand from sunup to sundown and pay you every day if you want. That's what Gerry says you need, right?"

Martin waited for Brady's "yessir," and then said, "So, that deal work for you?"

Brady worked the math, thinking that ten an hour was pretty

188

rank, but it sure beat hell out of zero. And lots of hours would add up fast. "Yes, sir, I'm in."

"Cool. 'Bout ten more minutes of driving and we'll go to work."

They rode silently for a few minutes, time Brady used to worry over the murder suspect thing like a dog with a new squeaky toy. He broke off that train when it came to him that he ought to know more about what the heck he was doing right then, riding off with a guy he didn't know on the basis of a referral from another guy he didn't know other than the say-so of a guy he had only known a month. *That sure is a whole lot of blind faith, Brady boy. Okay, ask.* "So, where do you know Gerry from?"

"Gerry?" Martin glanced at him, then back at his driving. "He used to be a cop, a good cop. Took pity on a Puerto Rican boy who didn't know no better than to think gangbangers and drug dealers were the coolest thing going, everything a man could want to be. Gerry didn't arrest that boy when he probably should have. Worked, too, the boy went straight."

"You?"

Martin shook his head, gaze fixed on the vehicle ahead of them. "My brother."

"Oh. Well, that's a good story. Does your brother work with you?"

"Nah." Martin rotated his fists on the steering wheel, the forearm eggs bulging and slithering, his eyes still focused straight ahead. "He's dead. Just going straight doesn't mean everybody from that life believes you're straight. Sometimes the past catches up to you. But he did have that time to get his life right, so he's with God now. And I owe Gerry Terence for that."

"Hey, sorry I brought it up," Brady muttered. He felt like a total fart at a funeral, one with a profound need to change the subject.

189

"Chaz Martin doesn't sound Puerto Rican, are you from there?" he said, wincing inwardly as he remembered Maggie and Susan asking him the same thing on his first day in Heron Point. Bet Susan hadn't asked from embarrassed floundering, though.

"Yep. Born in Ponce, moved here when I was eight." Chaz smiled. "And Chaz Martin is very damn Puerto Rican if it starts out as Chavez Mart-*een*. When we moved here, the kids took one look at Chavez and decided to call me Chaz. It stuck. And you can forget anyone saying Mart-*een* on the mainland. Your ass gonna be Martin."

"So, then how'd you get JTA for your company name?"

"Stands for Jesus Loves You in Spanish," Martin answered, glancing over at him. "Ain't I supposed to be doing the interview here?"

"Well, both of us maybe," Brady said with a sheepish laugh. He found himself admiring the guy's positive flow and the palpable self-assurance that seemed to be the source of his easy manner. "I didn't mean to get too personal."

"Nah, man, s'cool. Probably good you're interested, might mean you'll last more than a day." He turned left into a cul-de-sac and parked in the circle at the end. "Here we go, first stop on our list."

CHAPTER THIRTY-FOUR

To Brady's surprise, he grew to like his job with Chaz. It was the most exhausting work he had ever done, especially the first two days, before he became accustomed. The labor itself wasn't difficult or taxing, but the long hours of nonstop hustle in the heat and humidity were. Yet he began to enjoy the physical nature of it all—the honest bone-weariness at day's end and the simple pleasure of surveying a freshly manicured lawn, when the nostalgic smell of cut grass evoked the endless summer evenings of childhood. And the long drag of each day was offset by the week seeming to fly by in the midst of his wake-work-sleep routine. Best of all, he'd made a good start on his goal of enough money to pay Terence, make good his bounced check, hire a lawyer, or whatever it took to stay out of prison.

His evenings he spent digging through the Internet, compiling and collating every reference to Leo Burgess he could find. Though he saw Maggie's brother's help as an unrealistic hope, her suggestion had started him thinking. She was probably right in identifying counter-blackmail as his only ticket out of this. Problem there, he couldn't imagine finding any secret dirty enough to force Burgess into surrendering his son, which was exactly how the man would measure it. If Brady had pegged Burgess correctly, there could be no greater loss of face than Nick's arrest for rape.

So concentrate on hunting down the right kind of dope to stir up some controversy for Burgess. Create a little skepticism

191

against that unimpeachable reputation. Then his word versus Leo's would not be such a slam-dunk. He just needed to raise enough eyebrows to make Burgess unwilling to chance it. Whenever the enormity of the task ahead of him brought on a bout of despair, he reminded himself of what he'd seen during his year on the inside of the automobile business: people didn't get as rich as Burgess without a few shady deals here and a sleazy cover-up or two there. Just had to find them.

He had considered going to the police and suggesting they investigate Nick for the rape, with an explanation of why. Just tell them of Burgess's Godfather impersonation, which had to be illegal. Give them the old "where there's smoke, there's fire" spiel. But even if they believed him, something he saw as unlikely, it would result in Burgess swearing out his warrant in retaliation. That meant jail time for Brady, regardless of whether or not he got sentenced to it, because he was a long way from saving enough money for any bail bond. He'd have to wait in jail for his trial, and he could not bring himself to walk into a police station and ask for that.

He had an even scarier worry that kept buzzing around his ear like a mosquito that won't go away. Why hadn't the police talked to him about Lexy? After Nick's television spot, they had to, didn't they? He wanted to believe they just never bought into Nick's tirade, or that Terence had steered them away from him, but he was haunted by a recurring panic that they were playing a waiting game. Waiting for him to run, or waiting until they built an indestructible case against him. But how, with what evidence? He didn't do it. Unless the Burgesses supplied the evidence—Brady had witnessed their work firsthand. Though surely Burgess wouldn't frame Brady for the murder of his daughter at the cost of the real killer going free. Or even Nick, toad that he was. Would they? Yeah, right, more wishful thinking.

So he stayed glued to his laptop, night after night until his back ached and his eyes burned, praying that his skill at accessing just about anything ever put into any database in the world would unearth a silver bullet before his time ran out.

He found plenty of Leo Burgess on the Internet. Copious official records detailing land transactions, some business media articles on the bigger deals. He also came across a few society page mentions, even an architectural feature on Burgess's beach house. The article only dated back two years, which surprised Brady. He had assumed the mansion in Heron Point to be older. A picture of the previous Burgess home proved they had not exactly been living at the YMCA, though.

The most interesting item of all was an editorial railing against the sale of a particular land tract four years ago. The columnist called on Leo Burgess to abort the sale and donate the land as a preserve. She wrote it in open letter form, reminding Burgess that he already enjoyed more wealth than one man could need, and was it not time for him to give something back to this majestic paradise that had blessed him with such bounty? Over the top, for sure, but Brady liked the passion. He sidetracked long enough to read some more of her stuff.

Her name was Jeanette Voyes, and she was an environmental conscience with tiger teeth. Offshore dumping, wetland eradication, industrial waste, man, she fought it all. Her latest campaign targeted a mysterious silt build-up in the channels between keys. She had written a series on it, describing its deadly effect on marine grasses and the consequential decimation of native fish. It brought to mind a comment Pete had made, about an erosion problem he was fighting. Brady wondered if she might entertain talking to a homeless felon-to-be. Whether or not she could or would help him, her writing sure showed zero indication of being intimidated by Leo Burgess. Maybe he needed to find some tutorial info on oceanography first.

One news item that popped up—because of the Burgess name in the text—snatched his breath away, depressing him to the point of just quitting and giving in to Burgess. It was the local newspaper's report on the death of Pete Cully. Vehicular homicide, speculated the reporter. Pete had been struck and killed by a drunken motorist as he attempted to cross Shoreline Drive on foot, apparently because of an unspecified mechanical breakdown.

Reading it made him fiercely sad for Pete, and it re-emphasized how alone he was. What was the use of this war? He could have his job back, his debts forgiven, and no one around here gave a damn about his character or lack of it. Well okay, he did. Nor could he forget Pete saying something about the "good folks" from Carolina. Like a legacy Brady had to live up to, for some inexplicable reason. Somehow, without having ever discussed it, Brady had sensed that Pete would've stood up for him, even against his own employer. Pete had been the closest thing to a friend he'd found in Florida, though he was beginning to consider Chaz one.

As he waded through the tedious torrent of material on Burgess, he often lapsed into dwelling on the last time he saw Pete. Seeing the image of him kicking at J.D.'s tire marks on the lawn and telling Brady about Gerry Terence. Nor had he forgotten the odd look Pete had when he told Brady he might wind up in a ditch someday. He kept replaying the overheard phone conversation, wondering if he should repeat it to Terence. But Pete's death was obviously an accident, right? Nobody could arrange murder by drunk driver, could they? Maybe he would slide it into his next meeting with Terence anyway, just to make sure he honored that last request in case Pete meant it. For now, best to keep his head down, work hard, and stay at the research. Somewhere out there, if he dug deep enough, existed a grenade he could roll into Leo Burgess's tent. And he wasn't going to quit.

CHAPTER THIRTY-FIVE

Gerry Terence's horseshit meter had redlined. He never trusted weird timing of supposedly unconnected fluke events, and he damn well would not accept this one. Open and shut that the idiot who blew a point one-eight on the Breathalyzer actually killed Pete, and that guy was going to get a hefty prison sentence to show for it. But why had Pete pulled off the road and walked away from his truck? That question kept Gerry from swallowing the deplorable yet random misfortune theory.

Something happened to put him on the side of the road. Guys like Pete Cully did not run out of gas, and he was capable of repairing most anything, right there on the spot. So Gerry wanted an answer on that breakdown. If it proved to be simply bad luck, maybe he could let it rest. The idea of someone connected to all of the players in a homicide investigation having such a coincidental accident just gave him that familiar old "uh-oh, I don't think so" reflex.

He rang up a traffic cop who remembered him from his days in harness and talked him into running down the name of the mechanic assigned to the inspection, storage, and/or disposal of Pete's truck. That name turned out to be Doug Ridings, a guy he did not know well, but well enough to know how to bribe him. He merely offered to pay Doug's bar tab for an evening in exchange for looking the truck over for any mechanical failure and then talking about it. Since Gerry never considered himself a reformed drunk, more of just a lucky one, he didn't have any of the knee-jerk need to reform other drinking men who could handle it.

They met at Spahn's, and after the usual stilted greetings between two guys pretending to be closer than they were, Doug got right up in Gerry's face. "So, how did you know?" he asked, almost a whisper. His eyes glistened with excitement at being on the inside of intrigue.

"Know what?" Gerry countered, backing away from the whiskey breath.

"You know, that somebody jinked up the truck?"

Gerry grabbed the other man's wrist, clenching it. "Are you sure?"

" 'Course I'm sure." Doug snatched his arm away, looking offended. "I ain't been turning wrenches for no twenty years to go and make a mistake like that." He polished off his drink and waved for another.

Gerry should have felt triumphant, but he just felt tired. *Damn it, Pete, what did you get tangled up in?* "Run it down for me. What, how, maybe a when."

"It's kinda crazy, if whoever did it wanted it to look like an accident," Doug said, making a slashing motion across his fist. "They just cut the brake lines, plain as day, couldn't miss it. No way those lines could get cut that clean right there by accident."

"How did he keep from running off into the bay with his brakes gone?"

"Vehicles nowadays have emergency braking power, like this one, it runs off the vacuum system. So you'd have enough juice to stop it once anyway." Doug leaned back in, lapping up his chance to play detective. "Anybody knows cars, they'd know that. But whoever did this knew enough to pull the fuse for the warning lights. The driver wouldn't get any idea of something wrong until the pedal went to the floor. So I bet you'll find out it was done by somebody who knows cars, but ain't been around 'em for quite a few years. Late models, anyway."

Gerry sat back and kicked Doug's logic around, amused by the mechanic's smug expression. Fair enough, he thought, for even though it was far from being the only possible deduction, it did click. He waited as Doug ordered another Jack on the rocks. Gerry knew damn well the guy wouldn't be slamming down Black Jack at this rate on his own budget. Oh well, still a cheap price for the information.

The drink arrived and Doug's attention returned. Gerry asked him again for the time frame of the tampering.

"No way to tell, looking at it," he answered, shaking his head and sucking down the Jack. "But I bet the diagnostic computer in that truck would log a major system failure like this. 'Course, it would only register it from the first time it was started up with the lines cut. So all you'd get is a no later than. You want me to hook it up, see if it's recorded?"

"Do that. Call me when you find out."

"Can do." His face bunched up, the sun-leathered forehead folding like a road map. "We gotta tell the suits assigned to the case. You gonna do it?"

"No, I think it'd be better if they get it straight from you," Gerry said. He did not want it known that he was even interested, leave alone snooping around their investigation. Part of why he was getting Doug oiled, counting on him to be close-mouthed about his drinking. He also realized that Doug seemed to think Gerry was still on the job. No reason to explain all that now.

After yet another double Jack went down the hatch, he convinced Doug that four was enough and shooed him on home. He settled the tab, frowning at his own unfinished drink. He would like to have enjoyed his customary one-and-done glass of hooch, but watching Doug pour it down had made him queasy. Nothing wrong with Jack Daniels, Gerry had never met a whiskey he didn't like, it was picturing how Doug's mornings must feel. Brought up some rough memories. He collected his change, figured a tip, and left, returning to the office instead of going home.

He sat at his desk in the near dark of just his reading lamp, dealing out a hand of solitaire. He hoped no one ever caught him playing cards, since it fit the stereotype of the hokey B-movie private eye all too well, but it never failed to help him think.

Okay, Pete, who could you anger enough for murder? Or to whom could you have been such a threat? Someone with outdated automotive knowledge, or someone scatterbrained, who might forget an important step. The ghoulish joke of it all was that it would have been a botched murder attempt even had the brakes failed completely. Pete was just not driving fast enough to suffer a fatal injury. He could have driven right into the four feet of surf in the bay and walked off. Gerry had worked enough traffic fatalities to doubt that even a head-on collision would be deadly at those speeds. And the wannabe murderer apparently never thought it out, considering there were no roads near Pete's home or work with a speed limit over thirty. Sufficient incompetence to laugh at, if not for the fact that the sabotage put Pete in the path of a drunk driver. Gerry feared that the person responsible would never go down for anything heavier than attempted, but he was going to nail the peckerhead and take his chances.

So who, Pete? Family is the first place to look in this kind of sneakiness, but Pete had none. Gerry had caught a definite whiff of conflict between Pete and Leo, as well as the obvious one with Nick, but he couldn't imagine Leo bungling anything this badly, and no way Nick had the guts. Instinct said it was connected to the Lexy Burgess homicide, maybe a cover-up kill by the same guy. Okay then, Pete, what did you see, hear, or know that was worthy of murder?

His hand of solitaire was going nowhere, stuck needing a red ten. He collected the cards, shuffled, and re-dealt. He absolutely did not want to horn in on the Lexy Burgess investigation. Despite grudging appreciation for his work on the Zeletsky case, which ought to shake out any day now, none of his old buddies would take kindly to a private license sniffing around a homicide. Especially without a client, ex-cop or not.

He could give Brady Spain's name as a client, but that would be the precise opposite of what he wanted, drawing attention to Brady as someone who needed a detective. Like shouting, "Here, look at me, I'm a suspect." As yet, he had drawn a blank finding out if Brady was on the short list. He had wheedled enough to learn that the investigating team was dead-set on the theory of a lover's quarrel, chiefly because they had found champagne for two all set up and waiting by the tub. So they were running down everyone who looked like a possible bed-mate. Had to be nothing pointing at Brady as such yet or he would be sweating it out in the fishbowl already.

Gerry did believe Brady's claim of no sexual relations with Lexy, but he had met too many impressive liars over the years to assume his nose to be infallible. One thing for sure, though; if Brady Spain had the ability to lie that convincingly about his sex life, Gerry was going to like him very much as the guy who tore out Lexy's throat with a fire poker.

He gathered up his cards and put them back in his lap drawer, ready for home and bed. Maybe Pete Cully and Lexy Burgess would talk to him in his sleep.

CHAPTER THIRTY-SIX

At the end of his fifth day with Chaz, Brady drove back to the Suncrest through the heavy, humid September twilight, arriving to find a dusty red Corolla in his parking space. His mind careened at the possibility of a police officer coming in a two-door compact to serve a warrant. Surely not, he reasoned.

Leaving the Jeep in a visitor slot, he crossed the pavement in a half-circle to see around the Corolla. A woman was sitting quietly in a lawn chair by the door to his unit. Brady's pulse hammered in his neck, his throat swallowing convulsively against the sudden case of dry mouth.

The yellow glare of the security lamps caught the auburn highlights in her dark hair, giving it the deep luster of polished cherry wood. As he came nearer, he could make out that she had a boss figure—rounded and soft, yet tight and solid, the kind your eyes keep wandering back to so often, you wind up walking into a wall or something. She had gray-green eyes and a spatter of freckles across her strong nose. He knew she also had a light trail of freckles between her breasts, but absolutely none on her legs, unless he was hallucinating.

"Peggy Donellson," he exclaimed, not yet convinced this wasn't some seriously weird mind trip. "Is that you? What are you doing here?"

She bounced out of her chair and smiled at him, the happy one that turned her eyes up at the corners. "Yes, Brady Spain, it's me. Is that any way to greet someone who drove eight hundred miles to see you?"

"No, no. I'm sorry, it's awesome that you're here, I mean, to see you. I'm just a little wigged out. I'd give you a hug, but you really don't want to," he said, gesturing at his sweaty, muddy, grass-stained clothes.

"Yeah, really, where have you been, dumpster diving?" She wrinkled her nose and then smiled again. "But I'm going to do it, anyway. It's not like I'm what you would call shower-fresh after that drive."

"Okay, you talked me into it," he said, wrapping around her perhaps a bit tighter than he intended. Dang, she smelled good. Felt pretty righteous, too.

"Pee-yew!" She laughed, pretending to struggle against his clasp.

He broke away before he wanted to, before old muddy-lungs in the office called the cops on him for being too excited. He unlocked the room and led her inside. "Don't look at it, don't ask, I don't even want to talk about it. You never did answer why you're here."

She sat on the bed, thank God it was made up, and accepted the beer he offered her from the cooler that served as his refrigerator.

"Do you remember my cousin Zoe?" she asked. At his head-shake, she continued. "Well, she remembers you and she lives in Clearwater now. So she calls up to tell me about this news thing she saw and what did I think about you being investigated for murder."

"I'm—" Brady started, wanting to defend himself. He realized how stupid he'd sound and put his head in his hands instead. If he ever did commit a murder, it was going to be Nick Burgess.

"So I went on their website and watched the segment," she continued. "I know you're capable of a lot of crazy things,

Brady, but I'm sure you wouldn't kill someone. And even though we don't see each other anymore, you can't have changed that much."

"Thanks, Peg. I can't tell you how good that feels," he said, wishing he knew a better word to describe the massive morale boost of just sitting in the same room as her, hearing her voice. Still not quite believing she was here, and lightheaded with the feelings it awoke. "That's a hell of a drive you made to join my fan club. You'll be the second member, me being the other one. How the heck did you find me?"

She sipped her beer and glanced around his room, making him cringe inside at what she must've thought of it. "Well, I wanted to call you, find out if you were in trouble and needed help. Your mom had given me your home number and the name of the place you worked. I didn't want your cell to ring at work, so I pulled up their number. Then when they said you weren't there anymore, I knew things couldn't be going too well."

"But they don't know I'm staying here," he protested. Watching her talk, he noticed an elegance about her, a poised, confident air that he didn't remember. Probably just from looking at her through fresh eyes, having seen her only once in the past year. It made him see how she was every bit as captivating as Lexy, just in a different kind of special Peggy way. It also gave him a grasping sense of loss, like he no longer really knew her. "How'd you figure that out?"

She blushed and lowered her gaze to her fingers picking at the label on her beer bottle. "I tried to think like Brady Spain would. When I discovered your home phone was disconnected, which your mom doesn't know, by the way, I remembered that I kept all the receipts from special dinners and things you took me to."

She glanced back up and her blush deepened at his raised eyebrows. "Well, I did. And some were old enough they had your whole credit card number on there instead of just the last four digits. So I figured you would still have that card for the reward stuff you get. I called them and told them I was your wife and I had lost the card. The security questions the woman asked were a breeze, I know you so well. She said this was the last place it was used, no charges, just an inquiry. I told her I remembered it now, and I'd call her back if we needed to cancel the card. I hope you're not mad at me for doing all that."

"How could I be mad at you?" *Just totally blown away that you worked so hard at giving a damn about your blind ex-boyfriend.* "Though I am torqued at that fat liar in the office here for calling on my card when she said she wouldn't. Peg, why didn't you just call my cell instead of going to all this hassle? Not that I'm not happy to see you."

"I almost did." She set her bottle on the floor and pulled her legs up, tucking them under her in a yoga-like position. "But talking to your mom, even though she didn't exactly say this, I could tell she doesn't think you have anyone real close here that you can trust, like someone to get your back, as they say."

"Oh, shit, you didn't tell her anything, did you?" He bolted upright in his chair, picturing Mom getting just the jolt her high blood pressure needed to kick up to stroke level.

"Sure, I gave her the whole story." Peggy rolled her eyes and then laughed at his relieved expression. "You know better than that. Anyway, I realized that if I called, you would tell me everything was fine, don't worry, I'll call you later, all the usual Brady stuff. And everything can't be fine if you're on the news as a murder suspect. So I called the motel and the woman said you were registered."

She paused, wrinkling her nose. "She asked me if I was with the police, do you believe it? So I came on down without giving you a chance to tell me not to. Even if you have a new girlfriend, honest, I just want to help. I've even already got a room, though not here. I have to tell you, Brady, I was scared to check in here."

He laughed, wondering how, in the midst of the impossible odds he faced in the struggle to salvage the rest of his life, it could feel so lucky to be Brady Spain. "So was I, girl, so was I."

He moved over and sat beside her, picked up her hand, and held it in both of his. "You are some kind of unbelievably wonderful person, you know that? By the way, I've been reading up on criminal statutes, and the penalty for lying about being someone's wife is that you have to go out for a late dinner with him. Let me wash up real quick."

CHAPTER THIRTY-SEVEN

They selected a steak joint with red-checked curtains, faux-oak tables, and the deserted air of being a week away from bankruptcy, but then, privacy was why they picked it. While Peggy studied the menu, Brady studied her, this girl whom he had assumed he knew so well.

"Penny," she said, looking up and catching his eye.

"Thinking about you. About how fast a year goes by, but how long it is looking back. Are you still teaching?"

"I am. Even finished my master's this year, so now I make a smidgen more than I would as a Walmart greeter. But I don't like the new administrative team, and the district does, so I may have to move instead of transferring within the district." She picked up a breadstick and pointed it at him like a pistol. "Now talk, Brady Spain, before I have to get out my rubber hose. I want to know how all this happened to you."

He raised his hands in the classic surrender pose. "Don't I get a blindfold and a cigarette?"

She just aimed the breadstick at him again and shook her head. He knew he had been avoiding the subject. But the thrill he got from her unexpected company, this person whom he could trust unconditionally, who also trusted him, was a mood he wanted to prolong, not ruin with a bunch of raggedy-ass drama that would surely make him look like a loser. That drive, though, and all the work to be here—she had earned the right to hear it.

He waited until they ordered, Cobb salad for her and a Philly for him, then told her the whole sordid sequence of disasters. He could tell she felt embarrassed for him when he got to the part about the yard work, an emotion he too would have felt in his previous life, which seemed much farther in the past than a week. But living at the Suncrest and trying to stay one step ahead of prison changed a man's idea of embarrassment. In telling it he found out that, clichéd or not, it really did feel good to unload it all on someone who believed you.

"You really should tell all that to the police," she said when he finished. "Why haven't you?"

"Well, I missed my chance to do it before Burgess and son set me up as a liar," he said. "Now, no one is going to believe my word against theirs, and I can guarantee you Leo Burgess will have me in jail the minute I open my mouth."

"You can't know that. I still think you should talk to someone official, it's the only way you'll get to tell your side." She cocked her head and raised a suspicious eyebrow. "You're not getting hardheaded about this, are you?"

"No," he lied. "Why would you think that?"

"Whatever." She brandished her fork this time, a shred of lettuce dangling from its end. "I know you, Brady Guillermo Spain né Torres. 'Oh, I can't go to the cops, Peg, they won't believe me. Oh, I don't want a lawyer, it'll make me look guilty.' What you won't say is that you want to fight this out yourself, just you on your trusty white charger."

Brady sat back, pinching the bridge of his nose between forefinger and thumb to hide his eyes. Busted. He had not yet even admitted it all to himself, consciously.

Once he had his poker face reloaded, he stalled some more by working on his last bite of sandwich. Funny how he had thought of her as sweet but hopelessly small-town compared to the glamorous girls of the Florida beach scene. Yet here she sat, and the reality was that she made the women of Heron Point look neurotic and shallow. And behind those freckles hid an intuitive brain that proved faster than the ones in paradise. Made him wonder if everyone's perceptions of others were clouded by their own personal discontents.

"Well, at first I really did just want to get untangled any way I could," he said after swallowing. "But now I can't see a way out unless I do something. And I guess I do want a certain amount of satisfaction. My name clear, anyway. I still can't believe you actually drove all the way down here, it like totally made my day. Heck, my month. What made you so sure I would still be here, and not skipping town ahead of the posse?"

"Based on that news story, I figured you couldn't." She pushed her plate aside and picked up her napkin, twisting it around in her fingers. "Besides, like I said, I know you. You've never run away from anything in your life other than me."

He just stared at her, unable to speak. Kind of felt like getting slapped with a wet catfish, but she was dead-on as usual. And he was a dumbass.

"Hey, don't get that beat-up look on your face," she said, reaching across to pat his hand. "Just because you're done with me, it doesn't change the fact that I couldn't stand the idea of you going through something like this alone. Being accused of something this scary, something I knew you couldn't have done."

"Stop the presses. I never said I was done with you. Being a total moron is not the same thing as being done, okay? In fact, if you're not too over me and my brain-dead self, I don't think I'll ever be done with you. But I need you to do me a favor."

"That's what I'm here for." Her eyes had darkened to a jade green, a depthless shimmer in them that he couldn't read.

"I need you to go back home and stay there until I call you, okay?"

The shimmer gave way to a high-voltage flash of anger. "That

207

was a dirty trick, Brady."

"I know it was. But I really need you to. There's nothing you can do for me any better than you've done by coming. I need you to go because I'm scared to have you here." *And I want the chance to come to you, without any baggage, show up on my knees and ask for another shot.*

"But why?"

"You deserve the truth, but you have to promise that it won't send you off the deep end about what I've got to do, okay? These guys are so outrageous I don't trust them not to do something to you as a way of banging on me. I take that back, I do trust them to do exactly that. Like what they've done to me, or worse. And to me, that would be harder to live with than that prison cell I told you about."

Digger Carrero drummed his fingers against the edge of the table, putting all his attention into the rhythm, because he knew it would annoy the narrow-ass smart-bitch cop questioning him. He'd done this scene before, make a statement and listen to a bunch of stupid questions. Probably this same room, too. Couldn't tell 'cause all they junky-ass rooms looked the same, furnished from the same garage sale. He knew they only asked questions when they ain't got shit on you, and he wanted old redheaded beast sitting across from him to know he wasn't listening to no woman cop.

He sneered for the camera, wondering who all was watching, while she droned on and on about his car being placed at the scene of this, that, and the other. All of which told him he was here because of that whacked-out smiley cop who came to see him. Get out of this, he would hunt down old fat boy and dust him up. Then he remembered the eyes in that smiling face and decided it might not be so easy. Seemed like maybe those eyes weren't as fat, dumb, and happy as the rest of his act. *Shoulda never figured him for a mental without looking closer, Digger. You got to check out a man's depth.* His attention snapped back to the female when he heard her say some shit about first-degree homicide and a death penalty.

"The hell you talking about, homicide?" he interrupted, terror mushrooming in his chest. No way he was letting this skank put him in that frame.

"Gee, Albert, I guess you weren't listening," she said, bullshit innocence on her face and using his real name for the first time. "I told you, we've got witnesses who saw you cruising the neighborhood where Lexy Burgess was killed. You admit you have no alibi, and considering your history with the ladies, a jury wouldn't even leave the stand to think it over."

"No fuckin' way," Digger yelled. "You got to have evidence, and you ain't got none, 'cause I ain't do no homicide. I want me a lawyer. I ain't never even heard of no Lexy."

Bitch cop smiled at him, a nasty smile like a Doberman's. "I checked your sheet, Albert. You never know any of your victims. You went too far this time. I can't believe some of the plea deals you've gotten. You should've pulled a big number a long time ago. Maybe you'll get lucky again, talk it down to life without parole. Somehow I don't think so, though. Anything else you want to say before I call the public defender?"

She placed both hands against the table, did a brief fingertip drumroll of her own, and shoved her chair back to stand.

"Wait," he blurted.

She eased back down into her chair and leaned all up in his grille, just looking, not saying shit. He turned sideways in his seat and pulled his head as far away from her nasty ass as he could. Damn, his skin got all cold and tight-feeling at the idea of going back to the joint, having to wear make-up and perfume, and spending his nights on his knees. But he could do it, long as he knew he was getting out at the other end alive. No way he could do life like that, and he damn sure couldn't face the needle. And he couldn't be sure Roni would come and visit him on no murder stretch. So forget the PD, they just always want to plead to any damn thing. Better off to cut a deal with this old snake-mean heifer here himself.

"Look, you get off me on this bullshit murder if I give you something?" he said. "You know I ain't do it."

Now she finally leaned back, crossing her arms and looking at him like he was a dumb fuck. "I don't know, Albert, I think we've got you cold on this one. But I'll listen to anything. Whaddaya got?"

"How 'bout if I cop to doing a ponytail girl and maybe dime a couple of parole busters y'all ain't never found?"

CHAPTER THIRTY-EIGHT

Leo Burgess stood at the head of the steps leading down from the lanai, hands on his hips, surveying the disgraceful excuse of a pool party below him. No more than twenty guests in attendance, milling around and pretending that it did not feel like a fat kid's birthday party, while sixty pounds of prime beefsteak rotted away in the ninety-degree broiler of sunset in September.

After an initial flash of alarm that he had committed a social blunder by hosting it so soon after the deaths of his daughter and his maintenance man, he decided that was not the issue, disloyalty was. After all, Alexandra's tragedy had taken place almost two weeks ago, and Anna could not lie in bed forever. Pete was not even a member of the family. No, these people needed to be here paying their respects, appreciating his strength in a time of sorrow. He would simply make note of those who did not attend and remember where they really stood with him.

The most egregious offense was the glaring absence of any of the members from the executive team at Beach Haven Resorts. He had invited them as a show of his appreciation for their cooperation in the Brady Spain matter, planning to reassure them in person that the deal was still a green light, the county commission would rubber-stamp any zoning exception or permit Leo Burgess requested. Yet not even a token appearance from a lone representative.

He descended the five steps to the cobbled brick path, almost missing the last one and falling flat when he spotted Brady

Spain crossing his lawn, coming toward him. He tasted the bitter bile of anger rising in his throat. Who in God's name did this fellow think he was?

When Brady Spain got the call from Gerry Terence informing him of Albert Carrero's confession to the assault on Sara Zeletsky, he had to sort through a maelstrom of emotions and reactions. Jubilation at being free of Leo Burgess, gratitude toward Terence, residual anger at Burgess for holding him hostage, an urgent regret that Peggy had done as he asked and was now not here to celebrate. Plus a flutter of anxiety up his spine when Terence cautioned him that the police had not zeroed in on a suspect for Lexy's murder.

Already in the Jeep when he took the call, driving back to his roach hole after taking advantage of an option to work on Labor Day, he ripped a U-turn and sped back north toward Heron Point. Showing up at the Burgess estate covered in a day's sweat and grime couldn't be good politics, but too bad. Brady wanted to get in front of the guy right now and find out if the good news would bring a cease-fire. Underneath his euphoria, he recognized the hard truth that shaking loose of the bad check rap was only the first step in getting his life back to anything remotely like six weeks before, when he had moved into Heron Point.

He almost made another U-turn at the Burgess home when he saw a dozen cars lined along the curb and what looked like a grill-out shindig happening at the pool. Then he saw Leo Burgess standing alone at the edge of the veranda and reminded himself, *too bad. Let's get this done.*

He double-parked and cut across the yard, hustling to catch Burgess before anyone else came within earshot. Christ, but the man possessed a powerful, intimidating presence, especially for someone that old. It hit Brady that it was more than just Burgess's imposing size creating that aura; something about the stoutness of his size made his age feel like a source of strength and toughness, like with a giant oak or sequoia. The impending confrontation turned Brady's insides hollow and breathless, and there was no other word for it but fear.

"Mr. Spain," Burgess said as Brady approached. "This is a function for residents and invited guests, of which you are neither. There is only one thing I am interested in hearing from you, so that had better be your purpose here."

"Yeah, well, so I'm a gate-crasher, too." The challenge helped smooth Brady's jitters back into resolve, though his pulse continued galloping. "Figured I might be invited if this was a wake for ol' Pete, but I can guess he probably didn't score enough society points. I take it you haven't heard the news, then."

Burgess's brow drew down low enough that he stared at Brady through the shrubbery growing up there. "I find your impertinence most irritating, and I do not think it wise of you to antagonize me, with what you have to lose. To what news are you referring?"

"Nick's off the hook. They got the guy who attacked Sara."

The momentary spasm of relief that crossed Burgess's face looked like it packed such a punch that Brady thought the man's knees would buckle. Then the harsh face reset into its rigid lines.

"I am afraid you misunderstand," Burgess said. "He was never on the hook, as you put it. No one except perhaps you could imagine him guilty of such savagery. You have attempted to incriminate my son by lying about his presence that night, for what motive I cannot hazard a guess. Perhaps jealousy of a man your age who is more fortunate than you. Now you are in your current predicament because I refused to allow you to do so. Don't you feel quite stupid to have brought this trouble on yourself, Mr. Spain?"

Brady stared at him, openmouthed, imagining that his eyeballs were sticking out like a Looney Tunes character. Who was this guy kidding? "Well, that sure cleared up a lot for me," he said. "I'm glad you got all that worked out. But what I want to know is, are we done? You don't need to squeeze me anymore, and you bagged a free month's rent in the bargain."

"I suppose now you would like your money returned and all criminal proceedings dismissed," said Burgess, smiling like a vampire eyeing an open vein.

"I couldn't care less about the money as long as you'll drop the whole matter and call us all square," Brady retorted, stunned by the vicious contempt visible in Burgess's features. What more could he possibly want?

"First, I am going to tell you something," said Burgess, looming huge in the halo of the porch lights behind him as the dusk deepened. He waggled his forefinger at Brady.

"I suspect you see yourself as brave for resisting me in this matter. You are not. You are a scared little rabbit, unable to think clearly when faced with any threat. I find it amusing that you lacked the chutzpah to challenge the fraud charge. With the prevailing sentiment in courtrooms today, it is doubtful that you would have been jailed, though you certainly will be convicted of the offense. Yet you allowed yourself to be cowed by an irrational fear of a nebulous threat. So no, Mr. Spain, I will not drop the matter, for if nothing else it will create embarrassment, inconvenience, and expense for you. You have annoyed me, Mr. Spain, and you will pay for that. In addition, your foolhardiness and insolence have convinced me that you are capable of all manner of irrational behaviors. I believe I will join Nicolas in personally calling for a thorough investigation of you for the murder of my daughter. Now, I have guests to tend to, and you must leave."

Anna Burgess balanced the tray of canapés on one arm and reached for the doorknob with her other hand. Though they had staff there to handle food preparation, she always made up a supply of her own salmon and cream cheese hors d'oeuvres for party guests. She had not felt up to doing so for this event, but Leo had insisted, and in truth the ritual had improved her spirits. It did not change the fact that no party would ever feel festive again, without her Lexy.

She managed the knob and eased the door open with her foot to avoid jostling her tray. She paused there in the doorway when she noticed Leo at the bottom of the steps, talking with a young man she did not know. She set the canapé tray down on the occasional table by the door and closed her eyes to enhance her hearing.

Once she tuned into the conversation, she realized with a flinch that the stranger was Brady Spain, the boy who was supposed to help Nicky. She heard Leo ask about news and Spain's answer sucked her breath away. She waited long enough to be sure, but she never got a chance to savor the joy of hearing the answer to her prayers.

Feeling her mind darkening as vertigo crowded in on her, she ran out of the kitchen, up the stairs, and flung herself across the bed—the party, the hors d'oeuvres, and Brady Spain all forgotten. She could not bring herself to even ask God to forgive her for this. She had committed the most damnable of sins, willingly as an act of love for her son, but to find out it was a needless act removed all right to pray for absolution. It was her punishment for not believing in her Nicky.

Now the only penitent course left to her was public confession of her sins, to let others judge her in the hopes that she could earn back the privilege of asking for God's grace. She knew she should tell Leo first, but he would prevent her from carrying out her duty. She must go now; her sin demanded it.

CHAPTER THIRTY-NINE

Jeanette Voyes looked nothing like what Brady had imagined. After hearing her deep voice over the phone, he'd pictured a bulldog-faced wine barrel of a woman, banging out her purple prose on an old-fashioned Underwood as she smoked her way through half a carton of Camels a day. The woman who waved him over to a table at the coffee shop they'd agreed on turned out to be a short, slight, intense-looking Mediterranean type with dark curly hair and restless brown eyes. No Camels in sight, though the dark roast or espresso that sat steaming in front of her smelled strong enough to be just as deadly.

After introductions and seating, he thanked her for meeting him and then hesitated over picking where to start.

"So you believe you can help me find the source of our silt runoff," she said before he could get his mouth open. "How?"

Okay, start there. "I've taken a crash course in this stuff, so I may not have it all straight, but I think I do. Most of the biology part I've gotten from you, and I've been boning up on tides and currents. Have you ever considered Heron Point as your source?"

The restless eyes locked in on him, narrowing into slits. "There aren't any estuaries near Heron Point. Nothing that feeds into the ocean. No construction, no nothing."

"That's why I'm learning about currents. What would you say if I told you that the computer model shows it to be as a feasible scenario, given the prevailing current? Wouldn't it be worth doing a study?"

She took a measured sip of coffee, holding her gaze on him. "I would say, whose computer model?"

Brady felt a trickle of sweat running down his ribs despite the air conditioning. He was betting a lot on this woman he'd just met. "Let's say I know at least one of the models the National Oceanic and Atmospheric Administration uses would show that, if you knew someone authorized to access it. I'm equally positive the University of Florida's would corroborate the results."

She raised her eyebrows, setting her cup down. "And you know this how?"

He drew a deep breath. "Look, maybe I gambled wrong on you, but I'm betting you wouldn't have bothered to meet me without researching me first." He saw a twitch at the corners of her mouth and plunged on. "So you at least know I have the background to possibly be capable of doing what I'm not telling you I did."

Another twitch of the lips and a small nod. "And you're one hundred percent certain that a certified, authorized programmer will get the same results you would've gotten if you did what you didn't do?"

Brady grinned. As smart as he'd believed her to be. "Well, no. I can only promise ninety-nine percent, because I'm not an oceanographer. But I am one hundred percent good at what I do. So, worth getting a study done?"

She let out a bitter-sounding snort of laughter. "Sure, like I can afford to finance a study. Apparently no one else gives enough of a damn to do anything. I've busted my ass trying to get the DEP on it, but so far, no soap." She paused and stacked both hands under her chin, giving him the narrow eye thing again. "Who are you trying to hang?"

Brady formed a matching chin rest with his hands and held the eye contact. What the hell, he had called because she seemed tough and savvy, and she'd lived up to it so far. "A question first," he said. "Does Leo Burgess own your paper or any part of it? More to the point, does he own anybody at your paper?"

She gave him a lopsided grin. "Sounds like you've done business with Leo."

He laughed. She knew Leo. "Let's just say I learned the hard way how he does things. Whatever happened on that land sale you were riding him about a couple of years back?"

"So that's how you decided I would listen to you," she said. She picked up a swizzle stick and jabbed at the table with it, then nodded as if to herself and looked back up.

"What happened was consummate Leo Burgess," she said with another twisted smile. "He arranged an interview with another reporter where he explained how it wasn't a question of his financial gain, it was about the one hundred families of the construction crew who would get a paycheck if the deal went through. Then he trotted out all these studies showing how the land was not home to any endangered species, or any unique species. So who's going to listen to this one kooky environmental wacko in the face of all that?"

He felt himself mirroring her knowing grin by the end of the tale. "Sounds like the Leo Burgess I know and love."

"Well, that's a big fish you're going after," she said. "I have to admit I wouldn't mind gumming up the works for him. He does own a piece of my heart for what happened to his daughter, but that does not change the fact that he is the environmental equivalent of Pol Pot. And no, he does not own my company, and no, I'm not afraid of him. He certainly has influence, he's too rich not to, but the worst they can do is fire me. I'd have a job somewhere else the next day, and I could live off my blog anyway. There are too many readers out there who agree with my views, and ME's know that. Now, how is all this going to help stop the channel from choking to death on silt?"

He liked the tough talk, but he had to wonder how well it would stand up to the kind of coercion Burgess had orchestrated for him. Not that he had much choice: he didn't have the public forum or the depth of knowledge it would take to make this thing stick. If she said yes, he had to gamble on her backbone being as strong as the talk. "Have you ever seen Burgess's house?"

She shook her head, coiling the swizzle stick around a finger.

"Well, you need to drive by it, see for yourself. He moved enough soil around to make a hill for his house to sit on. Near the water's edge. I have it on good authority that he suffers constant erosion and runoff. Add to it this pool he has dug in twelve feet deep that's even closer to the water. There's your construction. Yeah, it was two years ago, but my reading tells me the build-up you're seeing in the channel is often a delayed reaction. And with the piping and draining system you have there for that pool, it'll take forever for the sand shifting and runoff to settle down."

"This good authority you speak of," she said. "Is it someone I can talk to?"

He pictured Pete, his gap-toothed smile and his ever-cheerful morning chatter. "No, he won't be available. But I think I can offer something better."

She raised her eyebrows in question.

"What if I know a guy, a federal guy, who loves taking down people like Burgess? He's not EPA, but he promises he can get the EPA on it if we have any reasonable scientific suspicions. That way you can skip over the local people, bypass the Burgess influence. What my guy needs is an expert to talk with them if he sets it up. That's where you come in. If you look it up, you'll see there are precedents for proving a single individual homeowner liable for ocean damage. And you'll like how much it cost some of these cats that got stuck with the bill. What do you say?"

She studied him for a minute, tapping her mangled swizzle stick on the table, and shook her head. "No, I can't be your expert."

"Why not?" he asked, thinking, *great, all this for nothing. She lied. She's scared of Burgess just like everyone else.*

"Because I can't," she said. She tossed the tortured swizzle stick aside and leaned in, all that intensity lasering into him. "Look, Brady, I would crawl on my butt through a mile of broken glass to save that channel. And I told you I would love to stick a thumb in Leo's eye. However, my job is to report the news, even write opinions on the news, but not to create the news. I cannot write a column about something I am personally involved in. That is what's called a conflict of interest."

"Well then, let someone else write it." He realized he felt more disappointment at her passing on a chance to halt the destruction in the channel than his failure to enlist a potential ally against Burgess. *Come on, woman, where's the commitment behind all that passion?*

"No, sir. It's my story now. You brought it to me, I won't give it up. And I think you're missing my point here. I don't have any credentials as a marine biologist or oceanographer. What I am is a damn good reporter. If you want Leo to take a hit, you want publicity. That's where I'm your expert. Now, what if I can provide a true expert in marine matters? Someone credentialed both professionally and academically? Someone who wouldn't be afraid to go up against an entire infantry battalion for a cause like this?"

Solitaire was just not doing it for Gerry Terence this time. He couldn't find the focus to even recognize the pips on the cards, never mind keeping track of which one played where. His brain

Hugh Dutton

was too punchy from hearing the bizarre tale of Anna Burgess walking into the county house at ten o'clock last night and announcing that she had come to plead guilty to the murder of Pete Cully. Exactly how she said it, too—not confess, not even make a statement or give information, but plead guilty. Lord help him, Gerry could not stop expecting a director to step out onto the stage and holler, "Cut." Just when he thought nothing could ever surprise him anymore, the ghastly farcical comedy of human behavior reached a new height of absurdity. So instead of solitaire, he amused himself by bending each card, one at a time, between his forefinger and thumb until it popped loose and fluttered to the floor.

Oh, he understood her motive, or could at least follow it, given the way she had calmly explained her actions to the flabbergasted sergeant taking her statement. But how in the hell did she arrive at that line of reasoning? Not that reasoning was the word for it. She thought Pete was trying to frame her son for rape? Well, horseshit. She thought Nick was as guilty as Cain, and she was afraid Pete could prove it.

He fluttered another card. Hey, almost across the room this time. His technique must be improving. Four of diamonds, he noticed when it landed face up. Anna would never face a murder charge, he felt sure. There was just no getting past the fact that she did not actually kill Pete. Hers was the worst attempt at murder in Gerry's memory. Except that it worked. Pete was dead.

Anna was safely locked away in a rubber room while the shrinks dug around in her skull. Maybe she wouldn't ever get out. From the way Gerry had heard the story she sure belonged there. One thing he dearly wished was that he could have seen Big Leo's face when he learned second-hand about his wife copping to a homicide. According to Gerry's source, Leo was not even aware she had gone down there.

222

Nor did the irony stop there. If Anna ever did face any charges, a jury would lap up the diminished capacity argument her lawyer would surely use, and not just because of the emotional trauma from Lexy's death. No, now her lawyer could righteously point out that any mother would take action to prevent her poor, innocent son from being framed for rape in some vicious evil plot of Pete's. Great. So Pete's character gets trashed and his killer takes a walk, all thanks to the work Gerry did in proving Nick innocent by popping the Carrero puke. Ain't that a cockroach in your salad.

Aagh. He could not decide whether to laugh or throw up. If he laughed, he feared he would never stop. The men in the white suits would come and get him and bundle him away in a straitjacket while he chuckled maniacally along. Maybe he could room next to Anna.

He fluttered another card. Jack of spades. *Sorry, Pete, old buddy. You wanted justice served for Sara Zeletsky and we did it, but doing so is going to give Anna a free pass. I'm guessing you wouldn't want to exact your pound of flesh from an old lady who's lost her marbles, anyway. The other thing you really wanted was Nick. What did you know that made you so sure he did it? It was something significant, because Anna believed it too. What died with you, locked away in that hardheaded skull of yours, bro?*

CHAPTER FORTY

The two detectives declined J.D. Macken's offer of drinks, politely, but in a manner that made him feel like an idiot for suggesting it. He sat on the sofa next to Ellie, facing his visitors, and noticed his wife sliding as far away from him as the sofa allowed. What an impressive marriage. No wonder he'd gotten sick of her. His palms felt sweaty, and he went for the sneaky swipe down his pant legs. He knew in the loan biz sweaty palms often meant the customer was ready to surrender and sign, and the last thing he wanted his guests to notice was any sign of surrender.

Today made the third time he'd talked to these two, but it was the first time he had a case of nerves over it. The previous questioning had been quick and matter of fact, no sense of him being a suspect. Even after he admitted to his affair with Lexy, knowing they would learn of it anyhow. But this one felt different, formal somehow, and their request for Ellie to be present seemed a bad omen. He had no doubt they would bring up the affair in front of her. He'd even considered refusing the interview, but didn't dare risk pissing them off. Ellie learning about Lexy weighed in as a chickenshit worry compared to lethal injection.

The woman cop, a sharp-faced redhead named Bearcy, jumped right into it. "Now, how long ago did you begin your relationship with Lexy Burgess, J.D.?"

"We've already covered that," J.D. said, feeling Ellie's eyes on him. He didn't look at her.

"We're going to cover it again," said the other detective, a guy named Godwin. He was a sleepy-eyed, beefy sort, hypertensive looking, like you would smell the sausage and onions if he belched.

"I met her almost two years ago, when we moved in here," J.D. said, picking his words carefully. Maybe he could confuse the issue enough for it to slip past Ellie.

"No, we want you to tell us when your intimate relationship with Miss Burgess began," Bearcy said. She gave him a smile that was supposed to look kind and friendly, but it didn't fool J.D. for a second. This was a hard woman.

"I guess I would say we became intimate friends about a month or so later," J.D. said, and hurried to add, "We want to do anything we can to help catch her murderer, but how is all this going to help?"

Bearcy let out a theatrical sigh and slumped her head down. All a bullshit act. She raised her face and said, "Okay, this isn't working for me, J.D. Let's try it this way. When did you start having sexual relations with Miss Burgess?"

J.D. felt his wife stiffen, and he risked a glance at her. She sat motionless, a tear trickling out of her tight-shut eyes, with her hands clenched into hard little fists in front of her. Time to get it over with, try to move on. "Five or six months ago," he said, his whole body sweating now except for his mouth, which had gone dry as a sand dune. "Right around the first of the year. But you haven't answered my question. How is that going to catch the killer?"

Bearcy smiled again, this one with no window dressing, just a straight-out vicious, flesh-eating show of teeth. "Because we know you're our guy, J.D. We know you did it. We're just trying to find out why."

Ellie sprang off the sofa and backed away, pointing at him

225

with a forefinger as rigid as a sword. "You bastard," she screamed. "I can't believe you were sticking her. Oh my God, I hope they give you the death penalty. You don't deserve to live."

J.D. was so blown out by her explosion that he had to turn his eyes away, and he caught the cynical, know-it-all glance Bearcy shot at her partner. And in that flash, he knew. He could not fucking believe it, but he knew.

"Is that why you killed her, Ellie?" Bearcy asked, her voice as gentle as the mother of a newborn. "Because she was sleeping with J.D.?"

Ellie whirled to face the redheaded detective, aiming the finger at her. "No. It was for love. What would you know about love, you hussy? She laughed at me when I told her I loved her. She wouldn't tell me back. She laughed."

Ellie collapsed into a cross-legged seat on the floor, sobbing into her hands. Her muffled voice came through in hiccups. "How could she let you touch her, let you degrade her like that? She was so beautiful. So beautiful."

J.D. wanted to stand, but he felt nailed to the sofa, certain he was blacking out. He and his wife both in love with the same woman. Impossible, except it was so Lexy. He could hear in his head her patronizing laugh at Ellie's offer of love, because he'd played that scene. And he could picture Ellie's murderous rage, because he'd felt that, too.

Through the roaring in his head as loud as an airport runway, he dimly heard Godwin droning, ". . . the right to remain silent. Anything . . ." and remembered that he and Ellie had already been read their rights. Why twice? Funny, huh, he had assumed the first reading to be directed at him. But not as funny as the cruel joke Fate had played on him. All his scheming and now, with one enraged swing of a fireplace poker, he had lost it all. No Lexy, no Ellie, and no inheritance. Poof.

CHAPTER FORTY-ONE

It took almost an entire week to get all the parties together—
Grant Thibideaux and his EPA contacts with Jeanette and her
expert—but Brady finally hooked them up. Thank you, thank
you, Maggie. Word of Ellie Macken's arrest for the murder of
Lexy Burgess had gone public. Brady was at long last out of the
crosshairs, but now he had too much heart built into the ecol-
ogy gig to let it die. Even without a need for leverage on Daddy
Burgess any longer. All the research and learning had lit a fire
in him, and now he obsessed about seeing this thing answered
for. And corrected. Never had thought of himself as the tree-
hugger type, but there you go.

He waved bye to Jeanette, who was already back on the phone
again, and found his way out of her office and back to his Jeep.
Woke it up and set off for his next stop, Gerry Terence.

During the brainless chore of driving, his thoughts wandered
to Grant, Maggie's brother. Boy, did she describe him right.
That guy was ready to dice Burgess into little chunks, slow
roast him, and eat him for lunch. Grant had seemed let down
that Brady hadn't found any shady finance stuff for him to dig
into, but he brightened up a bit when Brady told him of the
eight figure settlement the guy in Hawaii paid in a similar
environmental case. Must have been some father they had—
Maggie drinking herself to death in an effort to idolize men like
Burgess, and Grant running around stomping on them. Just
another happy, all-American family.

And how about Ellie Macken? Talk about your lurid headlines. He still hadn't gotten a reality grip on that drama. Hadn't even decided which was a bigger mind blower, the affair between the two women that no one suspected or the mental picture of quiet little Ellie whacking away with a poker. Though she did have the arms for it, he remembered. Which also reminded him of her heated comment about Lexy's availability, a clue he totally missed.

He caught an empty parking slot, bailed out of the Jeep, and bounded up the stairs to Terence's second-floor office. Wow, these weeks with Chaz had put him in killer condition.

Terence's door was locked, with an envelope taped to it bearing Brady's name on the front. Odd, Terence said he'd be in all afternoon. Oh, well. He pulled the envelope free, flipped it over to open it, and saw a handwritten note on the back. "Sorry, duty calls. Holler at me if you have questions. G.T."

Brady gave the door a shrug and took the envelope back down to the Jeep, sitting there to open it. He pulled out two sheets of paper, the first one a letter from Terence. It read:

In your call, you requested your bill for my services. There won't be one from me, but I thought you might be interested in writing a check for this. Not another one of your rubber checks either, pal. Anyway, apparently this is something he had planned on doing during his lifetime, since he had escrowed money for years in a sheltered account. And he left his entire estate to it, so I will see that it is done as he wished. We don't have enough yet, but added to the substantial insurance he carried, we have a start. The instructions are that no one person may give more than a thousand dollars a year, to avoid patron influence. I guess we know of whom he was thinking. I will inform you once the legal mumbo-jumbo is in place so you can deduct your gift. Best of luck.

Brady read it twice, then re-folded it and checked out the other enclosed page. It was a donation form for something called the Cully Foundation, a nonprofit organization established for the counseling and legal advocacy of date-rape victims. Brady smiled. Bet Pete would never allow it to be named the Cully anything if he were still around. Well, that was all right, then. It would be an easy thousand bucks to spend, if he ever saw that kind of money again. He tucked the envelope away in the dash and put the Jeep in motion.

He headed across town toward the Suncrest, figuring the time had finally come to say goodbye to the roaches and pack up his junk and split. At the intersection of Shoreline, he noticed a vaguely familiar guy walking along with his head down, a carryall in his hand.

Brady made his turn and drove past the man by the time recognition clicked. Last he saw that guy was in a BMW crashed up against a tree in his yard: J.D. Macken, playmate of Lexy, husband of her killer. He spun a U-turn right in the middle of Shoreline and pulled to the curb.

"Need a lift?" he called.

Macken's head jerked up. He stopped and touched a forefinger between his eyes, then pointed it at Brady. "Hey, I know you. Barry, right? Don't mind if I do, thanks."

"Pretty close. It's Brady, actually," he said as Macken clambered in and tossed his bag in the back. "So where are you headed?"

"Bus station, Brady. Sorry 'bout that, and thanks."

"You got it. What happened to your Beamer? Breakdown?" He timed a gap in the traffic and scooted the Jeep out into the flow.

"Naw, can't afford it anymore," Macken said, his gaze averted. "That puppy is sitting on a consignment lot, hopefully selling before it gets repo'd. Lost my job."

"How come, if it's any of my business?" Brady asked. *Wow, this dude has seen it all. His wife is in jail for killing his mistress because the two women were having an affair of their own while he carried on with both of them, and now his job. Whew.*

"Hell, I don't mind," Macken said. He unwrapped a stick of gum and shoved it in his mouth, tucking the wrapper in his shirt pocket. "Supposed to be good to talk about it, right? Already spilled my guts to you once. And hey, thanks also for being a stand-up guy that day. I was some hammered."

Macken brooded out the window for a moment, then said, "They screwed me. Told me it had come to their attention that I had a pattern of charging minorities a higher rate than white folks. When the whole damn bank does, and not on purpose, necessarily. But I got no chance of my word against theirs on that hot an issue. And I can't turn around and blow the whistle on them if I ever want to work again."

Dang, this sounds familiar. "What, Leo Burgess owns your bank?" Brady asked, laughing.

Macken turned and looked at him cockeyed. "How the hell did you know that? I worked there, and I only just found out because I had one buddy who wanted me to get the real story."

"I didn't. I thought I was cracking a private joke," Brady said. An idea began growing, snowballing in his brain. *Woo-hoo, Grant Thibideaux, you are going to par-tay.* "Now you say the whole bank does this thing with the rates. How does that work? Is it provable?"

Macken eyed him, suspicion knitting his brow as a visible process of animal cunning connected things in his head. "Why do you care, you ain't got a dog in this fight, do you?" Then his eyes widened. "Leo Burgess, huh? He send you here to fuck me over some more?"

"No, nothing like that," Brady said, snorting at the idea of Leo sending him anywhere besides jail. "Maybe I'm just curious to know more about his bank."

Macken kept the stare on him a moment, then a smirk tugged at his lips. "I'm on you, Brady. If you can find a way to twist his tail, give him one for me, okay? So here's your deal. Doing a mortgage, you can usually make more spread on a young buyer than an older one, right? Well, over half of our young buyers are minority, but almost all the old geezers are white, see? Now do the math. You break it down by race, the average rate for whites is always gonna come out lower if you don't figure age. Hell, nobody does it on purpose, it's not even a discrimination thing, it's just making rate where you can. It might not stand up in court, but it would make a hell of a big stink, and that alone can ruin a mortgage lender."

"And they canned you for it, knowing you can tell all this?"

"Aw, hell," Macken said, fanning a hand in the air. "By the time they get done, my name will be on all the high-rate paper and they can claim they got rid of the bad apple. No, they canned me because Leo said to. Can't have the husband of his daughter's murderer working for him."

"Yeah, pretty rough deal there," Brady mumbled, embarrassed for the guy but dying to know more. Too embarrassed to ask, though.

They waited at a crossroads while a gigantic yellow tractor-trailer stacked with glistening new cars jockeyed back and forth to squeeze into a narrow turn.

"Hell, it's all my fault," Macken said firmly after a moment. "You know I had a thing with Lexy, I blubbered my guts out to you that day. And Lexy, not to speak ill of the dead, Lexy loved stirring the shit more than anything. The idea of having an affair with a husband and a wife without them knowing about each other until it blew up in their faces would be irresistible to her. I'm just sorry it got her killed. I'm sorry for Ellie, too, because I brought Lexy into this and treated Ellie like shit, basically pointed Lexy at her like a gun. Ellie needed someone, and never stood a chance against Lexy's idea of fun."

"Man, that's pretty heavy stuff," Brady dropped into the sudden silence. Yeck, what could he say to the wreckage of so many lives? It called to mind Maggie's remark about a horrible disease catching up to them. The big rig finished its turn and Brady punched the gas. "Trailways or Greyhound? Might as well drop you at the right one."

"Greyhound," Macken answered, pointing. "I gotta go up to the women's prison, find an apartment near there. Hopefully a job, too. But I'll be back. Ellie's still here until her sentencing, I just want to be all set up."

"You're sticking with her?" Brady could not hide his surprise.

"I'm all she's got, Brady. And like I said, it's my fault she's here. Least I can do is be there when she gets out. Even her own mother won't talk to her. So I'm her family now, in a way I never have been for her before. Even if she's sworn off of us boys." He grinned.

Brady gave him a little half-shrug, half-nod, not ready to buy Ellie Macken as a tragic figure. Maybe a lover's quarrel wasn't as reprehensible as Anna Burgess and that whole rotten deal for Pete, but murder just didn't make his list of defensible acts. Even Lexy didn't deserve it. He did appreciate the intensity he heard in the man's declaration of allegiance to his wife. Sounded genuine, like maybe it was a recent revelation for him.

"Funny, ain't it?" Macken mused, rubbing his chin between a thumb and two fingers. "All this time I've been waiting to get rich off of her nutty old lady, and now I never will. Yet here I go, planning the rest of my life as a poor man and you know, it's the first damn thing I've ever done right."

Brady pulled up outside the bus terminal, and Macken reached across his body to grab Brady's hand. Shook it, snagged his bag from the back seat, and climbed out.

"Thanks for the lift, amigo," he said, leaning down into the doorframe.

"Sure thing, thanks for the ammo. Hey wait, I don't even know the name of the bank."

"Oceanic Bank and Trust." Macken grinned again. "Thought you'd never ask."

CHAPTER FORTY-TWO

Gerry Terence stood motionless in the familiar shadows of the palms lining Oak Street across from the blue corner house. This was it, and man oh man, he'd better be right. Hidden around the corner, two vice guys sat in their souped-up but hard-used Camaro, awaiting his signal. Zack and Ace were their names, which sounded like a late-night cable comedy act, but they were the closest to sane of anyone he knew on vice detail.

They had trusted Gerry's guess on the drugs and came to take down the resident of the blue house, one Cameron Degardo. But Gerry nurtured his own private agenda, one he was ready to risk twenty-five years of reputation on. He wanted Nick Burgess wrapped up and had chosen this night of the week on the hunch that Nick's usage rate made him a creature of habit.

"Gerry, I see one up there," Zack's voice came over the cell connection they were keeping open for the stakeout. "We're going in."

"No, wait, I don't recognize the car," Gerry whispered quickly, eyeing the Acura pulling into Degardo's drive. Most likely a customer, but not Nick.

"Look, numbnuts, we can't wait all night for you to recognize somebody," Zack said. "A buyer's a buyer, we only need one. And Ace is sitting here farting his lunch all over the car and I just don't think I can stand it anymore."

"Yeah, but you go in now, you get one dealer and one possession," Gerry wheedled, hearing Ace giggling in the background. "I'm telling you, this other guy's coming tonight and he'll buy enough to be tagged for intent. Then you've got two dealers and you'll get credit for taking down a network instead of one dealer, okay? So you children behave and keep your pants on."

"Okay, okay, but hurry it up," Zack bitched.

Gerry heard the phone rattling as Zack set it down, heard him saying something indistinct to Ace in the background. He willed himself to remain still, be patient. *Come on, Nicky boy.* He wished he could tell Angie the story, have her see him doing something good, something needed, and betting his whole stack on it. He knew he could call her up and tell her, and she'd probably listen, but it just wasn't the same as *talking,* like over dinner or in bed.

At last he heard the unmistakable twin-pipe rumble of the Porsche as it burbled around the corner and swept into Degardo's drive. Gerry crossed his fingers. If he was wrong, if this turned out to be two queens playing house on the down low or something, he'd never have an in with anyone on the job again.

"It's our boy," he said, loud enough for Zack to hear him and pick his phone back up. "Remember, time it right and we'll catch the buyer holding."

Zack didn't answer him, just disconnected. Moments later, Gerry spotted the two of them crossing the lawn, staying in the shadows. For all their zaniness, they moved nice. He had not told them that the buyer was a Burgess, unsure whether it would scare them off of his plan. He did feel sure they wouldn't care who they'd bagged once they were psyched up from the bust.

His angle of view didn't allow him to see all the details of it going down. He saw Zack and Ace poised by the door and saw it swing open, presumably Nick coming out. Zack took him down right there on the stoop as Ace went in, moving fast in a low crouch. He heard the shouting, the guys identifying themselves, but no shooting or sounds of a struggle, thank God. He waited, realizing that he absolutely did not miss doing doors.

After the scene settled down, the two-way on his cell chirped and Zack came on, loud and breathless. "Got him holding a whole half. You da man, G."

Gerry released the breath he hadn't known he was holding. He'd set this up without any concrete indications of Nick's buying habits, just his experience leading him to expect a rich punk with a monkey on his back to be a volume buyer. Not like Zack and Ace would have been disappointed if they only got possession on Nick, because it would still be a good collar on Degardo, but they sure would have razzed him for it.

More importantly, it guaranteed a felony rap for Nick Burgess. He might never spend a night in jail, people like the Burgesses rarely did. But intent was something that even a Burgess shouldn't be able to plead down to a misdemeanor. And once he had a prior in his jacket, no one in law enforcement would ever give him the benefit of a doubt, regardless of Leo Burgess. The next time Nick slipped up, which guys like him always did, he was going to be doing a stretch.

And that's the best I can do for you, Pete, Gerry thought as he wound his way through the trees to where he had stashed his car. *Whatever you had on him died with you, and your will tells me there's a rape story somewhere in there that I'll never know. I got exactly nowhere on the peeping, but this is the first step in taking him off the street eventually, inevitably. Sleep well, bro.*

CHAPTER FORTY-THREE

Brady slammed the Jeep's door, just for the sheer joy of creating an unseemly racket in front of the Burgess home. He followed the walkway up to the door that didn't feel nearly as imposing anymore, wondering if Anna would answer his ring. What would pop out of his mouth at the sight of the woman who put Pete out there in front of that drunk driver?

He had to wait a good ninety seconds to find out. He spent it admiring the lazy rollers crashing down on Burgess's beach, wondering how someone could willfully do harm to such a beautiful force of nature.

No Anna. Instead, a short little brown woman of indeterminate age pulled the door open. Indeterminate language too, since she merely looked at him in question and waved him in when he asked for the mister. Why did this place always feel like the set of a paranormal mystery series?

He followed her to the same luxurious office where the same hulking presence of Leo Burgess stood stirring what might as well have been the same drink.

"Thank you, Juana," Burgess rumbled. He watched her leave and turned to face Brady.

"Good afternoon, Mr. Spain. I make it a policy to never refuse a caller, but I cannot imagine what business you and I can possibly have to discuss."

Brady strode to the seating area where he'd met with Burgess a thousand years ago, slipped an envelope from his hip pocket, and tossed it on the table. "The money I owe you. No, let me rephrase that, I don't think I owe you anything. But it is the money I committed to when I wrote that hold check."

"You may keep it." Burgess pointed his stirrer at the envelope. "To use your words, I couldn't care less about the money. You are going to pay me with something much dearer."

The urge to laugh welled up in Brady's chest, surprising him. Guy used to scare him speechless. "Yeah, yeah, whatever. Believe you're out of ammo there, pardna."

Burgess's face darkened. "I hope that is not a tasteless reference to the tragedy that forestalled testimony by the victim of your swindle."

Brady stared at him, round-eyed. "Really? You just said that?" He shook his head. "Actually, the only reason I brought your money in person is, just like back on Labor Day, I had the idea that I would offer my condolences about Lexy. Because she mattered, regardless of what's between you and me, and she was your daughter. But both times your attitude has talked me out of it inside of thirty seconds."

He moved to the center of the room, stopped and stood, feet apart and hands hanging, amidst the rich burgundy leather furnishings that projected the same vibe of imperial prerogative as the indomitable man before him. But fear of Burgess wasn't in him any longer, not even the slightest tremor of adrenaline remaining. "I have a friend who told me this and at first I thought she was exaggerating, but she nailed it. Everything is about you. I gotta tell you, man, Lexy dying wasn't about you. It was about her."

"You are not fit to discuss my daughter," Burgess said, the familiar merciless glint of blue ice showing in his eyes. "If that is the purpose of your visit, you may leave."

"Oh, I will," grinned Brady. He'd gotten over feeling like a fool after Burgess's scared rabbit speech, thinking he'd lived through this bad dream for nothing, once he realized that it embodied the difference between them. A victory defined by exploiting the vagaries of the legal system was a bullshit substitute for what was right. Brady knew now that he would've fought like this anyway. "For the first time since I met you, I can go anywhere I want, anytime I want. It's a nice feeling to be done with you."

Seeing Burgess's raised eyebrows, he added, "Yeah, I know, you got this warrant you want to threaten me with. Well, let 'er rip. I've got a guy from Uncle Sam just hoping for a chance to intervene for me."

"If you are quite finished," Burgess growled, "I will not pretend to bid you good day." He waved his drink toward the door in an abrupt slashing motion that slopped the top third of it onto the bar.

"He's the same guy who's heading up the investigation into the lending practices at Oceanic Bank," Brady went on, as if Burgess hadn't spoken. "Yep, exactly. Investigating your bank. Oops, I guess that was a secret, it being your bank. Well, not anymore. You might get a little mud on you in this deal."

Burgess neither moved nor spoke, just eyed him impassively, and Brady saw why the guy had become so ultra successful. Talk about your poker face. After a stare-off that felt like a week, Burgess shifted his gaze to the door and back.

"I know, I know, get out," Brady said. "Make sure and read tomorrow's *Trib,* too. There'll be a really cool column on the EPA opening its own investigation of you. This one's about your Taj Mahal here being the source of all the runoff that's choking the channel. I don't know, maybe they make you tear this garage down, but it's going to set you back a little change either way. By the way, the article is written by Jeanette Voyes. You probably don't remember her, but boy, she remembers you."

"You are a little man, Mr. Spain," Burgess said, each word

bitten off bone-hard, his face turning an ugly magenta. "Running around in an infantile attempt to harm me because your little man's ego has been offended. If any of your rabble-rousing is actionable, I can promise you I will pursue it."

"See, that's what I mean." Brady laughed at the hopelessness of it. He'd come here with his mood wavering toward compassion for this man who'd tried to destroy him, who'd lost his daughter to a murderer and his wife to incarceration for committing a murder, but the guy's arrogance was staggering. Maybe Maggie was onto something with that whole bad blood idea. "It's all about you. But what you don't get is that this is not your planet, Burgess. You're just a resident. You can't just do whatever you want to."

He took a step closer to Burgess, then another, enjoying the reckless heat firing through his body. "Because you're right. I am a little man. So are Maggie and Grant and Gerry and Pete and Jeanette and all of us. I guess you think all the little ants look up to you, but I've got news for you. You kick over enough anthills and, no matter how big you are, they can put together an army to drag your ass off for dinner. So I think it would be wise for you to do that 'be in contact with my attorney' thing. You're going to need it."

Burgess strode to the door and held it open. "Since a civil request does not seem to reach your ears, I have one word for you, Mr. Spain. Out. I can assure you, you will regret this day."

"Trust me, brother, I already regret everything about you," Brady answered as he brushed past on his way out. He stopped in the hall and turned back. "Oh, I thought you would like to know, I made a call to your cronies over at Beach Haven Resorts to explain your problems with the EPA, figuring they might be interested in hearing how you won't be able to get any permit for anything for a while. I guess I scared them off that deal you had incubating."

Brady found his way back to the foyer without seeing Juana and let himself out. He sat in the Jeep a few minutes, collecting his breath and shaking off the irritation that came with hearing another dose of Burgess's endless supply of condescending crap. He noticed the voice-mail light blinking on his phone and grabbed it up, thinking Peggy. No such luck.

"Hi, Brady, this is Ed Schlatt calling. We want to thank you for thinking of us and passing on such timely information, though that isn't the reason for my call. In light of recent changes around here, we feel that we may have acted hastily in eliminating your position. We would like for you to return to Beach Haven Resorts, in the management position we have discussed. I am happy to inform you that the salary will be half again your previous scale, and perhaps we can arrange permanent accommodations as well. Look forward to working with you again, guy. Call me back."

His breath caught and he felt his eyebrows climbing his forehead. *Well, there it is, Brady: life on the beach with a six-figure income. Everything you ever dreamed of.* He sat motionless for a moment, there in the shadow of the Burgess mansion, then looked up at his reflection in the rearview mirror and realized he was grinning like a fool.

He let the grin grow into a laugh and tapped the seven on the screen, erasing the message. He adjusted his seatback for a long haul and glanced at the dashboard clock. If he drove straight through the night, he might get there in time to wake her up, have her fuss at him for seeing her with bed hair. Maybe even stop by and visit Mom first, see if she would fix him an egg sandwich and her famous cheese grits. He reached for the ignition and checked the clock again. Yep, he could make it. And he wouldn't have to try to survive another day in paradise.

ABOUT THE AUTHOR

A native of rural Florida, **Hugh Dutton** grew up in a succession of small Southern towns until the lure of the big city took him to Atlanta at the age of twenty. After two decades in business there, he hung up his wingtips for the more challenging career of parenthood. He lives in Hawaii, where he now devotes his time to his family and, of course, his books. He is also the author of a previous novel, *Supposed to Die*.